NOT QUITE HUMAN

The dark figure moved swiftly, glistening arms flashing. As Quas Starbrite skidded to a halt in midstride, he got his first good look at his adversary. His gut clenched in fear. Adrenalin poured into his body, and he wanted to run in panic from the black, faceless monster in front of him.

A shiny metal face without nose or mouth. A black, gleaming body, smooth and featureless. Articulated arms that had the force of a machine. And red, burning coals for eyes, eyes that didn't blink.

One arm clutched Lyra about the waist, her eyes wide with terror. The other hurtled toward him in a dazzling metallic blur . . .

QUAS
STARBRITE

James R. Berry

*Created by James Razzi, Richard
Brightfield and Jack Looney*

BANTAM BOOKS
TORONTO · NEW YORK · LONDON · SYDNEY

QUAS STARBRITE
A Bantam Book / September 1981

ISBN   0-553-14820-6

Published simultaneously in the United States and Canada

Bantam Books are published by Bantam Books, Inc. Its trademark, consisting of
the words ''Bantam Books'' and the portrayal of a bantam, is Registered in U.S.
Patent and Trademark Office and in other countries. Marca Registrada. Bantam
Books, Inc., 666 Fifth Avenue, New York, New York 10103.

PRINTED IN THE UNITED STATES OF AMERICA

0 9 8 7 6 5 4 3 2 1

To Ronan
a zesty cohabitant of this spaceship called Earth
and an explorer whose dreams aim at the stars.

QUAS
STARBRITE

Chapter One

He stood there, hating as he waited.

Far below, along the broad avenues that terraced the city, squads of Dark Horde warriors marched in stilted, staccato steps. More of the Fellowship—singly for the most part, but sometimes in pairs—strode with grim determination, their dark carapaces gleaming dully in the glow of a descending sun.

KraKon drank in the sight, his slim powerful body motionless as a statue, as he stood before the expansive window of his towering Tabernacle. He saw no waste of time or motion. Every step, every movement was calculated to achieve the highest predictability. Efficiency. Economy. Purpose. The bywords of the Fellowship.

KraKon's voice box hummed in satisfaction as a surge of contentment momentarily eclipsed his simmering hatred. For 2000 years he had worked to eliminate the random factors that so often mangled rational plans. And *now* his planet and galaxy were subject to *his* law. Subject to his Cybernetic Fellowship—the creed he had created to glorify majestic logic and obliterate the corruption of the senses.

His hatred revived as KraKon remembered that—elsewhere—other civilizations hadn't bent to the Fellowship. Still there were races, someplace, that hadn't submitted, that might *not* submit; intelligent beings who might offer opposition to the joys he offered. Races like . . .

An uncharacteristic excitement animated KraKon. He moved in stagger step to another wide window of his Tabernacle and glared with crystal eyes at the magnetic tramway that led from the spaceport to the city. Nothing yet, and in this rare instance delay only whetted his expectations.

He had felt a similar anticipation some fifty times in the last two millenia over what he had christened the *Visitation*—the moment when the first captives of a new alien race were brought for inspection; the time when he first saw the creatures who, every instance in the past, had become members of the Fellowship, willingly or not.

Now, after an unusually long span of seventy-five of his planet's orbits around Sola, he was to experience that heady sense of impending conquest once again. At last. At *long* last.

KraKon swiveled his head even further to glimpse an added length of track along which the silver personnel cart would carry the captives. He saw no movement save the staccato walk of Dark Horde soldiers, administrators, and workers, all scurrying like black ants from one destination to another.

KraKon, annoyed now at the delay of his pleasure, stamped one alloy foot, and the Tabernacle floor vibrated under the blow. The fresh surge of rage cooled quickly as he again mentally feasted on the coming pleasures and, at the same time, remembered how it all had started 2000 orbits of Sola ago. So long. . . .

But it seemed like yesterday when he was among the most powerful of his planet's political corps, still a biological entity. Then came a medical diagnosis that withered a desiccated personality even more: a pump muscle, weakened and diseased.

He got a mechanical version powered by a tiny speck of nuclear material. And with that artificial pump he gained an ambition that drove him like a madman: immortality.

Slowly, at first with private wealth, then with public monies, he funded cybernetic research—the replacement of fallible biological tissue with synthetic substitutes. His office became a tabernacle dedicated to the god of immor tality. When, seventy years later, his eyes began to deteriorate, he lured squads of specialized researchers with a promise of a fortune for each. They created his crystal lenses, electronically linked to the stub of his optic nerves, just a year before his biological eyes would have ceased functioning altogether.

Characteristically, these cybernetic organs and their subsequent improvements were better than nature's own. He could see, now, in the far infrared and near ultraviolet. True, the light intensity registered only in black and white. But color, it turned out, had been a distraction not a necessity.

Over ensuing centuries, as KraKon's power increased by simple longevity combined with ruthless opportunism, cybernetic developments stayed a pace ahead of tissue degeneration. New alloy-polymers with characteristics of muscle tissue were myoelectrochemically joined to nerve centers of his brain. His epidermis was replaced by a dark, enormously tough polymer. Liquids, enzymes, and hormones were pumped, secreted, purified, and oxygenated by electronic regulators. Biofeedback that produced a sense of touch, hearing, sight, and speech was governed by spectacularly efficient mini-computers melded directly to appropriate neurons. Smell and taste were contemptuously discarded as unnecessary and distracting.

The only remaining biological vestige of his former self was his brain. And in this arena, KraKon had won true neo-immortality, for a delicate medley of antithanic fluids prevented any deterioration of neurons. And, in less than four hundred of KraKon's years, the magic wand of cybernetics had transformed a biological being into a tough, nearly featureless black shell of a body that housed a shrewd and everlasting mind within.

KraKon snapped out of his reverie. Far in the distance, along the magnetic tramway, he spotted a glow in the infrared band, a slight heat given off by the cart carrying the first of a new race to the Visitation. The first aliens from another galaxy.

KraKon's black arms rose in exultation, carrying his dark ceremonial cape with them like the wingspread of a predatory hawk. His voice box purred with malignant joy. He whirled in ecstasy toward the door-wall of the huge room, his cape snapping at the sudden motion.

After so long the yearning for new acolytes had become desperate. But finally a new race—beings from beyond his *galaxy*—to be relieved of their futile senses. A historic moment that capped the Fellowship's first sortie into the universe at large. And once—KraKon's voice box hummed louder now—it had seemed so impossible. Once. . . .

The milestones leading to this moment flashed across his mind: the creation of his theocracy, the Cybernetic Fellowship, with himself at the pinnacle; christening himself KraKon, which in his language meant "Great Immortal One"; and maintaining absolute control over all cybernetic products, which guaranteed unquestioned loyalty from his minions. Another shrewd move had been the creation of administrative levels: the CryKons, subalterns one large step below himself, and the Dark Hordes, cybernized soldiers—cannon fodder—from the proletarians of his own planet and all alien races, led by KreeKons, the lowest of all executive posts.

KraKon edged to another window of his Tabernacle, savoring how far he had come.

Then he saw the dull glow of a setting sun and, unexpectedly, his elation over the Visitation was sucked from his mind. Desolation filled its place, a mood that rapidly metamorphosed into venomous hatred. His eyes glowed fiercely as he felt the familiar raging thirst for dominion over the universe. A dominion that, unknown to him, he had never achieved over something that mere cybernetics could never eliminate:

Memories.

Memories of a warm, soft companion with violet eyes from whom he had received compassion and comforting warmth he now hardly believed could exist. The fleeting memories of her melodic voice sometimes made him ache. His arms and torso were of polymer-alloy but through a perversity within his brain he sometimes *felt* her soft touch.

His olfactory sense had been abandoned as useless but torturing ghosts in his mind sometimes sensed the subtle

4

fragrances she wore, the perfume of her epidermis, the scent of warm sunshine on yellow-colored hair.

Over two millenia ago, frantic with disappointment, she had faced him in this chamber and had screamed, "You can create, but you choose only to destroy. Yourself. Me. Us. You're nothing but a vicious sadist now." Her sudden, unexpected loathing had rolled over him like a foul wind.

And as Sola was setting—as it was this instant—he was blinded by fury and had squeezed the life from her. Now she was a mere pinch of dust, her atoms mingling with trillions of others. And he—KraKon—was immortal.

Like the steady pressure of water against a dam, these memories strove toward consciousness, mocking his cybernetic body. At the worst of these periods KraKon would storm through his quarters, brutalizing his CryKons, issuing death notices on a whim, his black body animated by palsied motions. The CryKons had learned to avoid his wrath at all costs during these times.

The setting of Sola: red, tinged with yellow. Colorful. And KraKon, whose crystalline eyes saw only in black and white, registered these colors through some phantoms in his mind just as he had when his companion had screamed her invectives and died eons ago.

KraKon's voice box screeched in an ascending scale, the sound echoing weirdly throughout the room. He wheeled, his cape cracking. The silver cart had stopped before the Tabernacle building. Three Dark Horde soldiers tugged at two other figures while his chief CryKon, covered by a shorter cape than his own, commanded. KraKon's enormous rage subsided as he saw the two struggling figures forced into the entrance.

Just a few tantalizing minutes more. His cape snapped again as KraKon rapidly flapped his arms in exultation, his warped mind focused on the creatures from a distant galaxy. The *first* representatives of his coming dominion over the entire universe, a dominion that would forever shut from consciousness the perverse memories that so unsettled his composure. The memories he had conquered a galaxy to forget.

From the Tabernacle's antechamber he heard the hum as the elevator doors opened. His arms twitched as random neural currents activated sensitive solenoids within shoulders and elbows.

In a flash KraKon remembered with grim satisfaction how he had ordered his scientists, most of them at CryKon level, to find a gateway. To use their knowledge of gravitons and hyperdrive to uncover an entrance, a gateway, to the universe. Oh, *how* they had protested. Yet, how quickly they had found the secret after he had carved the brain from one CryKon scientist at a public death ceremony.

Now, seventy years after the secret had been found, the first aliens from another galaxy were just outside his Tabernacle. How grateful they would be to savor the gifts the Cybernetic Fellowship offered—immortality combined with the obliteration of useless senses. There, outside his Tabernacle's door-wall was the first of perhaps thousands of races throughout the universe to fall under his command.

High frequency chimes rang.

"Admit them into my chambers," KraKon intoned in ultrasound. KraKon turned slowly, as was his custom during the first moments of a Visitation, his back to the door-wall.

At the far end of the bare room two tall sections of the wall slid apart. A scuffling sound from the antechamber brought an ominous hum from the KraKon's voice box. Resistance? In his very Tabernacle?

His annoyance was joined by a sadistic pleasure at the thought of reducing these creatures to whimpering jelly. He had done it scores of times before. This instance would be no exception.

At a flick from the CryKon's dark hand, the three Dark Horde soldiers dragged the creatures into the Tabernacle sanctum. The CryKon, knowing his KraKon's preferences, had the soldiers spread the captives by their arms two body lengths from his master. The room quieted as the whimpers of one captive died out.

KraKon wheeled, his crystal eyes glowing.

He stared for a moment, then reeled backward as a blinding pain lanced through his brain. A wellspring of vivid memories burst into consciousness, like a floodgate suddenly opened. His hands sprang to his head and squeezed, as though pressure could exorcise the pain. His voice box ululated with keening whines.

In front of him, spread-eagled, were a man and a woman—both incredible examples of parallel evolution. They were uncanny replicas of his own race as it had been thousands of years ago.

The man: youngish, with a square jaw covered with stubble. Straight hair matted over his head, his body muscular. Double-jointed digits with opposing thumb.

And, the *woman*:

She had hair that cascaded over her shoulders and arms. Her face was a lyrical poem, with bright eyes, now wide with fright. Her breasts, bare through the shredded tunic, were round and full, her legs slim.

KraKon saw her in black and white. Yet he knew that her hair was golden and that her eyes were violet. He knew what she would feel like, taste like, smell like. He knew that her voice would have a lilting tone. He knew because. . . .

Eahoooo! Memories two millenia old and as vivid as yesterday. Memories that tortured his mind. Memories that drove him close to madness.

Rage squeezed these phantoms from consciousness as he told himself that this female had not stepped from 2000 years in the past, but had been dragged from another corner of the universe.

The pair, taut with fear, began murmuring as KraKon slowly lowered his alloy hands from his almost featureless head. They glanced around apprehensively as they talked, their conversation meaningless to KraKon. He stretched out his slim, black arm, his head not swiveling a millimeter. His CryKon handed him a linguistic cartridge, prepared during the preliminary interrogation during their flight through the gateway.

Still staring at the two creatures, slowly recovering his mental composure, KraKon inserted the cartridge into a receptacle in his forearm. The pair's language became intelligible.

"Rolf, he's crazy. I can sense it. Whatever he—it—is. What they've done so far, from the time they took us from our ship. What do they want?"

The man answered in deeper tones. "Don't panic. Got to keep our heads. It's a small chance we've got but a chance yet. At least the boy wasn't with us this trip—"

"*Silence*." KraKon's voice box intoned metallically, at the lower frequencies their ears could hear. The pair, startled, were suddenly quiet. KraKon noted a blood vessel in the man's forehead throbbing.

In ultrasonic speech KraKon commanded the Dark Horde soldiers to release the two. Observing how a strange life form moved often offered clues to their overall attitudes.

The man and woman both rubbed their wrists where the grasp of Dark Horde soldiers had bruised skin. The man, frightened but defiant, stared into KraKon's crystal eyes. The CryKon and Dark Horde soldiers stood as immobile as black suits of armor.

"We're citizens of the Galactic Federation. A kidnapping by pirates like you is to be punished. A hard punishment, too, if we're not freed now."

At first KraKon felt scornfully amused that these creatures had no idea of where they were. Then, as he recognized the extent of the man's insolence, a new attack of fury boiled through him. A *threat*? In his own Tabernacle? A *warning* by a germ of a life form not worth stepping on?

KraKon's rage exploded. In a lightning-swift flash of his arm he crushed the man's face with a backsweep of his hand. The crack of bones was even louder than the man's moan.

"Rolf!" the woman screamed. She knelt and stared at the mass of blood and bones that had been a face, gently sweeping back a shock of hair from the man's eyes. She rose slowly and stared at KraKon, her eyes blazing and lips curled.

"You scum," she shouted, and before anyone could move she attacked, clawing at KraKon's eyes with splintering fingernails.

The CryKon and Dark Horde soldiers stood in dread.

8

For someone to attack their KraKon was a sacrilege that took a fleeting moment to digest. Anything could happen now.

Before they moved, KraKon grabbed the woman's neck in his slim, powerful hand and lifted, his mind bubbling with revenge. The woman's feet left the ground, and she made low, croaking noises. Her face turned red, then purplish as her hands vainly clawed at KraKon's wrists. Her eyes bulged from their sockets.

But before life left her, KraKon flung the woman to the floor, next to her groaning companion.

He turned to his CryKon.

"Tear him apart. Molecule by molecule." In his fury KraKon's metallic speech slurred. "Synthesize every enzyme, hormone. Desex both. Begin cybernetic transplants. Make certain the woman remains alive."

The CryKon felt a tremor in his elbows and knees as worry over his own safety flooded his circuits with intense, random currents. He had never before witnessed such a traumatic Visitation as this. Never before had he seen an intelligent life form so belligerent or aggressive when hope was lost. And *never* could he have imagined an attack mounted so swiftly against his KraKon by a defenseless creature like that female.

Would they have trouble with this race?

The CryKon motioned to the Dark Horde soldiers to drag the humans from the Tabernacle. He began his own quiet, cautious exit. When his KraKon was in such a fierce temper, anything was possible.

"One moment," KraKon's voice box purred. The Dark Horde soldiers and the CryKon froze. KraKon's right arm rose ominously and a finger pointed like an accusation at the battered creatures before him. "Where does this race come from? What name do they give their planet?"

The CryKon didn't stumble over the answer. But it was close.

"New Earth, Master KraKon," he said, adding a ceremonial title to appease any rage that might be directed his way.

"New Earth," KraKon replied slowly, as though making the planet's name indelible in his mind.

Then, almost as a joyful afterthought, he added, "Before Sola rises tomorrow I will have begun plans to put that infernal world in complete thrall."

Chapter Two

Quas Starbrite was ticked off.

Not at anything in particular, but just about everything in general.

It had been one hell of a bad day, week, and month. And, if you wanted to go back far enough, it hadn't been a real sterling year either.

Sure, there wasn't a shortage of Spaceforce personnel who didn't envy him. With a cushy post as one of four aides-de-camp to *the* Supreme Commander of the Spaceforce, his future was secure. Envy aplenty—except for the eighty or so fellow officers of his Spaceforce Academy class with whom he had graduated three years ago. By now, almost all of them were spread over the Galactic Federation, on line posts, doing what they'd so arduously been trained for—maintaining order within the Federation while exploring, always exploring, for new planets to colonize.

They'd understand how he felt. Not like the swarms of fat-buttocked bureaucrats he worked with whose closest contact with deep space was the recreational area on top of the Spaceforce Command Headquarter's building. If he played by the bureaucratic rules his thirty-year stint with the Spaceforce would be a series of comfortable planetary assignments where the greatest inconvenience might be a dearth of wide-bottomed desk chairs.

OK. Maybe it wasn't as bad as all that. But he, Quas

Starbrite, hadn't spent eight years becoming an expert in a dozen skills, from galactic navigation to cruiser pilot— incidentally copping a license to pilot the Whippet, the neatest space fighter to spring from a designer's dream— so that he could shuffle papers and tap computer terminals.

Starbrite glanced at his duroplastic desk and with an irritated motion shoved aside a pile of forms. Somehow there always seemed to be paper. A historical imperative, someone had once joked. The piles seemed to rise yearly in direct proportion to the number of computer readouts in one's office and in inverse proportion to the real importance of a job.

Starbrite exhaled in exasperation and snapped up the interoffice memo he had received ten minutes earlier, its typeface the neat, artistically sterile figures characteristic of computer readouts. Somewhere, Starbrite knew, the memo's contents were sequestered in a computer's electronic memory, petrified forever by magnetic imprint on a length of tape.

He read the message again.

```
09876473 FRM: SC I. CROOST, SFCOMMAND GD27/
3510

INTENT TO: CAPT. QUAS STARBRITE PRIORITY
STRIPE

REPORT TO SUPREME COMMANDER IVOR CROOST AT
1600 HOURS OF GALACTIC DAY 27 YEAR 3510. INFOR-
MATIONAL CONTENT OF SESSION WILL BE SUPPLIED
IN REAL TIME. NO REPLY NECESSARY.
```

He flipped the message sheet onto his desk. It skimmed across the top, skidded over the edge, and seesawed to the floor some meters away. Starbrite let it lay.

Translated, the note's jargon meant that he'd been summoned for a confidential meeting, the subject of which old man Croost would tell him in person.

A sudden meeting, just a half-hour off. A bit unusual, actually, given the fact that, despite his high-sounding job of aide-de-camp, he hardly even glimpsed the commander once in a month of New Earth's turns. Maybe someone saw that his shoes weren't shined, Starbrite thought sarcastically. He imagined the start of the coming conference:

"Captain Starbrite. We've had a report that your shoes lacked the luster expected of. . . ."

Starbrite caught himself lapsing into self-pity. OK, he hadn't got what he'd expected after graduating, with honors, from the Academy three years ago: a line post somewhere in the depths of the Galactic Federation.

OK, so he was assigned to Supreme Command's Headquarters right afterward.

OK, so the job wasn't the best.

But, damn, it didn't have to be the worst sort either.

Starbrite swiveled around in his thickly cushioned chair and gazed out a wall of glass that covered one side of his office, wondering why *he* had been picked for a post of aide-de-camp. Then, for a fraction of a second, he was startled as a figure stared back at him, a man in a light blue tunic with short sleeves, cuffed at the end, and sporting the narrow, red, green, and silver epaulets that marked the rank of Captain in the Spaceforce.

Whatever the reason it certainly wasn't looks, Starbrite thought. The figure in the window had brown eyes set too far apart. A shock of brown hair fell over a wide forehead that emphasized cheekbones set too high. The entire face that looked back at him sullenly was tapered like a V, ending with a square chin cleft by a dark crevice. Not real good in the looks department, Starbrite told himself indifferently, suddenly focusing beyond his reflection.

His office had a beautiful, panoramic view of Terra, the capital city of New Earth and the hub of Spaceforce administration. It was a lovely city, built on gently rolling hills and encompassing huge parks, acres of trees, and one genuine forest in the center of the city. Tall buildings, terraced, tiered, and spiraled, soared toward the heavens, all grouped in pleasing harmony with the terrain around them. A clear river flowed through the city, and Starbrite often walked along its banks amid the sightseers and frolicking children.

New Earth.

Somehow it had worked. A planet modeled after a

legend, a template called Earth. *That* pitiful planet was now a shadow of a once fine and vibrant world, now inhabited only by a few troglodytes, descendants of long-dead survivors who had refused, or were unable, to take part in the Great Migration some eight hundred and fifty years earlier.

Starbrite sighed. Earth's desecration was in the far past but worth remembering. Who was it who kept repeating—yes, old Major Reener in the Academy History Section: " 'He who does not understand the past is condemned to repeat it.' " For that reason alone. Remember.

And *now*. An entire federation of planetary colonies spread throughout the near galaxy, seeding other worlds with civilization. An enterprise dependent on the resources of the Spaceforce. Dependent on so many of his friends. . . .

Like Tripsy Alcaldes. Crazy Tripsy they called him. Now exploring the space quarter near the Magellanic clouds, scouting, with the same carefree energy he put to any task, for additional habitable planets. He had one planet already bagged, with the first survey teams working on it right now.

Then—Starbrite grinned—Rhinna Treaver. Lovely Rhinna, a classmate for whom Starbrite had gained a high respect and fond affection. Now a Spaceforce pilot, already bloodied in one battle with a band of piratical maniacs on a fringe planet in the Constellator Quarter. Gutsy Rhinna. No one in the graduating class could down her in the simulation chambers. Her scoring was close to ninety-eight percent, an academy record.

But there were losses, too. Trensk Kattern, dour and something of a recluse but with a stupendous natural knack for galactic navigation, killed by a group of renegades on that hellhole of a world in the Alcans system.

All comrades. All *doing* something. Not like. . . .

Starbrite mentally rattled the memo again, glanced at his chronometer and came back to New Earth. Ten minutes to go, time to freshen up. A conference with the Supreme Commander of the Federation's Spaceforce wasn't something to take too casually—not if he had any future other than pushing memos and punching computer terminals.

14

Starbrite rose, took a last lingering look at the sky, and went to the private washroom of his richly furnished office.

Private washroom.

Hell, Cherese Holdts had crashed on Xeerst-III and lived for six months without a change of clothes or a bath before rescue. And Lorianne Peotyers had survived three months in a life ship designed with a one month's support system when her ion engine blew. And take. . . .

Starbrite entered the immaculate washroom. Recessed panel lights automatically illuminated the carpeted interior. He slammed the door.

A trim, wrinkled man with a pointed white mustache surrounded by green plants. That's how Starbrite thought of Ivor Croost, Supreme Commander of the Galactic Federation's Spaceforce.

His office was crammed with plants that flowered, plants that dripped and drooped, plants that exploded from wide pots into towers of bushy leaves. His passion for plants had turned his office into a miniature botanical garden.

Croost was a crisp soldier, his uniform a model of sharp creases, form-fitting tunic and tailored jacket. His face was lined with a thousand worries. Two clear eyes the color of a mountain stream gazed at a world that could no longer surprise or disappoint.

Starbrite knew that Croost had spent over fifteen years heading the fleet that had brought civilization to the Nether Quadrant—still a sparsely settled and troubled corner of the populated galaxy. He had pacified a dozen internecine wars, helped colonize a half-dozen planets, and with consummate diplomacy, policed an incredible galactic area.

He was known to be as shrewd as he was incisive. Starbrite recalled the story when, five years before, a Spaceforce intelligence agent had reported to Croost's office. The agent had evidently been suborned by the low level but omnipresent insurrectionist movement that for forty years had plagued the Nether Quadrant.

That agent had attempted to assassinate Croost. But

before the attacker could fire his own lasegun, Croost shot him dead with his personal weapon.

Two years ago, when he had delivered a high priority message to Croost's office, Starbrite discovered how the Commander had saved himself. The envelope fell under Croost's chair and when Starbrite picked it up he saw a tiny but powerful lasegun nestling in a niche built into the chair's underside. Easily reachable and nicely hidden. Croost, an experienced soldier, was a man who never took chances. Starbrite never forgot the lesson.

"Thank you, Captain Starbrite, for coming on such short notice," Croost said in dry tones, as though Starbrite really had a choice. Still, friendliness was more than he had expected. Croost wasn't known for being cordial to junior officers. For no reason Starbrite could fathom, he felt his heart pick up a beat.

"Thank you, sir," Starbrite answered, no trace of nervousness in his voice as he sat in the chair Croost waved him to.

A huge, drooping leaf touched Croost's desk and he brushed it aside with what seemed genuine affection before leaning back in his chair. He steepled his fingers together and pursed his lips. The points of his neatly trimmed mustache twitched slightly, right side first, then left, with a compulsive precision. Starbrite kept his face impassive, but he felt a building excitement.

"I'm embarking on a sensitive enterprise, Starbrite. One in which you'll be assuming a specialized role," Croost announced.

Starbrite didn't quite leap from his chair. But mostly because he squeezed its armrests so tightly. 'Jackpot,' he thought, his mind a whirlpool of anticipation. His voice remained steady as he answered, "Thank you, sir. I was hoping for a—well—a more active assignment."

"Active? I'm not quite sure how active this particular mission will be," Croost answered, his eyebrows rising into perfect arcs, as though the idea of activity somehow amused him. Croost suddenly leaned forward to underscore the significance of what was coming next. "Your assignment has an importance that cannot be underestimated. That is why you will report to one person. Me. Exclusively. No other order can supersede this one. Understood?''

Starbrite nodded, weak from the knees down, wondering what tasks he would be entrusted with. He added a strong ''Yes, sir.''

Croost nodded, satisfied with Starbrite's understanding, then glanced at his chronometer. ''We'll be having some visitors soon. They'll be with you on your coming trip.'' Croost paused as a breeze from an open window made his plants rustle. Starbrite swallowed hard at the idea of a mission. After three weary years things were looking up.

After a long pause Starbrite realized that Croost was waiting for him to speak. ''The nature of the assignment, sir? Our destination. Can you fill in some details now?''

''A full briefing will be handed to you tomorrow. It's being prepared by computer processing right now. Meanwhile, a verbal précis should do.''

Croost sat back once again and nibbled on the inside of one lip, as though rehearsing his words. His mustache twitched again. ''Starbrite, have you noticed anything peculiar in the reports you deal with concerning the Nether Quadrant? Anything about—difficulties?''

Starbrite's brow furrowed. A test? Could a wrong answer scrap his chances for this mission? He began thinking. Military action in that quadrant concerned only a small fraction of the work that passed over his desk each month. Yet . . .

''Just that there's been more trouble involving the Spaceforce over the last two years. I mean more trouble than usual,'' Starbrite said thoughtfully. ''No one *big* thing, really. But an increasingly steady stream of incidents,'' he added, remembering a report of stolen weapons from a Spaceforce Cruiser, a short vicious battle involving a Whippet and a civilian cargo carrier thought to be smuggling.

Croost nodded contentedly and Starbrite felt annoyed at the wave of relief flooding over him. He wasn't taking a test, after all. Or was he? ''And the *nature* of this trouble, Starbrite? Anything about that?''

Starbrite thought again, impatient with himself, and replied. "It's all consistent with discontent, sir. Excluding the cases where pure personal profit was the motive. I hadn't thought of discontent as a generic reason. But it *would* fit."

"Correct again, Starbrite," Croost said, his voice tinged with warmth. Starbrite again felt a rush of pleasure at the approval and hated himself for it. "Actually, the incidence of insurrection—or at least the preliminary symptoms—are enormous. Unusual too, in a newly settled area such as the Nether Quadrant."

Croost paused for a moment and stared abstractedly at a huge bush of a plant, as though for inspiration. "But why?" he asked, staring at Starbrite, his eyes as neutral as hailstones.

Starbrite squinted. Croost had the inside line on military intelligence, an area Starbrite wasn't closely in touch with. "I simply don't know, sir."

Croost paused for a moment then said, "Neither do I, Starbrite. But I'd like to. I'd like to know where the Federation's policies are hindering rather than helping the settlement of the galaxy. I'd like to know what causes inhabitants who would most benefit from order to rebel against the very source of stability."

Starbrite, puzzled now, nodded sagaciously. "And you want me to find out, sir?" he asked, surprise plain in his voice. He hadn't the slightest qualifications for such a mission. He knew that and so must Commander Croost. Sure he'd like a line post. But doing something he was trained for.

Croost answered, "Your task will be to accompany a civilian party that has the qualifications for just such a research mission. Something as an aide-de-camp, a position you're familiar with."

An openhanded slap in the face would have wounded Starbrite less. He swallowed, vainly trying to suppress his huge disappointment.

Croost added dryly, as though in compensation, "No mistake, Starbrite. It's an important role. These civilians must be made to feel comfortable in what will essentially be a military ambiance."

The communicator buzzed and Croost paused, fixing Starbrite in an icily indifferent stare. "You'll be meeting the chief members of your group now."

"Vac Orion is here," an aide announced.

"Orion, Starbrite, is a valued friend. He is in charge of the mission—though, as I said, you'll be responsible primarily to me."

The door opened and a burly man with a genial face and a tuft of hair springing over his forehead entered. He walked over to Croost, hand extended, with easy familiarity.

"Vac, this is Captain Starbrite, the man who'll make your journey comfortable."

Starbrite suppressed a groan as he shook Vac Orion's hand. He sensed that Orion, while affable enough, would be a burden. The man didn't seem to have the tough competence to face the possible hardships a far galactic corner could offer.

They sat and Croost proffered a chrome-plated smile. "Vac is a neurological anthropologist, Captain Starbrite. He and his team will be interviewing inhabitants. Well, perhaps Vac can tell it in his own words."

Orion gave a broad, boyish grin, his cheeks a rosy red. Like a Santa Claus, Starbrite thought. Like a bumbling Santa Claus.

"My area is the study of the relationships of nervous systems to social patterns that various civilizations adopt for survival," Orion explained with no hint of academic condescension.

In a carefully even voice Starbrite asked, "You expect to uncover the reasons for a deep-seated insurrectionist tendency through this specialty, sir?"

Orion's eyebrows peaked into small triangles, and his face became deadly serious. "Freedom is a growth from dependence to self-containment. Insurrection is an *angry* severance of relationships before this growth is complete. Often, an organism—just like a society—can't survive such premature independence. Then, that society or organism sometimes dies. Certainly its growth is stunted or malformed."

Orion paused for a moment, his explanation gathering

momentum. He crossed his legs and squinted at the ceiling
for a moment, then continued.

"Many reasons can contribute to a planet's wish to
abort its ties with our Galactic Federation. Some reasons
are neural in nature, others are cultural and still others
historical. I expect to study all three and provide Commander Croost with some kind of explanation for the
phenomenon of long-term, low-level sedition."

The speech satisfied Starbrite's curiosity. Orion, he
realized, wasn't in the least stupid or incompetent, just
inexperienced and probably inept at the hazards and incon-
veniences of space travel.

"And the rest of the team, Vac? I understand that
Lyra will be coming on this one," Croost said indifferently.

Starbrite shot a quick look at the commander, wondering if he would be functioning as a tour-guide director
as well.

"Lyra won't be along as an organic part of my team,
though I trust her judgment," Vac answered. "She needs
a vacation and also wants to so some observation around
the Nether Quadrant. Evidently there's something of interest
there to her, and some of her stargazing friends she hangs
out with. My trip came at just the right moment."

Starbrite felt a shattering dismay. Stargazing friends?
Lyra? An astrologer, perhaps? Someone who'd tell his
fortune from the configuration of the constellations? Terrific! Perhaps he could set up a kindergarten on the ship for
orphans who also needed a vacation.

Orion glanced at Croost with an ingenuous smile.
"She'll be here soon, in fact. Wanted to meet you again
and—" Orion beamed at Starbrite—"our military escort."
Starbrite's jaw muscles bunched.

As if on cue a buzzer on Croost's desk rang again.
"Send her in," Croost commanded without listening to the
message.

The office door opened and Lyra Orion stepped in.
Starbrite looked at her once and then glanced quickly
again.

Resignation, was the thought that ran through his
head. Becoming an official servant to a group of pampered

20

civilians who traipsed through deep space without an inkling of the problems involved was too much to stomach. Especially if he had to pick up the whole tab for their inexperience. Starbrite exhaled quickly.

There wasn't a starship trade concern that wouldn't hire an ex-Spaceforce Academy graduate on the spot. His alternatives polarized: nursemaid or resignation. The latter would take two minutes at his computer terminal.

He rose as Lyra Orion, pointedly ignoring him, walked over to Croost, her slim hand extended.

Quas Starbrite, fury plain on his face, turned toward the door.

Chapter Three

Not that Lyra Orion was hard to look at. Hardly a male in the Star Fleet wouldn't have given a month's allotment to spend a week escorting her through Hades. Hair like golden silk billowed down to her shoulders. Her eyes had the deep violet color of an overhead sky at sunset. A gentle swelling of her tunic tapered to a waist that was one easy armful around. Her face was a melody of soft curves and her fleeting smile at Croost hit Starbrite like an unexpected free fall through space.

He was aware enough to admit that, depending on one's viewpoint, Lyra Orion's manner indicated she was either competent or superficial; determined or willful; decisive or stubborn. In any case, she was completely independent.

In fact it was this last characteristic that decided his resignation. Escorting civilians on a basically military expedition was within barely tolerable limits. But aide-de-camp to a pampered albeit beautiful woman wasn't—especially if she had no head for tolerating suggestions and, yes dammit, orders if a situation got tense. Starbrite was still smarting with indignation and wasn't about to give her the benefit of any doubts. No way.

In the moment it took him to look toward the door, Starbrite pictured his searching out the best crafts emporiums on a given planet, carrying boxes of finery while trotting behind—*Lyra*, wasn't it? Outfitting her room, scouting out astrologers for her to play with, responsible for fulfilling her slightest whims. Intolerable.

"Starbrite, meet Lyra Orion." Croost's voice had a snap to it that cancelled Starbrite's impulse toward the door. Croost added almost as an afterthought, "Our last participant should arrive shortly."

Starbrite nodded to Lyra Orion and got a quick, impersonal nod in return. Croost brushed back more long, tapering plant leaves and once again looked on the assembly as though it were a crew conference in a Spaceforce warship.

"You know that this mission is authorized by military order. It will be carried out as inconspicuously as possible and with distinct civilian overtones. This will reduce attention and possibly avoid aggression by malcontents."

Croost's mustache twitched in sequence again. He pursed his lips briefly, as though about to confide an important secret, then added, "The commander of your transport will be Jost Adrian."

Starbrite's heart jumped. Jost Adrian. Already a legend throughout the Galactic Federation, his exploits defending the newly settled planets in the Nether Quarter thirty years ago were enough to bring him fame. For five years, while seconded to the Star Fleet, he had outmaneuvered, outsmarted, and defeated a determined organization of outlaws and renegades, who were overrunning these outpost civilizations and establishing their own parasitical alliance. He had lost both legs during a particularly vicious battle but had resumed command of his small fleet within six months after being fitted with prosthetic limbs.

That famous exploit was just one of a string of stirring accomplishments. Starbrite recalled the story of how Adrian had picked up a dozen life craft from two giant colonizer ships after they had been blasted by loot-hungry pirates. Through sheer force of personality he maintained order on his ship, though it was crammed with people, got them safely to their target planet, then blasted off to seek revenge. Not one of the attackers survived. As a bonus he had towed the two colonizer ship hulks to where the remaining supplies could be ferried to the colonists.

Starbrite breathed deeply. Nursemaid? No way. He'd be a scullery hand on a skow to serve under Adrian.

The communicator buzzed once again, and Croost's aide announced that Adrian was there. Croost was about to speak when the door to his office burst open.

Adrian's sudden presence was like a supernova. He was a huge, muscular man with an aura that enlarged his presence threefold. His voice was a basso explosion. His movements were huge gestures that were at once expansive and graceful.

"Croost, you old dog. What're you doing still shoving papers instead of settling the galaxy like ya should?" Limping slightly, Adrian strode over to Croost, reached across the desk, and gave the sitting commander a bear hug. Starbrite winced, half expecting to hear the crack of a bone.

Adrian was no man to be intimidated by protocol or position. He was iconoclastic, irritated with procedures and scorned petty bureaucrats. But he was someone who got things accomplished with the least effort and the most efficiency.

"Settling the galaxy is something you'll be doing until your engines burn out, Jost. As for me, I've let my incompetence drag me to the highest administrative level possible," Croost said with a wintry grin.

"Incompetence?" Adrian roared, waving his arms. "If we needed administrators at all, something I'm not sure of, one would be enough if it was you." Starbrite noticed a small flush of pleasure on Croost's face.

Jost Adrian: a master at governing crews, with a knack for just the right word at the right time. If leaders were born, Adrian was among the chosen few.

"Jost, you won't be going alone," Croost said. "I'd like you to meet—"

Adrian swept toward Vac, Lyra, and Starbrite. "Vac Orion," Adrian said, not waiting to be introduced. "Know your work, *Settlement as an Alternative to Aggression*. Welcome aboard my ship the *Cetus*," Adrian said warmly as he grabbed Vac's hand and shook it.

Adrian turned toward Lyra. "You've got to be the

prettiest astrophysicist who ever studied an equation,'' he said in warm tones. Lyra, flushed in spite of herself.

Starbrite, gave her an appraising glance. He had guessed she was a pampered child, without aim or profession. Pretty enough, but coming along as baggage. Astrophysicist? That explained the ''stargazing friends'' remark. Possibly, just possibly, he wouldn't have to be so much of a nursemaid after all. The mission was looking up.

''Quas Starbrite. *Captain* Quas Starbrite.'' Adrian towered above Starbrite, arms spread wide. The arms clapped his shoulders, and Starbrite felt himself being shaken like a feather pillow. He grinned weakly.

''From what Commander Croost there tells me, I've got the smartest young spacer in the Galactic Federation coming along.'' Adrian's eyes twinkled merrily as he released Starbrite. It was like a vise unclamping.

Starbrite felt a warm rush of pleasure. To be welcomed like that by Jost Adrian was something to remember for a lifetime; he felt like a little school kid getting a gold star on his homework.

But Starbrite also realized that Jost Adrian was shrewd. His expansive bonhomie masked a highly determined mind. He no doubt had read Vac Orion's book and asteroids to planets, he'd studied lots more of Orion's work. He had also learned that Lyra was an astrophysicist and probably knew something about her other interests, too.

Starbrite, seated again, breathed out slowly. The idea that he was on the verge of resigning now seemed like a childishly self-destructive impulse.

''Just a few more minutes of your time.'' Croost was again his composed and urbane self, completely recovered from Adrian's madcap arrival.

''I trust your mission won't take more than a month or so to accomplish. Hyperspace hops to the Nether Quadrant will eat up a week or so. Then a bit of—''

''Might be longer, Commander,'' Vac Orion interrupted. ''It's hard to tell in advance how many interviews will be necessary, how widely spread they'll have to be, or how many planets in the Quadrant we'll have to visit to ferret out the reasons for forty years' worth of low-level sedition.''

"Good dose of lasercannon might be all that's needed to bring thugs in line," Adrian added ominously. He grinned, but Starbrite guessed that he was completely serious. He was a man who acted by instinct rather than theory. A good method in its place, but—

"Jost, this is an *exploratory* mission," Croost admonished. "We want to know fundamental causes, to effect necessary changes. Peaceably if necessary."

"Learning's a good thing. No doubt about that," Adrian responded, "So long as it doesn't interfere too much with getting things done."

Lyra, Starbrite noticed, was studying Adrian closely with her soft violet eyes. Her face was tinged with puzzlement. Or was it faint amusement? Starbrite ran a hand through his hair. He didn't have a real clue as to what her genuine reactions were. Toward Adrian, Croost, or himself.

Adrian swiveled his chair toward Starbrite. "Anything to add, lad? Speak up, for now's the time."

All eyes turned toward him. Starbrite couldn't remember when he had felt so conspicuous. Lyra cocked her head slightly, as though taking his measure from the coming reply. Whatever he said couldn't antagonize. Yet, it couldn't be *all* platitudes, either. Starbrite compromised.

"It's been my experience that knowledge and action are rarely if ever incompatible," he said grinning sincerely. An actor, he thought. I should have been an actor.

"Maybe it's just that knowledge gets you into situations that action gets you out of," he added, realizing that it would take a professional philosopher to unravel that sophistry. But it would do for the moment. At least his comments couldn't ruffle any feathers.

"By Jove, we've got a thinker aboard. Space Academy must be churning out better cadets than ever before," Adrian roared. Starbrite sensed that Commander Croost was pleased. He glanced at Lyra.

Her expression hadn't changed much. But the slight difference might have been caused by her sucking on a lemon. Perversely, Starbrite was relieved. No fool, that woman, he thought and, unexpectedly, was glad she was coming along.

The remainder of the meeting was absorbed by details. Jost Adrian's ship, the *Cetus*, would leave in five days. Vac would brief his own small research team. Starbrite's duties at Command Headquarters were suspended from that afternoon on.

It was only as they were leaving that Lyra spoke to Starbrite.

"And your function, Captain" she asked. "I'm not clear about that."

For a moment Starbrite was flustered. Good question, he thought. Why *am* I included in this mission?

"This mission is civilian in content, but with military authorization, Miss Orion——" Starbrite offered.

Lyra finished quickly. "And you're along as an omni-present observer to assure that the military authorization isn't violated."

"I'm here to make your trip as comfortable, pleasant, and efficient as possible," Starbrite answered formally. Damn. She was *suspicious*. Of *him*. "At least, that's the only reason I've been informed of," he added sincerely. Lyra Orion's expression softened slightly. But only slightly. She nodded and without another word left with her father.

Five days later, Starbrite reported to Terra's spaceport. It had been a busy time filled with briefings, selecting equipment, and talking with acquaintances who knew something about the Nether Quadrant. The printed orders Croost promised hadn't told him more than the Commander himself. The briefing had emphasized that he was to report any unusual events to Croost, but what these might consist of remained a puzzle.

The *Cetus* remained in fixed orbit 400 miles above New Earth since its massive weight would have caused its hull to warp on a planet with any real gravity. Smaller shuttle and ferry craft carried passengers, baggage, and cargo to the mother ship above.

Starbrite paused before boarding the shuttle, exhilarated

at being space-borne again. He breathed the fragrant air and felt the warm wind of New Earth, only slightly regretful about leaving these things behind. The sky was a light blue, and the gleaming shuttle ship, itself a huge craft, pointed like a silver arrow toward the heavens. It was a moment that never failed to enthrall him.

Space: an infinity of distance and time, a vastness that contained adventures and secrets that humankind hadn't yet dreamed of. Each space trip he'd ever made was a new and exciting quest, a trip to a fresh unknown, and now Starbrite savored the anticipation of a space voyage to an area of the galaxy he'd never seen—the Nether Quadrant.

Inside the shuttle Starbrite relaxed on his form chair as the craft lifted off, launched by cryogenic magnets out of the grasp of New Earth's gravity, then maneuvered by rocket to the *Cetus*. He forgot about all others in the party. This was always a moment that Starbrite preferred to experience alone. The pressure of acceleration forced him deep into his form chair, an incontrovertible sign that he had left landfall and was again destined for deep space.

Within two hours the shuttle ferry had docked with the *Cetus*. Jost Adrian welcomed them aboard, a privilege that Starbrite knew was exceptional. Typically, the captain had little time for such formalities.

"Show the lad to his quarters, then give him a tour," Adrian had told a lieutenant when Starbrite stepped from the air lock. "And make sure you include the hyperdrive."

Starbrite felt a jolt of appreciation. The hyperdrive mechanism was the most delicate and precious part of a starship, off limits to everyone but the most trusted aides. For Starbrite to be allowed inside the hyperdrive compartment was an enormous compliment. Most starship captains would prefer to bare their necks to a knife-wielding stranger than allow a lifelong friend near the hyperdrive coils.

Jost Adrian grinned broadly as he saw the smile of pleasure on Starbrite's face. "Important trip. Let's get it off to a good start." Then he had turned abruptly to finish preparations for leaving orbit.

The *Cetus* was half a Km long and a quarter wide at its tips, with three tiers or levels. In profile, it appeared like a squat triangle. It wasn't a configuration that was most efficient for cargo carrying, but the hysteresis fields generated by the hyperdrive coils enveloped a triangle more effectively than any other form, more easily shifting the craft into null-time.

After stowing his gear, Starbrite stood in the hyperdrive chambers and stared at the tall, glittering coils. He vaguely understood hyperdrive theory; one had to be a master at vector angenetics to really comprehend the most elementary mathematics of faster-than-light travel. But it all focused on the twelve gleaming coils in front of him. Suddenly Starbrite frowned.

Hyperdrive had opened up the galaxy to a point. But the mechanism had a weakness.

Large ships like the *Cetus* could carry hyperdrive generators that hopped them about 5000 light years at a time. But the mechanism was limited to ten such hops per trip—five going out and five returning. More than ten hops distorted the crystalline structure of the massive but sensitive drive coils, each of which had to be replaced after 50,000 light years of time travel.

Long ago, experimental starships had carried a spare set of drive coils to increase their range. They disappeared. Theorists speculated that the spare coils resonated with the activated coils and degenerated with equal rapidity.

One more problem: manufacture of hyperdrive coils was an enormously laborious and specialized task. Expensive, too. In fact, the process was one of the Galactic Federation's major expenses. No outer planet could yet afford to spare the thousands of technicians needed for their manufacture. So, a starship couldn't refit its coils on a distant planet and probe further into the galactic unknown.

Starbrite stared at the beauty of the twelve squat coils. Each was bathed in a transparent tank of liquid helium, which brought their temperature to near absolute zero, at which point they became superconducters. They were beautiful but limiting. Until something better came along, humankind was bound to a mere 25,000 light years from New Earth, barely one half the diameter of its own galaxy. And billions of *other* galaxies populated the universe, each holding its own mysteries. To Starbrite, the limitation of current hyperspace drive systems seemed like a tether. It was a problem that had gnawed at him for more than a decade.

He gave a quick, resigned sigh that brought a look of curiosity from Lieutenant Questin, the officer who had given him the tour. "Can we see the observation deck now?" Starbrite asked, knowing that protocol demanded a visit to this area soon.

"Ship's captain is expecting you and the others at 20:30 hours, starship time." Questin checked his chronometer. "That's in two hours. We'll have half a day or so after that for our first hype hop," he added, using civilian spacer slang for a hyperspace jump.

They left, Starbrite glancing again at the delicate machinery that had freed spacers for a distance of 25,000 light years in any one direction. A mere pinpoint of space when viewed against the immensity of the universe.

Then Starbrite napped. He rose, refreshed, in time to wash, dress, and arrive at the observation deck to meet Captain Jost Adrian and the others.

Just in time, too, to witness the first of the disasters that were to plague the *Cetus* and their entire mission like a chronic disease.

Chapter Four

A geyser of red, yellow, and orange gases erupted from the *Cetus*'s hull with a shudder that shook the entire craft. The ear-splitting shriek of tearing titanalloy penetrated even the horrendously loud blast of the alarm. On the *Cetus*'s outside deck, one story below the observation tower, a shuttle ship twisted at its moorings, its thrust rockets spewing out exhaust gases that seared and melted the bulkheads of its nest pod.

With one final screech, the shuttle ship tore free. The enormous thrust emitted from its tail catapulted the ship from the pod, its nose gyrating in vicious circles. The exhaust gases, no longer confined to the pod area, sprayed over the hull of the *Cetus*, their vivid colors fading as they expanded in free space.

Then with a sudden, random lurch, the shuttle ship twisted on its side and blasted toward the observation deck.

Instinctively Starbrite and all those who saw the ship ducked. The topside of the shuttle, its nose pointing upward toward deep space, suddenly filled the observation windows. And, for one incredible instant, Quas Starbrite had a clear view through the shuttle ship's port windows into its control room.

There, only a few meters away, Lyra Orion sat in an acceleration chair, her mouth open in a scream that Starbrite's imagination heard plainly.

Accompanied by a loud crack, the shuttle disappeared from the top portion of the *Cetus*'s observation ports, leaving only a spray of hot gases that momentarily distorted vision like water running over a window. A long gouge in one of the thick, polymer port windows was a memento of how close the *Cetus* had come to losing its observation deck.

The entire incident, from first spout of hot flame to disappearance of the shuttle ship, had taken less than thirty seconds. Quas Starbrite, as everyone else, stood a brief half second more in shock as the ship sped off into space, becoming smaller by the moment.

Then, each man reacted. Questin, quick as a leaping cat, sprang to the trackradar. With the deftness of a symphony conductor, he manipulated the myriad dials that would keep the shuttle ship on the viewscreen.

Jost Adrian punched the button that silenced the ship's alarm with a massive fist. He grabbed the ship's intercom mike with his other hand and bellowed out orders to seal the shuttle's nest pod.

Vac Orion rushed to the port window, hands clenched and knuckles white, looking helplessly at the pinpoint of light marking the shuttle ship's trajectory, trying to keep it in sight.

And Quas Starbrite stared ahead, looking at nothing, his face muscles knotted with concentration, his mind racing through the available alternatives. There weren't many to pick from. No way you simply stopped a space cruiser, turned ninety degrees to her flight path, and chased a smaller ship. The laws of inertia didn't work that way. Once something as large as the *Cetus* was moving, it took hours of hard deceleration to stop its mass—or even alter its trajectory.

But those laws were kinder to a less massive ship. "Where's your mosquito?" Starbrite barked to Jost Adrian. There was no hint of deference in his tone now. Adrian shot him a glance mixed with chagrin, puzzlement, and then understanding.

"In a pod, on the for'ard hull," he said, moving

toward the entranceway. "Get a crew there. Ready the mosquito for instant flight," he bellowed to Questin.

Questin, staring at the viewscreen, gave a slight nod. The man seemed unperturbed by the accident as he calmly adjusted a communications mike over his head. Adrian whipped toward the entranceway, barely limping now, Starbrite at his heels.

During the next few minutes of their headlong rush through the long, cavernous corridors of the *Cetus*, Starbrite couldn't help but bitterly wonder at how fate reversed circumstances with a wanton arbitrariness. It seemed incredible that a mere ten minutes before he had been ushered onto the observation deck by Questin, a dour, slightly morose man who talked in monosyllables. Questin was bald, with a gold earring in his left lobe, his tunic perpetually open at his chest. He moved with quiet, subtle gestures, with none of Jost Adrian's expansiveness. Starbrite knew that Questin had been Adrian's chief lieutenant for decades and while on the deck had again wondered at the strange contrasts that drew one man to the other.

Now, Starbrite's and Adrian's feet pounded hollowly on the *Cetus*'s bulkheads, the sound of their labored panting sharp and crisp among the echoes. Starbrite grinned sourly, remembering how, in the lounge, he had felt his spirits soar. The view of a disappearing New Earth had been stupendous. The planet seemed to hang in space, its blue oceans only partially obscured by brilliant white clouds. The outlines of various continents were plainly discernible. Surrounding the planet was a medley of sparkling stars that seemed like glittering points on black velvet.

It had been a sight that Starbrite lived for. Space. Freedom. Beauty. He had felt at home, now, on the observation deck in a way that he could never adequately describe even to himself. He had hardly noticed Vac Orion, Jost Adrian, or Questin. It had been his moment to savor without interruption.

A pod on the *Cetus*'s hull had caught his attention. Many such pods peppered the ship, each one housing a smaller transport craft of some sort or another. Each such ship was linked to the *Cetus* by an air lock and mooring strips when docked. Otherwise, the various craft were virtually autonomous.

Lights were on inside a shuttle ship below the observation deck, and as he now paced after Adrian, Starbrite remembered his annoyance at the distraction. Inside the ship he had caught a glimpse of Lyra Orion, standing as though she, too, had been enthralled by the sight of deep space.

It was then that Starbrite had felt the sickening lurch of a quickly changed gravitational field.

Such fields, he knew, were typical. The hyperdrive coils also doubled as ersatz gravity generators, a vital technological step that made space flight infinitely more tolerable, even to experienced spacers. At the start of a long flight, delicate adjustments in power supply had to be made between the coil chargers and the engine drive. Such adjustments caused quickly fluctuating gravitational fields that could be frightening to the uninitiated.

Lyra Orion was obviously in this class.

Starbrite had seen her stumble against the shuttle ship's control panel as the gravity field dipped, overcompensated, then shot to normal again. It might have been her hitting a catapult lever that caused the engines to power—through Starbrite knew that there were several fail-safe backups to prevent such an accident.

Or it might have been that the gravitational variation caused the short circuit of a malfunctioning relay set at hair trigger. At least, that had been his immediate thought when the shuttle ship's engines ignited with a shuddering roar and a flood of flaming gases.

At first violent vibration, Lyra Orion had clawed her way into the acceleration chair, grasping its hand rests with the strength that impending doom imparts. It had been that instinctive reaction that had saved her from being tossed through the craft's interior like a marble in a shaken box.

* * *

Their pace-eating trot through the *Cetus* had seemed interminable to Starbrite, even though the kaleidoscope of mental images of the accident and what preceded it had taken barely two minutes. Suddenly Adrian, his face flushed, jerked to a halt. He threw back the lock lever of a bulkhead door and yanked. "Bay twelve. It's here," he roared as he darted inside, Starbrite behind.

Four other men worked feverishly inside the bay, checking the mosquito's fuel, release catapult, and communications system. Starbrite hardly glanced their way but mentally thanked Questin for the moments they had saved.

"Into the pressure suit while I give a last check," Adrian said, disappearing into the air lock. Starbrite cursed each second as he squirmed into the suit, helped by two of the crew. Adrian returned, sweat dribbling down his face.

"Good as it can be. Tromley's just confirmed the communications channels." Even as Adrian talked a squat crewman with a face as wrinkled as a dried prune crawled into the chamber below the mosquito's pod.

Without another word, Starbrite leaped through the hatchway and into the small, powerful spaceship.

It was all familiar to him. The control panel of the mosquito—essentially a short-range scout and rescue craft—had been standardized by Galactic Federation ordinance. He sank into the command chair, beginning takeoff procedures almost by reflex. The endless drills at the Academy were paying off handsomely.

"Communication's on," Starbrite shouted into the featherweight head mike as he touched the engine relay button. The air lock doors clanged shut. "Launching," Starbrite barked, leaning back in the soft chair, prepared for the enormous acceleration shock the mosquito delivered.

One second he was staring through a port window out at the deck of the *Cetus*. In the next instant he had sunk far into his chair and saw only stars. Red dots scrambled in front of his eyes. Then his pressure suit inflated, equalizing blood supply throughout his body. As initial acceleration slackened, his hands roved over the controls without thinking, without hesitation.

"Course heading requested," Starbrite said with exaggerated clarity. More training. Old-timers had drummed into the cadets from the day they arrived to the day they graduated the importance of clear transmissions. More lives were lost, so the legend went, because of garbled radio transmissions than in the Great Migration from Earth. Keep your transmission *clean*.

"Vector up three degrees, heading horizon for four," came the monotonously precise voice of Lieutenant Questin. Starbrite manipulated two settings and felt a strong tug as course correction rockets fired.

"Speed reading of target with comparison requested," he said with equal calm. Someone overhearing would have guessed from the tones that Starbrite's flight was a training exercise.

"Two hundred Km's and accelerating. One fifty Km's acceleration gain," Questin answered. Lyra Orion's ship was heading away at 200 Km's per minute and accelerating. Starbrite's speed was now only 150 Km's per minute, but accelerating at a faster rate. In short, he was catching up.

Now for the biggie, Starbrite thought. "Distance to target requested."

There was a moment's hesitation.

"Nine hundred and fifty KM's immediate. Current acceleration will bring you to target in twelve minutes."

Starbrite nodded in silent appreciation at the transmission but recognized another problem. Questin's voice was already fainter. His own ship had lower power radar scanners and microwave transmission. He had to rely on the massive radarscope capacity of the *Cetus* to guide him to Lyra's renegade ship. And he had to do it quickly—otherwise he'd run out of radio range.

He bucked up acceleration, and Questin was on channel within seconds.

"New acceleration data. You'll close in three minutes. Total distance between targets now fifty Km's." Questin added, "You should pick up the engine thrust flame about now. You're right behind her."

As if on cue Starbrite spotted a flickering pinpoint of light directly ahead. He was now traveling faster than

Lyra's ship and eased back on acceleration to avoid over-shooting his target. A few moments later he was tandem to the craft. With delicate control Starbrite nudged the mosquito to within a few meters of the shuttlecraft.

"Parallel with shuttlecraft," Questin's voice announced.

Starbrite flicked the switch for the autobeacon and spoke. "Lyra. Activate fine tuning autopilot. Red/white toggle switch upper right-hand corner of control panel. Pull toward you," he said with exaggerated clarity.

Chances of Lyra hearing his instructions were excellent. The radio beam of the autobeacon broadcast on a frequency that activated a speaker in the control room of any nearby spaceship. Once activated, the circuitry would also broadcast any comments spoken in the cabin. More than one spacer's life had been saved by the device during a rescue operation.

Lyra's shuttle had a large-scale autopilot that had kicked in during the most violent of the craft's maneuvers. Except for that computer-automated device, the ship would now be flipping end over end. Still, the craft's nose cone gyrated in sickeningly eccentric circles, movements the fine-tune autopilot would remedy.

As Starbrite watched, the shuttle ship's flight path smoothed, the gyrations becoming smaller and finally disappearing. Lyra *had* heard. Starbrite's dim estimate of their chances for rescue escalated a millimeter.

Minutes ago he had made a decision. He couldn't take a chance on her craft being undamaged and landing them back on the *Cetus*. Not with the violent launching it had made. Lyra would have to come to him. Starbrite grimaced. He would have preferred the opposite.

"Lyra. Don a spacesuit and get into the top-deck air lock. That's near—"

"Understood. See it from here. Clearly labeled. Spacesuit, ugh, there got it. Take a few minutes." Her voice, Starbrite thought, could best be described as a steady shake. She was avoiding panic with iron determination.

"Good girl. You'll be OK in a few minutes."

Lyra's voice cut in sharply. "Yeah, maybe. Ugh—got the suit on. What's next?"

"I just scoop you up. You'll have to shove from one ship to the other. Through the air locks. It sounded simple, but Starbrite knew it was an extraordinarily dangerous maneuver. Even a slight pulse in power or a tiny fluctuation of the autopilot could send the two ships crashing together with enough force to bend their hulls like clay.

"Right. Zipping up now. See you soon," Lyra's voice said over the cabin's speaker.

Starbrite hoped so.

He flipped on the exterior halogen spotlights, their bright beams illuminating both hatchways. In another minute he was in his own lightweight spacesuit and heading for his air lock. He dogged the port leading to the ship's interior then spun the wheel that loosed the exterior hatch. It slid back and Starbrite felt the air in the small chamber whoosh past his suit and into the vacuum of space.

He saw the hatchway of Lyra's ship slide open, her space helmet looking like a bright crystal ball in the brilliance of the lights. She wormed her way through the hatchway, went into a crouch, then sprang toward the mosquito.

It was at that instant the engines of the shuttlecraft sputtered briefly, a precursor to a total malfunction. The sputter made the ship lurch slightly, not enough to endanger the mosquito.

But the movement caused Lyra Orion to miss its hatchway by two full meters. In her inexperience, she had shoved off with too much force, hitting the hull with enough momentum to bounce off like a spring. Her arms waved wildly trying to grasp something more solid than the vacuum of deep space.

An old axiom flitted through Starbrite's mind: *If anything can go wrong, it will. And at the worst possible time.*

As he had done a hundred times during training, Starbrite reached to the underside of the air lock's hatchway. His gloved hand wrapped around a familiar handle, and he twisted once and pulled. A gun-shaped device, nicknamed "the fishline," came free and Starbrite felt a flush of gratitude that Adrian followed Federation safety ordinances to the letter.

Lyra was at least fifty meters away by now, her movements slow and lethargic, as though she had given up hope and was resigned to dying in the vastness of space. Starbrite sighted down the long tube of the fishline, aiming at her rapidly shrinking figure. He squeezed a trigger and felt a recoil as a long flexible line shot from the barrel, a fist-sized bulb appearing at its tip.

The bulb was an enormously powerful magnet, designed to cling like a leech to polyferro patches built into all spacesuits. A lost spacer, or free floating equipment, could then be reeled in like a fish.

The line snaked from the barrel and jerked to a halt, taut and straight, the magnetic bulb straining to reach the polyferro patches in Lyra's suit.

Straining because at its longest extension, the fishline was a half-meter short of actually touching Lyra. Starbrite groaned as he saw her slow down, feeling the tug of the two powerful, attractant magnetic fields. But the tug weakened as Lyra, tumbling in slow motion, drifted out of range of the bulb's magnetic field.

Starbrite stared in disbelief, then through sheer discipline cleared his mind of the desperation he felt.

He leaped from the hatchway, his shoulders, torso, and legs erupting from the exit like a rocket. As he stretched his arm and body toward Lyra, he also spread his legs wide apart. By the maneuver he added a full meter to the length of the fishline. His boot tips, caught on the underside of the hatch exit, locked him by a literal tochold to the mosquito's hull.

That added meter saved Lyra. The magnet at the end of the fishline snapped onto a polyferro patch on the leg of her spacesuit. He felt the pull of her inertia, easily countered it with a tug on the fishline, and, hand over hand, pulled her toward the mosquito, her body drifting lazily toward him. He eased back into the air lock, trembling at how close Lyra had come to being a corpse ambling forever through the heavens. If his feet hadn't caught, if the line had been just a bit shorter, if her speed had been faster. . . .

A thousand "if's" but all of them academic now. He grabbed her foot with two hands and guided her into the mosquito's hatchway. It was a tight fit for the two of them in the air lock, and Starbrite was barely able to dog the hatchway. It took another minute of careful maneuvering to open the port door to the mosquito's interior. They tumbled inside the ship in a welter of arms and legs.

Starbrite dogged the interior hatch by reflex, and shot to the control panel in free fall. He jerked off his helmet, banded himself to the control chair, and rapidly began tapping out instructions to the ship's navigational computer, instructions that began the inertial rocket thrusts that would bring them in a long, sweeping hyperbolic curve to a rendevous with the *Cetus*. They must be something like a thousand Km's from the mother ship by this time, Starbrite reckoned. A dangerous distance.

He tried to transmit to the *Cetus*, getting in return, a static-filled roar. In the background was a weak, completely indecipherable voice that Starbrite guessed was Questin.

Starbrite felt himself sink back into his chair as the ship began its lazy turn toward the *Cetus*, a long arc of a trajectory that certainly would have to be corrected as they neared their target.

They were out of contact with the mother ship for at least the next fifteen minutes or so. That was bad. But they were on a close-target trajectory and nearing the *Cetus*. That was good. So was the fact that Lyra Orion was aboard. All in all, Starbrite thought, noticing the aftershock tremble of his hands, the situation was definitely in the black, rather than the red, column.

A small, persistent shudder ran through the mosquito. It began as a mere vibration that rapidly became powerful hammer strokes. Starbrite's chair shook as though it would tear from its moorings. The port windows of the mosquito vibrated into a blur. Without thinking, Starbrite smashed his fist against a red lever, almost missing its wide handle. The mosquito's thrust engines quieted; the shuddering ceased.

It was then that Starbrite mentally pictured the arrow pointing to the black column of their situation race to the lowest end of the red scale.

"Trouble?" Lyra asked wearily from behind him.

Starbrite nodded glumly, totally exasperated. The steady white-noise hiss in his earphones dropped away and he could make out vague, barely distinguishable words. "Questin here. Starbrite . . . position . . . course off by . . . degrees. Change course now . . . to . . . Km's."

Then Questin's voice died and the hiss returned, a freak of radio transmission that had permitted a few snatches of voice contact.

No contact with the *Cetus* now. No course corrections or position guidance. Bad under the best of circumstances.

But not nearly as disastrous as the fact that they no longer had engines.

Chapter Five

Starbrite glanced up from the control panel and saw Lyra Orion's look of cool appraisal. Now that acceleration had ceased she hung in free fall, one hand grasping the guide rail near the air lock. Her silky hair flowed behind her, undulating slightly when she moved her head.

"Trouble, Captain Starbrite?" she asked again, as though what they'd been through before had been practice.

"Engines out of sync. The vibration would have torn us apart," he answered.

Gotta be a reason. Cause and effect. Gotta be a reason. The refrain circled in Starbrite's head. Sweat poured from his forehead as he tried to pinpoint the most obvious cause, the single reason that could be most easily fixed. The cause you better well pray was responsible for the effect.

Otherwise the mosquito they were in would become their tomb.

For no apparent reason Starbrite remembered a Space Academy course in linear problem-solving in which the instructor spoke almost entirely in aphorisms. "The simple is at the heart of the complex. So begin easy, avoid hard," or, "No more reason for deadly problems not to have simple causes than simple problems to have unsolvable causes."

Wiring.

Certainly the simplest possible reason for engine syncopation. Certainly the easiest thing to check.

Practically everything in the mosquito was electronically governed. Wires led like nerves from one part of the craft to the other. And in such a basic craft, practically all wiring was easily accessible for quick servicing.

Starbrite flipped up the four latches that held the console cover over the instrument panel and lifted it off. Two cables holding a score of color-coded wires led from the engine feed control to the rear of the ship. Connections at the console were sound.

Like a dog following his master's scent, Starbrite followed the cable to where it plunged from the mosquito's cabin, through the bulkhead and into the engine compartment. A service hatch led to the engine area and Starbrite threw back its retaining lever.

He smelled the source of their problem before he saw it.

Inside the engine compartment the cloying aroma of cigarelles filled the air: a pungently sweet tobacco some spacers still smoked aboard ship but only in compartments that had special air scrubbers. Warning bells clamored inside Starbrite's head.

He followed the cable's serpentine trail by the dim light inside the engine compartment, the smell growing stronger by the meter. Then he saw the problem—

Or, at least, the reason for the problem. A cigarelle had melted the insulation of two wires inside the thumb-thick cable.

Burned insulation leading to a short circuit. An accident born of carelessness; rare but possible.

But not in this case.

Not when the cable covering had been neatly sliced open. Not when the cigarelle butt had been meticulously stuffed between the exposed wires. Not when it had been lighted at its top so as to burn down over a period of thirty minutes or so before shorting out the wires.

And, a short circuit between *any* wires would do since each one was vital to some aspect of the engine's function.

46

Starbrite yanked out the butt and spread the wires so the exposed sections no longer touched. He searched frantically for anything to slip between the bare strands to prevent another short from vibration.

He ducked out of the compartment, frantically searching through his tunic pockets, muttering curses.

"Got a match?" he snapped at Lyra, barely noticing the look of amazement that spread across her face. "Anything to insulate wires."

Lyra unlatched the clumsy gloves of her spacesuit and tore off the cuff of her tunic. Starbrite snatched it from her without a word and ducked back into the compartment. In seconds he had stuffed the cloth between the shorted wires.

Starbrite breathed a sigh of relief: in this instance a simple reason had been the cause for a complex event. From long habit, he gave the engine compartment a quick, searching glance. He scanned the fixtures, halted, then, like a homing beacon, snapped back to one shiny valve.

A rash of goose pimples spread over Starbrite's body.

He yanked himself forward for a closer look. A pressure relief valve that linked the liquid oxygen and hydrogen tanks to the engine's combustion chamber was bent at a strange angle. The valve, no larger than Starbrite's thumb, was covered with scratches. It had been whacked from its setting with some tool. A slight movement from behind the engine tubes caught Starbrite's attention.

A heavy space wrench, powered by a small flywheel, drifted slowly in the compartment. In all probability someone had used that wrench to ruin the valve.

Someone very familiar with this kind of engine, someone very clever.

Because, Starbrite realized, without that valve equalizing excess fuel pressure after prolonged accelerations the fuel tanks would rupture. He and Lyra would be incinerated in space. He was faintly surprised that the tanks hadn't blown already.

The mosquito they were in, Starbrite thought briefly, was more likely to become their funeral pyre than their tomb.

In this case there was nothing to repair. The valve, a

simple, elegant component, had proven so reliable that no backup vent system existed.

As Starbrite backed into the cabin, he experienced a reluctant admiration for whoever had sabotaged the ship. Quick work, and efficient. If engine syncopation hadn't got them then an explosion would. Someone wasn't taking any chances.

"Any sign of radio transmission?" Starbrite snapped.

"Some. Couldn't make out what Questin was saying," Lyra replied evenly. She added in a more tremulous voice, "We're awfully far from the *Cetus,* aren't we?"

Starbrite grinned. At that moment he knew that whatever happened next, Lyra Orion was someone he could crew with contentedly. No one, no one he'd ever met before, would have used the word *awfully* in that way.

" 'Awfully' would be a terrific way to state it," he said, punching out the computer code to start the engines again. He hit the button that inaugurated their home beacon so that the *Cetus,* with its more powerful receivers, would have a radio as well as radar fix on the mosquito. For whatever good that did them.

Starbrite turned to Lyra. "Got a shorted wire that's fixed. Also got a malfunctioning relief valve. Chances are the engines will explode if we accelerate for too long."

"Can you tell exactly when the engines will—malfunction, Captain?"

Starbrite shook his head and motioned for Lyra to take the copilot's acceleration chair. "Nope. And why not call me Quas? Time to dispense with formality," he added, wondering why he was wasting time on social amenities in a situation like this. As Lyra settled into the padded chair, Starbrite continued.

"Bursting fuel tanks depend on a dozen factors. How strong the tubes are, their age, maintenance, hours of use, and a score of other things. But the tanks won't take much more acceleration without being vented. I'm sure of that."

Starbrite punched a numerical sequence into the navigational computer; then he added a trajectory change. He gave the course readouts a last glance and turned to Lyra.

"Here we go," he said, avoiding Lyra's puzzled

glance. He thumbed the engine start button on the computer console. A roar filled the cabin and the mosquito lurched forward, sinking them deep into their chairs. Starbrite had manually overridden all safety measures built into the acceleration mode. A dial shot into the red zone as the engines labored under emergency acceleration conditions, and an alarm bell rang through the cabin.

Starbrite's jaw muscles tensed as he read off the seconds on the large chronometer over the instrument panel.

Beside him, Lyra gasped. "Then why accelerate, if—engines—burst?" She gasped again as the pressure of her own chest made breathing a monumental task. Starbrite cursed briefly, then concentrated again on the chronometer. He couldn't remember everything, he told himself. Short, rapid breathing by expanding the abdominal wall rather than the chest was the way to get air during such hard accelerations. He had forgotten to warn Lyra.

She'd just have to bear it.

One minute passed, then two. Beads of oily sweat formed on Starbrite's brow as the enormous acceleration continued. The engines howled. Three minutes. Lyra was gasping painfully now, gasps mingled with mewing cries as she tried to get oxygen into her lungs.

Four minutes. Starbrite's arms felt like dead weights. Lyra had quieted. Rivulets of perspiration crawled down their faces.

Then, with what seemed the greatest effort of his life, Starbrite willed his hand to flip a toggle switch on the arm of his acceleration chair, shoving his arm forward with all his remaining strength.

The engines died. Acceleration stopped.

Lyra gave a huge, choking gasp. Starbrite ignored her, his head against the cushioned chair, eyes closed, waiting for an explosion. An eternity passed in thirty seconds. He opened his eyes.

"Safe for the time being," he said to Lyra. She was staring at him, fire in her eyes.

"I couldn't *breathe*," she bleated accusingly. It would have been a shout but she couldn't make the effort. "And you said acceleration would explode the ship. What's going on Starbrite?''

No more "Captain." Not even "Quas." Well, he couldn't blame her for being mad.

"I said *prolonged* acceleration would build up too much pressure. Or long-term mild acceleration. When the engines are shut down there's a bit of normal venting that takes place. Not too much, but some. We're still in the safety area if the engines haven't blown by now. At least this time.''

"*This* time?" Lyra sputtered, eyes wide.

Starbrite ignored her and turned their receiver, trying to pick up calls from the *Cetus*. At least they were into their parabolic curve toward the ship, moving at a rate that might just put the two craft in the same vicinity at approximately the same time. Like a grain of rice heading for a grapefruit in a giant hall.

Nothing but a hiss came over their receiver. Disappointing, but not surprising. He was sure that Questin was transmitting, that he had the mosquito on the *Cetus*'s viewscreen. Suddenly he longed to hear Questin's voice and to get a sure-fire course correction toward the *Cetus*.

"We've got to do it again. But not for so long this time. The dead engines vented partially, but each burst of acceleration will add to the overall load. Eventually they'll give,'' Starbrite told Lyra, wondering why in hell it hadn't happened yet.

"How do you know when they'll explode? How far can we get?" Lyra asked, less hostile than before, relieved at being able to breathe without effort.

"Can't answer that directly," he replied. "More by feel than anything else—which is as good as any instrument in these circumstances, and I can't tell you how it works.''

"But Starbrite, you—"

He interrupted. "If you've got a better idea let's have it. Short, hard bursts toward the *Cetus* with risk of explosion are better than no bursts and us missing the ship.''

"*Our* missing the ship," Lyra replied softly, a grimace on her face. Starbrite shot her an angry look. She grinned.

"Grammatically, it's *our* missing the ship, not *us* missing the ship. One uses the possessive with a gerund."

Starbrite stared.

Lyra shot him an apologetic grin. "Sorry Quas, I got worried that we had bought it." She gave a gamin shrug of shoulders. "But now that we're perfectly safe I'm not so frightened."

Starbrite relaxed and suddenly felt like laughing, understanding her gallows humor. "We've got a fair chance. Panic, though, will be the first thing that will cut any chance to zero."

"Not to worry, Quas. I'm not so panicky now."

"I was talking to myself, Lyra. I'm scared too."

"*Cetus* here . . . you on viewscreen . . . course . . . closer."

The radio call from the *Cetus* was barely discernible, but it sounded like a celestial choir to Starbrite and Lyra.

"Acceleration time again," Starbrite murmured. He shook his head before Lyra could speak. "We've *got* to get closer. Soon. Otherwise we'll miss the *Cetus* entirely. I know we're about on the right course. But we've got to get clearer transmissions to fine-tune our trajectory."

It wasn't so bad the second time. Starbrite explained how to breathe during acceleration. And he gave the engines full power for only two and a half minutes before shutting them off. They waited for the explosion that didn't come, knowing that they were rapidly using up whatever reserve of luck they had.

This time transmission from the *Cetus* was steady, though faint.

"Vector targets three points off yaw, acceleration lag by five." Questin radioed. The trajectory data sounded like an archaic language to Lyra. Starbrite punched out a correction course in their navigation computer.

"Adrian will have a ship in the vicinity," Starbrite told Lyra. It wasn't guesswork, just that firm law of space always had a rescue ship around when another craft was in trouble. And Questin, undoubtedly, knew they were in trouble.

"One more time," Starbrite said, biting his underlip.

"Get ready to leave the mosquito. *Instantly*. Reattach gloves, and hold onto your helmet. We'll fasten them in the air lock, if need be."

Starbrite gave it one and a half minutes this time, engines howling as the enormous thrust shoved the pair deep in their chairs, the ship vibrating with its enormous effort. Then, he felt a tiny lurch, a small skip in thrust that only an experienced spacer would notice. Starbrite slammed off the engines, knowing with vivid certainty that they only had moments to escape the ship.

"Out. *Fast*," Starbrite yelled to Lyra, leaping toward the air lock. He grabbed her hand in mid-flight.

Starbrite yanked Lyra into the air lock and slammed on her helmet. As he was about to put on his own, he noticed that Lyra was poised to open the outside hatchway as soon as he signaled. They were one tug away from deep space.

A roar rushed through the mosquito. The craft leaped sideways. Starbrite saw the walls of the chamber twist sickeningly, then felt a stunning blow against his skull. Grayness enveloped him. And as it did, Starbrite knew that they had lost.

Dizzy . . . so dizzy. Black dizziness covering him. Floating in a gray-black sea to his death.

Adrian in a spacesuit.

Starbrite blinked, the blackness dimming again to gray. He knew he was alive because of a head that throbbed with each heartbeat. In front of him, not ten meters away, was Captain Jost Adrian. Floating, holding onto—

Starbrite's hand went to his chest and found the thin fiber lifecord used to link spacers together. It coiled neatly when not in use, its tip easily fastened to another suit by a self-sealing hook that could be peeled but not tugged loose.

He traced the faint outline of the cord. He saw Adrian again, in profile, his face clear through the globe of his helmet. At the other end of the lifeline, a few meters beyond Adrian, was another spacesuit. Lyra.

Starbrite blinked, then opened his eyes wide. Adrian

held the lifecord at its midpoint between him and Lyra. Starbrite flipped a switch on the chest of his spacesuit.

"Captain Adrian. Starbrite here." The words were a croak. But the comm set worked perfectly. Starbrite saw Adrian's head jerk around. They looked at each other across a few meters of vacuum, then Adrian gave a reassuring nod. His hands fumbled at the lifecord and he held it up for Starbrite to see. A knot was tied in the center, indicating that, somehow, the cord had been severed.

There couldn't be much more luck in reserve, Starbrite thought. Somehow, Lyra must have got his helmet on and attached the lifecord. Then the cord must have been cut by a flying piece of metal, and Adrian had arrived in time to tie it together. This was a rescue tale that deserved to be recounted in spacer bars.

He felt a nudge at his back and instinctively relaxed. With Adrian so close there had to be other crew members helping. He felt the tug of gentle acceleration, saw the lifecord tighten. They were being ferried by rocket drive units attached to spacesuits.

He got a good glimpse of Lyra's helmet. It was blackened from the explosion. Why his own helmet was still clear was one of those unpredictable freak events that occurred during an accident. Her legs and arms waved gently as she was tugged to the rescue ship. Alive, she was alive.

Starbrite felt another wave of dizziness sweep over him. He relaxed. No need to stay conscious now.

A miracle. And even as consciousness left, Starbrite knew that he had exhausted a decade's worth of luck and a lifetime's quota of miracles in the last hour or so.

Chapter Six

A small circle of light on a dossier titled: "*Space Academy Profile and Rating: Quas Starbrite.*"

The pages rustled as hands dipped into the pool of light and flipped rapidly through the report. At the third page, following a dozen paragraphs regarding Starbrite's academic record, the hands spread the papers over the surface of a small folding table. At the middle of one page was the subheading: "*Psychological Profile.*"

The circle of light narrowed and intensified as the reader pulled the lamp closer. Using one finger as a guide, he scanned the pages, then returned to a selected few paragraphs for more careful reading:

> While psychological tests offer a context profile of a given subject, personal evaluations of flight and academic instructors must be utilized to obtain a true portrait of the individual under study. The following comments are a virtually unanimous compendium of such personalized observations.
>
> 1. Captain Quas Starbrite reveals an extraordinary capacity for improvisation and lateral thinking while his linear appreciation of a situation remains above average. This capacity stems from a native intelligence coupled with a high degree of selective imagination.
>
> 2. The subject displays a high degree of adaptation to rapidly changing circumstances and situations,

with qualities of initiative and imagination seemingly unimpaired by new sets of parameters, even if suddenly imposed. This quality lends itself to highly flexible thought modes regarding many various tasks.

3. The subject indicates what in vernacular speech is termed an intense stubbornness. This factor leads him to trust his own self-perceived abilities even though they are countered either by group pressure or individual rank. This factor, however, is modulated by his ability to incorporate new information into his operative modalities. Nonetheless, this factor of inner-directiveness has led to some conflicts with authority and can be considered a fault in static circumstances. It is a highly desirable trait in dynamic or endurance situations.

4. The subject appears normally determined to achieve reasonably attainable goals. However, this determination is coupled with the aforementioned inner-directiveness. Combined, they lead to highly motivated and persistent behavior during times of crisis. This behavior remains highly coordinated during such stress periods.

NOTE: These conclusions and observations must be considered in conjunction with the standard psy-personality tests administered by psyche scanner and the Academy's psi-psyche department.

The reader scanned the last two paragraphs again and in a sudden fit of frustration slammed a fist on the papers.

A knock sounded. The reader started, then hurriedly stuffed the report into his tunic as the door opened.

''Landfall at Benera soon. We'd better get ready,'' the intruder said. The reader nodded and rose from the tiny cabin desk found in all the *Cetus*'s crew rooms.

Benera: One of the oldest settled planets in the Nether Quarter of the inhabited Galaxy. For almost forty years the colony had yielded to the ministrations of human beings, furnishing food, lodging, and livelihood. It was a planet that welcomed the overflow of human beings; that offered adventure and challenge to a race that desperately harbored a drive for territorial domination which, if frustrated, turned back on itself like a malignant disease. But a quality that when directed toward the galaxy brought the conquest of land to yield crops, of ores to yield products, and of nature to yield the secrets of the universe.

Space settlement: the only antidote human beings had found for the incessant strife that had reduced the entire planet Earth to a hulk. Humankind now had an enormous galaxy to war on, to absorb its ambitions.

Except that something had gone wrong.

Benera. The focus of several short-lived rebellions that were still poorly understood and the cause of great concern among New Earth's administrators. Realistic fear. For what was happening in the Nether Quadrant was a miniature replica of what had taken place on Earth. Humans killing humans, often in ingenious ways, over causes that still made no sense.

And Vac Orion was determined to find out why.

"Aggression has many varied causes. Some are external to a society. Some are internal, psychological in nature." Vac turned to Starbrite. They were in the observation deck, ready for the shuttle flight to Benera.

"Just how do you go about it? The—" Starbrite groped for words and gave up. "I mean, how do you look into people's minds to find out why anyone does anything?" He asked bitterly, remembering the smell of cigarettes, the scratches on a bent valve.

"We really can't look into people's minds. Not directly," Vac replied. "But we can learn a lot from listening. That's what my team and I are for. Backed up by an instrument or two."

"Sounds simple enough," Starbrite said dubiously.

"But it isn't. Not really. In fact it's rather complex," came the mellow voice of Lyra. Starbrite turned, wondering how long she had been listening to their conversation. He had a warm, familiar feeling toward her. It had happened before. People who had survived near catastrophe often had a common bond that was indescribable, a feeling of ease with one another that couldn't be explained.

"And you'll be helping, too?" Starbrite asked, genuinely puzzled.

"Lyra's here for other reasons," Vac answered. "She has her own research to do." He turned to his daughter. "Not that I wouldn't value her suggestions. And they'll come anyway. But this is vacation time for her."

"Hardly," Lyra said. "Not when we have the most unusual manifestation of gravitational flux so far seen. And with the instruments on Benera—"

Adrian interrupted. "Aboard. Let's get aboard. We'll make it in two shifts." Adrian turned to Vac. "The rest of your research team will be on the second shuttle," he roared, shepherding everyone toward their own shuttle ship. Even with the two craft lost—a shuttle ship and a rescue mosquito—the *Cetus* had five left.

Starbrite, moving along with the others, reminded himself how little he knew of Lyra's work. He had learned that she had become interested in some sort of atypical space phenomenon that was especially prominent in this quarter of the galaxy. Even that was from overhearing some brief asides between her and her father. Well, on Benera he'd have the time to find out more. Starbrite realized he was anticipating the landfall more than he had realized.

Starbrite's debriefing with Adrian and Questin had been terse. They had met a few hours after Starbrite regained consciousness, a med patch over his temple hiding the gash he'd received.

"Sabotage? Well that's a bloody relief." Adrian regarded Starbrite's surprise with unblinking eyes. "Accidents like that would mean I was slipping, that the crew was slack. Sabotage is a hard reason. Not a clean one, but explainable."

"Who?" Starbrite had asked coldly, remembering how close to death he and Lyra had come.

"Someone after you most likely," Adrian replied slowly. "Because of your slot on Vac Orion's research team maybe."

Starbrite shrugged, genuinely amazed. His position as military escort was innocuous. He said as much to Adrian.

"Maybe someone doesn't think so. A killer who'd

get you and an innocent lass like Lyra Orion. Indicates a heady determination, eh?''

Adrian glanced at Questin who, arms crossed, sat against a table edge in Adrian's spacious cabin. He seemed more thoughtful than worried, distant but unconcerned. ''Desperation more probably,'' he answered, not hesitating to amend Adrian's thoughts.

Adrian nodded appreciatively, as though Questin had settled some unspoken question. ''Half our crew is new since our last landfalls. Normal turnover these days. Any one of six or seven hands might be involved. Or more.''

''Or old crewmen, too. Men will do a lot for wealth. Sometimes even for an idea,'' Questin added.

''Check it. Who had opportunity. Who had motive,'' Adrian commanded and Questin, his face a stone mask, nodded.

Starbrite wasn't satisfied. ''The shuttle ship. How'd it blast from the *Cetus*? The mosquito was sabotaged. The other—''

Adrian, his eyes glittering stones, looked from Starbrite to Questin. It was then that Starbrite realized just how much of the star ship's daily routine was in the lieutenant's hands ''Deliberate? Accident?''

''Shuttle ship's lost. Can't say for sure without looking over the craft itself.'' Questin, Starbrite thought, was a master at short answers.

Adrian reflected for a moment and with a grunt came to a logical conclusion. ''We'll know if it was done deliberately when we find who fixed the mosquito. Concentrate there. Meanwhile we'll assume the shuttle ship's loss was an accident. No gain in doing otherwise.''

Questin's head barely moved in acknowledgment and the meeting had broken up. The *Cetus* was a civilian ship so there'd be no formal court of inquiry. Adrian and Questin would use more informal methods to probe the incident. Informal but probably no less effective.

Starbrite had then encoded a report to Croost, remembering wryly that he had once wondered what he might ever have to say. He had sent it off before their hype hop to Benera.

* * *

They boarded the shuttlecraft, the *Cetus* remaining in planetary orbit. In two hours they had landed at the planet's principal spaceport, near the bustling city of Arctara.

And, as always before, Starbrite was struck by the extraordinary incongruities that coexisted on the Galactic Federation's settled planets where the ultra modern existed beside the rustic and even primitive. The technical facilities of the spaceport were gleaming with advanced navigational, docking, and repair equipment. Yet the sturdy reception hall was made of wood, hewn from the planet's abundant supply of timber.

Plumbing on an outer planet could, at times, be balky, but radio or radar contact would be guaranteed by the latest primary and backup systems. Transportation to a planet was by hyperdrive. But on one planet, Starbrite remembered, residents moved along its city streets mainly on roller skates.

This mix of sophisticated and primitive never ceased to astonish Starbrite, and, in fact, he had come to enjoy the variety and surprises each new planet offered, the various ways settlers of different planets coped with similar problems. Each inhabited world rapidly took on its own—well, *taste*: a kind of attitude that made it unique.

Benera was no exception. Arctara, the capital city, had a semitropical climate and was built on a bay of the planet's only sea. It was slowly converting to "modern," having erected several duralloy factories. The city was already a bustling metropolis, yet it retained the charm of a small town. Even the docking crews waved happily at the new arrivals.

Yet here was where Vac Orion was to probe the origin of intense sedition. Another strange incongruity. Genuine hospitality on one hand and hatreds that led to unnecessary and wasteful wars on the other.

For Benera was a bountiful planet whose only dependence on New Earth was for supplies it couldn't yet manufacture—and there were a huge variety of such items it needed. Its only obligations were to impose Civil Law of the Galactic Federation's codes; and, of course, reciprocate the subsidized goods New Earth sent it with a preferred trade of some vital minerals and specialized manufactured goods—mostly communication chips—which the planet's work force had become extraordinarily skilled in making. There was talk of establishing facilities to make the sensitive hyperdrive coils, which would turn Benera into a wealthy planet indeed.

But, somewhere, something had gone wrong. With a forceful economy in its future, Benera had periodically revolted. And the clean streets of the city and the white sands of its shore had seen the red of blood.

As they were shuttled to their quarters in the heart of the city, Starbrite glanced at Vac Orion, wondering what he was thinking. Vac's eyes were narrow as he seemed to absorb the atmosphere of the streets, of its populace, of its very buildings. He was already at work.

And Lyra?

Starbrite swallowed. She had never looked so lovely. A bright yellow tunic-skirt set off her tan skin to perfection. Her face was animated and her eyes sparkled with pleasure. She appeared to enjoy the strange and unusual sights, sounds, and smells of another planet.

Later, at a reception in their hostel, the citizens of Arctara again displayed their generous hospitality. The civil authorities had been alerted to the overall purpose of Vac Orion's mission and took pains to assure him and his team of their cooperation, as though to underscore that while there had been discord it was deeply regretted.

After numerous final toasts with the heady Langue drink, made from a plant found only in a small part of Benera, the reception broke up. The dinner had been stupendous and especially appreciated after the bland diet spaceflight offered.

Starbrite had had little chance to talk with Lyra or Vac, even though seated at their table. They were separated by several officials of Benera, all of whom seemed intent on talking with Lyra, Vac, or Adrian. Especially, Starbrite thought, with Lyra.

Later that evening Starbrite and Lyra shared a quiet moment on the roof of the hostel. Arctara glistened below them, a medley of sparkling lights and alabaster buildings, now almost rose-colored from the last rays of Benera's setting sun. The bay stretched before them in a gleaming semicircle of yellow sand. The largest of the planet's three moons edged above the horizon, a silver-white disk slowly growing in circumference. A warm breeze caused a long gossamer scarf Lyra wore to flutter gently; the air brought a mixture of rich smells of the bay, sand, the city wafting over them.

For a long while Starbrite and Lyra Orion stood at the building's parapet, each absorbed with the beauty of the moment. Behind them the sky darkened and began to fill with pinpoints of glittering stars.

There were always stars, Starbrite thought. Like majestical signposts. It was the one thing space travel could count on. And there were always more stars to be seen—stars that perhaps had intelligent life surrounding them, stars that had never been visited. Always the stars, most of which seemed beyond the space of time, beyond man's capacity to travel, beyond the limits of hyperdrive.

"What's that Quas? Muttering to yourself is a bad sign, you know."

Starbrite glanced at Lyra. She had an impish grin on her face. "Just thinking." Starbrite stretched, a full, muscle-relaxing stretch and breathed in the clear, scented air of Benera. "I've always wondered what's out there. Beyond our reach."

"I feel confined too. As though somehow, well"—Lyra paused for words—"as though I was restricted to a small island that I haven't fully explored. But wanting to visit other islands.

"It's possible you know. We don't understand a fraction of the universe's secrets," Lyra added softly, not breaking the spell that they had both fallen under and were so much enjoying. Starbrite looked at her quizzically. "That's what I'm doing here on Benera. There are other ways to bypass time than hyperdrive. I'm convinced of that."

Lyra turned to the bay, the soft wind blowing her long hair gently. She shook her head to free her face from a few strands and closed her eyes, chin uplifted, feeling the warm breeze on her face.

"Gravity. That's the mystery that has to be unlocked. That's the secret I'll learn someday. Unlocking gravity," she said gently, her eyes still closed. Then opening her eyes, she looked at Starbrite and grinned. "Remember. I told you here. Gravity's the key."

Starbrite smiled back, knowing that she was perfectly serious, though her tone was light and teasing. He glanced at the moon, now a full orb that seemed to hang just above the horizon. The rooftop was now dark except for the faint silvery light the moon shed.

"How can gravity unlock gateways to other galaxies or even to the far quarters of our own?" he asked, segueing gently into another mood.

"Gravity warps time," Lyra answered, as though incanting a magical spell she had repeated a thousand times before. "A lot of gravity warps time more. Infinite gravity warps time around so that it stands still." She paused. "I could say all this with complicated formulas. I'm used to that. It sounds funny to turn formulas into words. Very unprofessional. I could be excommunicated from the priesthood of theoretical science for that," she half teased again.

"Makes sense to me. At least I understand more than I would from a formula." Lyra looked at Starbrite and in an intuitive flash he understood her self-mocking banter. She was afraid. Afraid that he'd ridicule an idea, a hope, that was precious to her.

She sensed his appreciation and flushed with cautious enthusiasm. "If we could enter infinite gravity, time would have no more meaning. One could go from point *A* to point *B* instantaneously. Of course there *are* a couple of problems," Lyra added lightly.

Starbrite knew some of the problems all right, but for the moment put them aside. "Black holes are one source of infinite gravity. As far as I understand anyway," he said.

Lyra nodded. "Black holes are the great gravity wells of the universe. Inside them light stands still. And," she added quietly, "*nothing* travels faster than light, and that includes time. If light is infinitely still, so is time." Lyra stared over the bay, as though contemplating the vastness of space left to visit.

"Black holes are the gateways to the entire universe. If we could use their infinite gravity, all galaxies would be within our grasp," she continued. "All the universe would be ours to explore. All those civilizations out there that are waiting to be discovered. All the—" She stopped suddenly and laughed. "I get carried away sometimes. A bit sentimental I suppose."

"Not sentimental. Rhapsodic. I often feel the same way," Starbrite said.

After a long, relaxed pause between them he asked, "You mentioned something about gravitational abnormalities in this galactic quarter. Is that part of the reason you came with your father?"

"Apart from the need for a short vacation it's the entire reason. Anything to do with gravitational abnormalities is fascinating to me. And this quarter has shown some real doozies."

"Such as?"

"Oh, gravitational flux, changes of intensity that are simply so enormous as to be unexplainable by conventional theory. Sooo"—she drew out the vowel in another captivating mannerism—"that means that something *unexplainable* is the reason. And I've come to find out what. Or try, anyway. Anything we can learn about gravity—and there's lots left to understand—might indicate a way of utilizing black holes as gateways to the universe."

Time, plenty of time Starbrite thought as a dozen questions flooded his mind. But one question burned like a desperate hope: how to tame a black hole? How could anyone enter such a seething maelstrom of compression and leave again?

Before Starbrite could speak, he heard the swing of the stairwell door. "Quas Starbrite? You're wanted below," came a rasping voice.

Starbrite turned, mentally cursing the interruption, trying to see who it was. A crewman or a Benerian native he supposed. Adrian wanted him, or Vac, or someone with a message from Commander Croost. He sighed.

"Be back in a minute," he said. "At the most, two."

Lyra nodded, smiled, and folded her arms against a slight chill in the air. She turned again to the bay, drinking in the myriad sparkling stars.

It was only later, much later, after it had all ended that Starbrite, in a moment of self-loathing at his own stupidity, remembered that Adrian hadn't known that he and Lyra were on the roof. Neither had Vac.

In fact no one had known they were there.

No one except a man with a rasping voice. And the thugs in his party.

They had known.

Chapter Seven

He had watched them carefully, so he knew when Quas Starbrite and Lyra Orion had left the reception and gone to the roof of the hostel. He squinted in thought. Now? Perhaps this was the best time of all.

His sharp eyes quickly scanned the room and finally picked out a native of Benera. He sauntered over and whispered a few words, and the man nodded, his jaw tightening. When he knew that haste wouldn't be noticed, he moved hurriedly to a communicator.

Several minutes after Starbrite and Lyra had stopped at the ledge, the head of a figure rose above the parapet of another building not fifteen meters away and a bit to the side of the hostel. The figure's face was a gleaming black, without nose, mouth, or ears. It scanned the opposite roof and focused on the pair with crystalline eyes that amplified even the barest light.

The figure reached down to a belt, unhooked a cup-shaped instrument, and fit it into a slot in the metal alloy that was his head. The conversation between Starbrite and Lyra sounded clear and sharp, even the low, soft murmurs they occasionally made.

For the most part, the figure thought, their communication was trite, banal, and irrelevant. It began to lose patience. Then a few words from the female suddenly caught his attention.

"... There are other ways to bypass time than

hyperdrive. I'm convinced of that," she had said. The figure waited, but the female looked toward the sky. The figure couldn't understand that—wasting so much time without good purpose.

Then more words of no real meaning. More wasted time and wasted effort. He grew impatient, then suddenly alert again.

"Black holes are one source of infinite gravity. As far as I can understand, anyway." That was the male speaking. Dangerous. The figure strained to comprehend every syllable they were now exchanging. The female spoke again.

". . . Black holes are the gateways to the entire universe." They were correct; the female must be stopped.

The figure was alert now to all their words, storing the conversation in his memory core. Then he stirred in sudden frustration. The woman had said something his translation cassette hadn't made clear.

". . . And this quarter has shown some real doozies." He replayed the phrase. "Dooo . . . ZZZZ . . . EEEEE . . . SSSS." The translation cartridge blanked out at this word. The figure made a mental note to uncover its significance later. Even a single phrase might prove invaluable when evaluating the knowledge these two enemies possessed.

Enough for now, though. Time to take them in. The figure beamed a radio signal to the opposite building. The willingly conquered, those aspiring to the Fellowship and believing promises of eternal life and power, were ready. The figure went to a lower flight of the building. From there, through an open window, he shinnied over a thin, incredibly strong line to the building opposite, to personally direct the capture.

That's the way a chief CryKon should act. To make certain no mistakes were committed.

Not now, not a month or so before the entire Galactic Federation would be swept into his KraKon's domain.

Starbrite headed toward the stairwell door, a triangular structure jutting up from the hostel's roof more annoyed at the interruption with each step. It was ajar, a strip of yellow light shining from the crack it made.

The faint light, coming from an inside wall panel, blanked out then shone again. The difference in the light's intensity was slight, but Starbrite, remembering the sabotage attempt during their flight, almost instinctively became wary.

He felt foolish for seeing shadows where none were likely to be. Foolish at being paranoid, at suspecting that a figure behind the door could be the cause of a faded light beam.

But he didn't feel so foolish that he didn't act on what he sensed.

Starbrite quickly pushed open the door a few centimeters, as though entering. Then, just as quickly and in rapid succession, he slammed the door closed, flung it wide open, and dashed into the stairwell.

A black hood fell over his head. A sharp, vicious blow landed on his skull. An arm circled around his neck and tightened.

But because of Starbrite's maneuver the timing was off. The hood didn't reach his neck, where a strong, circular steel spring bottom would have choked him to insensibility.

The blow glanced from the top of his head, rather than solidly connecting with its side.

And the person whose arm circled Starbrite's neck was off balance, leaning forward over Starbrite's slightly hunched back.

And these three factors made all the difference in Starbrite's survival.

At the Space Academy, part of the curriculum was a course in an ancient art called jujitsu, a style of unarmed self-defense, where scores of dirty tricks were honed into an art. Starbrite had enrolled in several advanced classes and ultimately became a member of the Academy's jujitsu sport team. He hadn't been the best on the team. But the team was about the best in the Galactic Federation. That meant that Starbrite was good. Very good.

Good enough not to have to *think* what to do next.

Starbrite bent his knees and pitched forward. His hips shifted to the right, placing his attacker's weight on his left. He reached over his left shoulder with both hands and grabbed his foe's hair, yanked down the man's head, heaved up on his left side while lowering his right, and snapped the attacker over his shoulder.

And, he held onto the hair.

The man screamed. At the same time Starbrite heard a fainter screech, one of terror as well as pain. Lyra!

And then Starbrite realized they—whoever *they* were—were as much interested in capturing or killing Lyra as himself. Perhaps even more so. Or entirely so. Or . . .

Starbrite heard steps running across the roof toward the stairwell. Almost inevitable, he realized. Whoever had set this up had underestimated their enemy, sending only one man for him. But they had sent several after Lyra. . . .

And then Starbrite realized that he was a mere accessory, Lyra was their prime target, and he felt a goading urge to meet them head-on. Gallant, but stupid.

With one ferocious knife-edged blow of his hand, Starbrite silenced the man lying in front of him and in one mighty heave threw his body down the first flight of stairs. The others were almost to the door as Starbrite hid behind the tiny triangle that the inward-opening door would form. Sweat beaded his forehead. He thought about Lyra and clenched his teeth at even a moment's pause—but a pause that would gain time and reduce odds. Maybe.

Just as Starbrite flattened himself against the wall, the door burst inward, slamming against the wall and stopping centimeters from his face.

"Where's Larents? Don't see Larents," someone said.

"Went below?" another person asked doubtfully. They ran down the first flight, found the body, and turned it over.

A howl of anger arose from the stairwell.

Starbrite waited until the first burst of rage was over. And while they frantically mulled over what to do next, Starbrite leaned over the stairwell and dropped his stylus several flights below. In the hollow, enclosed space, it created a loud, bounding rattle.

"Down there. The scum's down there. He's getting away." Whatever else they said was drowned out by the rumble of feet racing down the stairwell.

Starbrite exited back onto the roof. The entire scene had taken perhaps one minute, possibly two. And, Starbrite reasoned, he had another two or three minutes before those two thugs again appeared on the roof.

Time to reconnoiter, to get a quick perspective. He slipped silently over the rooftop, listening, looking, his senses at hair-trigger reaction level.

Scuffling. Murmurs. All from one corner of the rooftop. He eased toward that direction and peered around an abutment. Three figures, one especially indistinct and dressed in what appeared a shiny black tunic. He spotted the bright tunic dress Lyra wore, almost invisible through the welter of arms and legs surrounding her.

Again Starbrite resisted wading in, feet and fists flying. He felt drops of sweat roll down his cheek and, with a quick, irritable gesture, quickly wiped more beads from his brow, thinking hard—solving a problem rather than being defeated by it.

Starbrite didn't wade in.

Instead, he whistled. A shrill, cheery, attention-getting whistle, as though hailing someone across a street.

The figures froze, then looked in his direction. He whistled again, even louder this time. No one, Starbrite reasoned, would expect a foe to attract attention so willingly. Besides, they would think him already dead or captured. Enough men had been sent to accomplish that job.

He whistled again. "Must be Larents calling," came an especially loud whisper.

"Why doesn't he come over then?" someone asked.

"Go see. Now." Starbrite heard the sibilants clearly. One man walked over quickly.

He was felled by a blow of clasped hands that would have downed an ox.

Under ordinary circumstances Starbrite would have simply rushed the other two. He had little doubt that he would win a hand-to-hand fight. But there was Lyra. And he couldn't risk her being hurt by one while he fought the other. More confusion was called for, something to separate the pair, something to add to his odds even more.

This time he shouted, disguising his voice several times to make it appear that more than one person was in his party.

"Got that one. The other two are over there. Get 'em."

He moved his position. "Get ready to rush them, call in Trisam and Veerent. Circle around." A gruffer voice.

He charged. "Follow me. Two of you keep back for reserves." His own voice now.

In later years when Starbrite remembered what happened in the next few seconds it was always with a shiver, an icy fear at how innocent ignorance had almost turned him into a mangled jelly of bones and flesh.

The remaining thug looked up, startled. "Scam time, go," he shouted, started to run.

That's when the figure in black moved. His glistening arm flashed as he grabbed his cohort by the back of the neck, lifting him as easily as a paperweight. And then, as though flicking away a cigarelle, he tossed him over the roof.

Starbrite skidded to a halt meters from the figure, the hairs on his neck stiff. And it was then that he got his first good look at the third adversary.

Starbrite's lips curled involuntarily. His teeth gritted. The fingers of his hands stiffened, forming tense claws. Andrenaline poured into his body and—more than anything else—he wanted to flee from the sight. To run in panic, to bellow in fright and pound away from the black, faceless monster in front of him.

A shiny metal face without nose or mouth. A black glistening body, smooth and featureless. Articulated arms that had the force of a machine. And red, glistening coals for eyes. Eyes that didn't blink. Eyes that stared in his direction without movement, without passion.

It was someone—no, *something*—too powerful to attack with his own body. He had witnessed what *one* of those arms could do. The other still held a gagged, petrified Lyra by her waist, her eyes wide with terror.

With an insolent indifference to Starbrite the figure backed away, turned, and began to carry Lyra toward a stairwell at the other end of the roof.

That told Starbrite two things.

First, the *thing* wanted Lyra above anything else. It could have attacked Starbrite, but only by forfeiting the certainty of retaining Lyra. It had enough confidence to ignore Starbrite, to know that within the arc of its arms Starbrite was helpless.

Second, that the creature was a biped. And it was this second fact that Starbrite capitalized on.

Balance. A word drummed into his mind from constant training on the jujitsu mats. Lose balance and you lose the battle. And balance is precarious state for bipeds, easy to lose and hard to retain in a fight.

Starbrite's mind raced. His hands undid the corded belt around his waist, essentially a braided rope that was doubled and threaded through the loops at the top of his pants. Two tassels at the end completed the design. A formal belt for receptions now become a weapon.

Starbrite fashioned a lasso from the end of the belt. Then, still fighting an urge to run, he moved after the creature. Lyra, carried by her waist, hardly made a movement.

Starbrite was within three meters when the thing's incredibly sensitive hearing heard the slight crunch of his footstep. It paused and began to turn. Starbrite knew he had to move then or not at all.

Starbrite dodged behind the creature, dashed closer, threw the loop around the thing's neck, and moved quickly back. Then he heaved, every muscle cell in his body straining.

The metal hulk in front of him stumbled backward, still holding onto Lyra. Starbrite circled and heaved again. The thing staggered backward, then stumbled. It fell in a sitting position, both hands grappling for a grip on the belt. Lyra rolled free.

And Starbrite learned something else.

However strong the creature was, it was also incredibly light. Starbrite hauled back again, dragging the black body a few meters from Lyra. She was on all fours now, trying to rise. Then Starbrite began circling, the belt taut, the thing's body making strange rasping sounds as it slid across the roof's surface.

"Far exit. Get downstairs," he shouted. Lyra rose and stumbled toward the exit.

Starbrite spun even faster, gasping for breath as the thing's body began to skim above the roof's surface by centrifugal force.

Starbrite's tunic was soaking. His muscles ached and he gasped for breath. The belt, looped around his hands, bit into his flesh. Still he circled faster, staggering but somehow keeping his own precious balance. At each rotation he saw Lyra moving closer to the far exit

He heard a low-pitched but loud hum as the creature's arms flailed grasping at the rope. The hum rose to a pathetic, wailing drone as the thing rose high off the ground, higher than the protective ledge around the roof.

It was then that Starbrite loosened his hold on the belt. The creature hit the parapet, tumbled onto its top, and skidded off into space. The last glimpse Starbrite had of the biped was a dull black hand vainly clawing at the ledge's edge before disappearing.

Exhausted, Starbrite stumbled after Lyra. The two other attackers had descended the stairwell. It was sheer luck that they hadn't yet returned, luck that they were still searching for him somewhere below.

He felt an arm and jerked back, ready for a last defensive thrust of fist that would barely have dented a pillow.

"Lean on me, Quas. Door's opened downstairs." Lyra's voice had never sounded so welcome. Starbrite nodded, his lungs burning and they stumbled down the stairwell.

But he felt something else beside a tiredness that seemed like the weight of several gravities. And that something else was sheer, atavistic fear. Fear of the unknown— of a creature that superficially resembled a human being but resembled more closely the robot monsters in stories that parents still sometimes used to frighten children.

Chapter Eight

The Nether Quadrant's dissidents were as persistent but elusive as a staphylococcus infection. Most Benerian officials deplored the violence of the movement and were unquestionably allied with the ideals of the Galactic Federation, albeit sometimes irritated by particular directives. They were, by and large, embarrassed and angry at the attack on Lyra Orion and Quas Starbrite. And they listened with tolerance to Starbrite's description of an enormously strong biped topped with a featureless face. Starbrite might have been better believed if he had left out any mention of the creature that looked like an ancient suit of armor. Especially as no trace of it had been found.

The official version of the incident was sincere, but to Starbrite, inaccurate: an attempt by local hotheads to stir up bad feelings between representatives of New Earth and Benera. Somehow, he *felt* that the black biped's presence was connected to something more complicated than an insurgency. He couldn't have said why or how. But that didn't change his gut reaction.

These vague suspicions were reinforced a few days later by Vac Orion. They were in Vac's room at the hostel. He appeared preoccupied, his typical gregariousness replaced by a studied deliberation.

At first they rehashed the rooftop fight, Starbrite glad to again exorcise the loathing he felt every time he remembered that *thing*, trying to recall anything else that might be of use. "It seemed so—well, *human* in some ways," Starbrite said to Vac and Lyra. "It *reacted* as a person would. Anger, purpose. Yet, it wasn't, well—"

"It *wasn't* human," Lyra filled in. "Its hands were cold. All the time. They were hard, made of something stiff." She shuddered and folded her arms across her chest as though to protect herself from a bad memory.

Vac sighed. "We've had official apologies. The local Conduct Force assumed it was a radical wing of the dissident movement." He looked first at Lyra then at Starbrite. "I don't buy that somehow. But in any case—Vac gave a dour smile—"we should get off this planet soon."

"You're through already?" Lyra asked, surprised.

"Got enough data to suggest that whatever is at work is exogenous, an outside force. I need more data from another outpost planet to cross-reference what the team has learned here."

"Exogenous? Any examples?" Starbrite asked, still grasping for all the implications of Vac's statement.

"Once on a small planet called Thresty, we had instances of violent outbreaks. Something like instant mass hysteria. That turned out to be caused by a superabundance of cosmic rays. At certain times the planet's magnetic field dimmed a bit and let more very heavy cosmic rays through. That triggered off an alteration in blood chemistry, which in turn affected emotions. Entire groups became paranoid. Through social feedback, that paranoia became highly intense, leading to otherwise normal people joining highly destructive bands."

"Cosmic rays were the exogenous factor?" Starbrite asked.

"We had to study several factors. Social behavior as well as nerve reactions, which were influenced by blood chemistry."

"Nerve reactions?" Starbrite asked doubtfully. "Isn't that far afield from mass hysteria?"

Vac looked patiently at Starbrite, as though he had answered that question many times before. "Not if you think of the human brain as one giant nerve," he said. "At best you can consider the brain a conglomerate of nerves.

But its effective operation is more like *one* extraordinarily complex nerve, one influenced by many factors—perceptions, emotions, cosmic rays, wishes, memories, desires, wants.''

"And a lot more things," Lyra interrupted, "including patterns that make life more comfortable."

"A highly important factor," Vac added, nodding an acknowledgment to Lyra. "Combine the two—social patterns with biological operation of the brain and subsidiary nerves—and you can understand the reasons for most behavior."

"Including insurrection?" Starbrite asked.

"Sometimes it's simple. But if a given event is more complex, then we have to know. That's why I'm here. Social and political analyses haven't indicated enough reasons for what's happening. But I've just begun to hit on something no one has found yet."

Starbrite paused, realizing that Vac Orion was telling more than he had wanted. "What is that? The thing you've hit on?"

"Nothing definite, Quas. Just that the outside factor is—well—*directive*. It causes people on Benera to act in ways that aren't likely, or even possible, given their life patterns. There's a lot more stress here than you'd believe. Much of the lavish hospitality and gaiety we see really stems from a defense against something fearful. And I'd guess that even most Benerians don't even know what it is. But there's more fear here than reasonable. And I don't understand it," Vac concluded, his voice low and musing.

Even Lyra looked surprised, as though her father's mood was something new to her. But whatever troubled Vac Orion on a professional basis also troubled Starbrite on an intuitive level.

And somehow, he had no doubt that that strange, metal-clad figure was connected with his unease and Vac's suspicions.

Vac grimaced. "There's one other thing. I just *feel* as though something is wrong here. Highly unprofessional, but I'd be a fool to ignore what years of training have developed—my intuition."

Vac rose suddenly from his chair. "Now, I've got to look over a few more surveys. Talk to the team that I've brought along. And"—he smiled—"a bit of shopping. Prosaic as hell. But you can't buy chronometers better than they make on Benera. Or so they tell me."

Earlier, Vac had arranged with Adrian to lift off for Golline, a neighboring planet in this Galactic Quarter. He left the fine details of the voyage in Starbrite's hands. In principal, Vac would have handled most technical arrangements. But since the near catastrophe aboard the *Cetus*, Starbrite and Vac Orion had been drawn together through mutual concern for Lyra. Gradually they had come to respect each other's abilities. More importantly, they had come to enjoy each other's company. Starbrite by now was more than an escort. He had become a working part of a team that had been forged by near catastrophe.

And as Starbrite left with Lyra he knew with certainty that neither of them would escape danger simply by leaving Benera.

Every spaceport city in the Galactic Federation had a chandler section, an area full of shops catering to spacers and their spaceships. Benera was no exception, and soon Starbrite was wandering among shops brimming with supplies. Benera's chandler area was crowded, its streets narrow, its shops busy, and Starbrite loved it. The acrid smells of machinery, the whirring noises of motors being tested for such diverse items as chronometers or fuel pumps, and the smooth feel of polished metal were all things that Starbrite was familiar with and fond of. You could almost build a complete starship and outfit its crew from the odds and ends found here, Starbrite thought. He picked up an ancient, but still serviceable, space helmet, wondering who had used it, then replaced it next to a dozen others of equal vintage. He spotted several crew members from the *Cetus* wandering through the area, fingering goods from the deep bins, idly adding odds and ends to their personal equipment.

It took Starbrite a while to find the particular shops he wanted, those specializing in deep-space gear. And he was lucky. For the items he was searching for were on the rare side, certainly known by most spacers but still not as available as more typically used gear.

"Yeah, got two in back. Whatcha want them for, buddy?" the owner of the store, his face covered with stubble, grunted. "Haven't had a call for those things in years."

Starbrite fended his question with some vague explanation. The storekeeper moved to the rear of his shop and spent half an hour rummaging through what seemed like a warehouse full of boxes. "Got 'em. He returned lugging two cartons, neatly wrapped in durafoil.

Starbrite's next stop was a weapons shop; this time he wanted items that were readily available but harder to buy. Laseguns of all descriptions—high energy delivery as well as simple needle-beam penetration—lay side by side with knives and laserifles.

Starbrite would have preferred to remain totally anonymous here, but he had to present an ID authorizing purchase of weapons, even though he risked alerting whoever had Lyra and himself in their own sights. Slight though the chances were, Starbrite chafed as he flashed his Spaceforce commission card, watching for the owner's reaction. The shopkeeper barely glanced at Starbrite's ID, as though the identification procedure was a banal formality he'd prefer to forget.

Starbrite chose a small weapon with a powerful punch over a short range. The owner asked no questions, knowing from experience that whatever answer he got would most likely be a lie. Starbrite paid for the gun and left, holding the smaller package against the two larger ones.

He glanced at his chronometer and hurried on. He and Lyra had made an appointment for a drink at one of Benera's cafe's. Privacy was something Lyra was going to have to do without for the time being; she was being covered by the Conduct Forces of the city as well as two crewmen who Adrian had watching her every movement.

Even with several pairs of friendly eyes watching every one of his and Lyra's moves, Starbrite found himself looking forward to the next hour or two. Except for a brief conversation of generalities about her work, he knew little of the details she used to investigate the "gravitational anomaly" she had once referred to. And it wasn't education only that interested Starbrite. He enjoyed her enthusiasm, the pert way she held her head, and the way her eyes crinkled when she explained something.

He also appreciated her lack of condescension. Many scientists, he had found, deliberately became obscure, substituting masses of precise explanation when a simple sketch would have sufficed, as though they were reluctant to share secrets with those who had not been initiated into a secret priesthood.

Lyra wasn't like that, and he appreciated her frankness and ingenuity. That was a large reason he wanted to see her again; simply to enjoy the *flavor* of her company. But also, too, to learn more about her work.

A nagging feeling had started soon after the attack on the rooftop. And that feeling told him that somehow Lyra's scientific interests were related to the hostility directed against her. But what—or whom—did her theories threaten? And how?

Starbrite sighed in exasperation at not having the answers, and clutched his packages tighter. Well, there were many ways to find answers to those thumpers. One could tackle them from an intellectual stance, hoping that knowledge would furnish comprehension. Then there was a more direct and physical route—and his packages might just fill in some important details that way.

Starbrite was uncharacteristically late. They had agreed to meet at a spacer bar, one officers and higher-ranking crew members frequented. Starbrite had picked the spot after sighting it on a two-hour tour of the city the day before, thinking that here there was least likelihood of violence. Spacers were a tightly interwoven breed. And someone disturbing the peace of a spacer bar—especially if he or they weren't spacers—ran the risk of great physical damage. The bar had a rough-hewn atmosphere compared to the sleek pleasure establishments that he guessed Lyra was familiar with. But it was, without a doubt, safer.

And Starbrite was frank enough to admit to himself

that he felt more at home in quarters where the drinks were served in huge steins rather than slim vessels and where boisterous, heartfelt laughter and hearty backslaps were common. Space was not just an adventure, but a challenge. And a dangerous challenge, one faced by dedicated women and men who on their time off knew how to enjoy the pleasures life had to offer—or at least tried hard.

"Ya really know how to impress a lady, Quas," Lyra quipped as he joined her table. "Another few minutes and I'd 'a joined one of the other tables for an evening of raucous fun." Lyra, even though sitting, put a fist on her hip in mock imitation of a barmaid. "And what will the captain take for some refreshment?"

Starbrite almost laughed outright, captivated by Lyra's ability for clowning. "Make it a large bale. That'll quench the thirst of this spacer," he said. "Though there are other thirsts it'd take someone like you to extinguish." Almost immediately Starbrite cursed his lifelong inability to be subtle, especially with women. Not like a dozen other friends in his Spaceforce Academy class, who seemed to have the right phrase for almost any occasion.

He blushed, and Lyra smiled sadly. "Lots of time coming to talk of other things than revolutions, insurrections, attacks, gravitational anomalies, and research projects."

Starbrite turned, seething at his own gaucherie and shouted louder than necessary to a nearby waiter, "A bale, large-sized." A beverage made of half beer and half ale, he drank it almost exclusively.

He turned to Lyra, glad to have something to ask, something he'd been meaning to find out since they had landed on Benera.

"How are you going about looking into those gravitational anomalies, especially since you're so far from New Earth?"

"Being far from New Earth has nothing to do with it, Quas. The sector of the galaxy has had big variations in gravitational flux for, oh, some forty years now. In fact bigger than we've ever seen anywhere near New Earth.'

They paused as the waiter, annoyed at Starbrit

abruptness, slammed down a huge stein of bale. "There ya go laddie. Enjoy."

Starbrite nodded and gave a hearty and sincere thanks. The waiter, mollified, passed on with a platter of drinks to nearby tables.

Lyra sipped at her drink, put it down and continued. "We've got gravitational probes moving throughout this sector. Scientific spaceships, really, that detect gravity waves and their intensity and radio back the results on command. The first was established forty-five years ago by my grandmother. She was one of the first scientists to start to explore this sector." Starbrite detected a note of pride in Lyra's voice.

"Where is she now? Your grandmother."

Lyra shrugged. "No one knows. She and my grandfather were on a flight from Benera to another planet, Stilettse, when they disappeared about a five-day ion drive away. The spaceport got a garbled message, but my grandparents and the ship disappeared. They were my father's parents."

Starbrite was nonplused. He realized, suddenly, that Lyra in exploring this quarter of the Galaxy, was somehow tracing her family's roots.

"No idea of what might have happened to them?" Starbrite asked, though he himself could think of a dozen things. Meteor strike. Engine blowup. Life support system failure. Navigational error. And, on those old ships of fifty years ago, even on-board fires had killed many a crewperson.

Lyra's lips pursed together sadly. "The garbled message that Benera's spaceport got was too faint or confused to tell much. But we do know that there was some kind of emergency, something that happened fairly fast. The voices had a quality of—well, urgency. That came through even if their words didn't."

"And your father was safe?" Of course, idiot, Vac was safe. Otherwise, he wouldn't be here, Starbrite thought. But Lyra answered the real question he had asked.

"They had left him on Benera. I think they were ing on a second honeymoon, really. They were quite ng when they disappeared. Dad was brought up by friends of my grandfather's. And those friends were related to Commander Croost. That's how we came to know him so well. He visited a lot when Dad was younger. Then Dad married. I remember Commander Croost as a child.''

Starbrite sipped on his bale, wanting to know about Lyra's mother, but not wanting to reopen any old wounds that might exist. Lyra saved him the worry.

"Mom was killed on New Earth. While hiking. A silly accident. But she was the one who got me interested in gateways—a way of beating limitations of our hyperdrive coils.''

"She was a scientist, too?''

Lyra nodded. "She was always exploring. And science is another way to explore the universe. Now it's my turn. Gathering the information that's sent back from our gravity probes, trying to make sense of the raw data. Trying to figure out a reason for the large variances in gravitational flux.

"And you might be interested to learn that those huge variations in the intensity of gravity waves are a lot more pronounced in the last years, and even in the last months. Somehow, the incidence of this—well, phenomenon is increasing. And''—Lyra held up her hand with mock patience—''I don't know why. But the instruments on those probes must be going wild.''

It was an innocent fact that fixed Starbrite's attention. "Lots of those probes out there?'' he asked, nodding to the roof as if to indicate the cosmos at large.

"Several dozen. Some of them launched by my grandmother. Most of them still working. The engineering if fantastic. Really great instrumentation. They have an automatic monitor that senses anything out of the ordinary and activates a readout. Those probes can register data for decades, and then when something out of the ordinary happens, their information is automatically stored and sent to receiver posts on planets like Benera.''

"And they just register gravity waves?'' Starbrite asked.

Lyra shook her head. "No. Lots of other things cosmologists are interested in. Star spectrums, cosmic ray flux, solar winds, X-ray bursts. All the playthings scientists love to learn. All of those things are observed. Regular little laboratories speeding throughout space. Love 'em,'' Lyra added, smiling. "Sure beats going out and spending a lifetime doing it yourself."

Starbrite grinned in return, about to say something inconsequential when Adrian interrupted them like a charging bull breaking up a pleasant picnic. He had known Lyra's itinerary to the minute.

"There you both are," he roared. "Time to move bones. We're lifting off within the day."

Starbrite and Lyra looked at each other, a bit sadly, as though the personal ease they'd found between themselves was suspended for the duration.

Duration of what? Starbrite asked himself. He stood, holding his packages protectively, profoundly angry at whatever was siphoning off energies that might be well directed to more profitable things—like getting to know Lyra better.

As he followed Lyra and Adrian from the bar Starbrite was surprised to realize that he held a grudge, at something unknown and ephemeral.

Unknown and ephemeral at this moment.

But not by the end of this trip, he swore to himself, and smiled grimly.

Chapter Nine

Starbrite felt that *something* would happen during the trip to Golline. And there was plenty of evidence to fuel his suspicions. In fact, all Starbrite did was extrapolate from the difficulties they'd had in the past to know there were bound to be problems ahead. Lots of them.

Not that Adrian hadn't prepared. Starbrite guessed that underneath Adrian's boisterous geniality was a shrewd wariness that matched his own. Even before takeoff, he saw Questin hovering over Lyra, and he knew that Adrian's second in command was to be her personal bodyguard for the rest of the trip. And there were crew member backups that Questin could call on with a press of a button in his belt communicator.

Starbrite found that he was carefully watched by other of Adrian's officers. Friendly, courteous officers—but as alert as Questin. Adrian was as infuriated over the violence that had happened on his ship as Starbrite.

"It's a roaring pity when a captain can't trust each an' every of his spacers," Starbrite overheard Adrian say to Questin. "There's a space dog on this starship, and I'll find out who by the trip's end."

"Too much turnover, Jost. We haven't shipped with half the crew," Questin had retorted. "But there are some I can count on for their lives. They owe and are ready to pay, if need be."

Starbrite had been on the observation deck of the

Cetus and silently walked away, embarrassed at even accidentally overhearing a conversation between a ship's captain and his executive officer over internal problems.

By one day's drive the *Cetus* had settled into flight routine, the sharp clicks of the navigational computer audible in the Captain's deck, a welcome reminder that the brain of the *Cetus* was operating faithfully. Golline was an annoying thirty-day trip. Too close to utilize the hyperspace drive, which was hardly ever used for a trip less than two months of ion thrust, and then only in the worst of emergencies. Far enough to eat up a precious fifteen days acceleration, then another fifteen days decelerating.

A hint of trouble came the first day out, when Starbrite was on the observation deck with Questin. He was drawn toward the command post, the heart of the ship, as though to a magnet. It was a time, for Starbrite, of easy thinking and far wondering, the sight of glittering stars through the thick ports of an ever-present reminder of the majesty of the space they intruded on—human beings daring to voyage through such unknowns, to taste a glory that even gods would covet.

Questin was at the intercept scope, a lasebeam radar that swept the area around their starship. He had become more taciturn than ever, his shaven head glistening with a perpetual sheen. A rakish foulard was at his neck, and a loose-fitting tunic covered his chest. Tattoos decorated each arm, and his gold earring glistened in the dimmed lights.

Starbrite, off to one corner, ignored Questin, not wishing to taste the abrupt, even rude, manner he sometimes showed. Then he heard Questin give an annoyed click of his tongue.

The whir of the telereplay made Starbrite turn in curiosity. Whatever the intercept scope caught in its lasebeam was recorded electronically and could be later replayed.

Questin glanced at Starbrite. "Take a look, Captain? Needs a second eye maybe."

Starbrite nodded and went to the telereplay screen. Without a word, Questin ran through a portion of the intercept scope's data. Starbrite guessed that it was a section holding whatever the scope had picked up a few minutes before.

White snow flickered on the telescreen. More snow. Starbrite grew annoyed. Then a gray shadow on the lower left-hand side—a fleeting shadow that lasted less than a second. White snow filled the screen again. Starbrite turned to speak.

"Wait, Cap. Look close," Questin said, indifferent to Starbrite's pique at his abruptness.

Starbrite's annoyance disappeared as the shadow, darker this time, again covered the lower half of the picture, then faded quickly. Questin flipped off the telereplay.

"Any ideas?" he asked simply. Starbrite noted a puzzled tone in Questin's voice. The lower half of the replay screen represented the rear of their starship. Starbrite had an idea, but one too absurd to express. At least he would have thought it too absurd even a few days before. Still, he hedged, knowing that Questin was an unmatched expert in electronics. The man had proved that during their flight to Benera.

"What's the intercept's range?"

"One-day ion drive for sharp image. Still, it'll spot vague outlines of anything even two days behind. Or ahead."

"Vague image like that. . . . Maybe it's a shuttle heading toward Benera." Starbrite guessed wildly.

Questin's head gave a short jerk of disapproval. "Not with an image that large. Vague but large don't add up to distance. Adds up to something else." Questin sat back in his command chair, eyes squinting. The click of the drive computer sounded like a gunshot. Still Questin said nothing.

"Like what?" Starbrite asked testily. He'd passed all the exams he needed to become a captain in the Star Force, and he didn't need a civilian like Questin to give any more tests.

"Don't bristle so, Cap. You can still learn. 'Till ya die learning's available. To me, Cap, that image means someone's close on our ion beam. And with a fouler at full force. An' why'd they have that? Means trouble—more trouble than maybe we've had so far."

Questin shot Starbrite a sharp glance, his eyes bright and alert. "And I'm thinking that it means more trouble for you than for me, if recent days are an example."

Starbrite was astonished. It was the first time Questin even seemed aware of any problems, much less conscious of their implications. His respect for the man's perceptions grew to match his appreciation for his technical abilities.

"Fouler? What equipment's that?" he asked evenly. No need for formal apologies. He was sure that Questin knew what he was thinking.

"Fouler's an electronic gadget that soaks up our electronic probe. Fouls up the intercept radar. Can't tell how far something is behind. Usually can't even spot it. But the operator's inexperienced. Lets the power of his fouler vary too much. So we got a shadow image."

"Of what?"

Questin hunched his shoulders a millimeter. "Of who, more than likely," he answered slowly. "Some hotheads from Benera following us for no good reason of their own, maybe. Someone playing games, maybe. But whatever, it's not normal." Questin turned again to the intercept scope. Starbrite knew that he'd milk every bit of data from the instrument it was possible of delivering.

But it was unnecessary worry after all, Starbrite thought less than an hour later, at once relieved and chagrined by the simplicity of the explanation for that shadow image.

Adrian met him while moving down a corridor of the observation deck. "Something you might like to be in on," Adrian boomed, holding up an electronic module the size of a small box. "Our intercept radar's blinked out. Questin spotted it. It's a malfunction and we need an EVA to slip this new module in place of the old."

Common enough, thought Starbrite, even with the best of this era's equipment. A simple task, really. Just yank out the current module and shove in the new. Unscrewing a few bolts was all the mechanics necessary.

Starbrite nodded to Adrian, happy to break the normal routine with any kind of activity, especially something outside the *Cetus*. Floating above the ship, tied only by the thinnest of umbilical cords, the U-cord, *tasting* the freedom of deep space in all its purity. And Starbrite was an EVA expert even among professionals.

Strange, he thought, heading to his cabin to change into the skin-tight underclothes one wore with the spacesuit during EVA's. Some spacers actually hated leaving the ship, floating free and easy through space, like seamen who detested swimming. It was an attitude he could appreciate, but never quite understand.

As Starbrite changed, he spotted the packages he had bought on Benera. He turned to leave his cabin and then paused, undecided, his finger on the door's switch. He returned, undid the wrappings, and took out the packets. An old cliché ran through his mind: "Better safe than sorry." The saying, trite as it was, fit the circumstances. He undid the wrapping and slipped the packet into his space bag.

Having got this far, Starbrite hardly hesitated to include the needle-point lasegun. The gun, twice as long as a finger but hardly larger in diameter, fit nicely into one of the side pockets of the space bag. Grimacing at his own caution, which Starbrite knew often took the form of an obsession, he left the room to meet Adrian.

"Lertner'll be here soon," Adrian called cheerfully at Starbrite. "Takes to EVA's as a fish does to water." Starbrite wondered if Adrian was ever depressed. Or even deflated. "Be here sooner, 'cepting that he's had a bit of indigestion."

No go. Absolutely not, Starbrite thought to himself. Indigestion could be any one of a multitude of gastrointestinal disorders, all of which were messy and potentially disastrous when in a spacesuit.

"Best if I do it myself, Captain. I'd prefer it, in fact," Starbrite said. To think of an excursion from the starship spoiled by someone else's problems was annoying at best.

Adrian didn't like it. Solo EVA's weren't extraordinary, but it was typical to have a two-person team. He bounced the fist-sized replacement module in his open hand a few times. "Seeing it's a five-minute job, an' you've got lots of know-how, go ahead," he agreed, giving a reluctant grimace. You'll be linked to the ship by a U-cord, anyhow." Adrian tossed the module to Starbrite.

EVA: each one was a fresh, exhilarating event, a time of absolute freedom, of unlimited liberty for the senses. The troubles and anxieties that Starbrite faced seemed to pertain only to the hulk of the *Cetus*, a few meters away, rather than the vastness he now floated in. The *Cetus*'s ersatz gravity had no effect here on the outside of the hull, and using the jet pack attached to his spacesuit, Starbrite maneuvered expertly toward the struts holding the intercept radar's module.

He reached the struts with regret, knowing that now technical responsibilities overrode personal enjoyment. With the flexible gloved hand of the suit, he pulled himself around to get a view of the box.

He squinted, first in puzzlement then in alarm.

The module showed black streaks radiating from its side. At the epicenter of the streaks was a circular burn mark. The alloy of the module had been melted, destroyed by—

Starbrite shouted into his voice-activated communicator. "Sabotage. Module's shot with laseblast." He waited a moment for a reply, began to shout again, then realized what was missing: a hiss. The communicator gave off a faint hiss when operating. This one was dead.

Starbrite felt adrenaline pump into his veins and a hammer blow of fear in his stomach. Once again, a setup. In the air hatch, or before, a quick twist on his communicator antenna, one of a dozen ways to incapacitate his communicator.

Starbrite loosed his hold on the module strut and turned in space, getting a panoramic view of the *Cetus* and its surroundings before darting back to the air hatch. The jet pack hissed softly inside the spacesuit as bursts of gas spewed from its tiny nozzles, spinning Starbrite in a slow circle. The rear of the *Cetus*'s triangular shape edged into view.

What Starbrite saw nearly paralyzed his reactions and he was only barely able to squeeze the jet-pack controls and stop his spin. He hung there in space, gazing at the black figure less than thirty meters away, closing the gap at a rapid pace, propelled by its own jet pack. It was headed for Starbrite, its arms outstretched as though to envelop him in death's embrace.

Another two seconds, Starbrite told himself, and he'd be locked in the grip of those powerful hands and arms. It took him one full second to fight off panic and half as much time to bound from the *Cetus*'s hull.

An alloy hand missed his boot by a half a meter, and Starbrite had no doubt this was the . . . *thing* . . . he had encountered on the rooftop in Benera. Propelled by its own momentum, the black figure hurtled past Starbrite and grasped a strut, halting its flight with a sudden jerk.

Starbrite grabbed into his space bag and felt the lasegun. A blast from the weapon would at least incapacitate the thing till he could regain the air lock.

But he wanted it alive. Unharmed. Starbrite swallowed, and with that gulp, panic evaporated. It was time to switch roles, from being the hunted to becoming the hunter. A risky role, but one with a lot more rewards than constant flight.

Starbrite pulled from his space bag one of the items he'd bought on Benera. It looked something like a lasegun with a barrel the diameter of a grown man's wrist. On its top was a receptacle only slightly smaller than a child's head. He grasped the handle, careful not to squeeze the lever trigger that emerged from a slot on the thumb side of the handle.

Starbrite felt the sharp jerk of his mesh U-cord. Its slight elasticity caused him to rebound toward his enemy. The dark figure still held to the strut, knowing that Starbrite was helpless before its enormous strength. And it now began to stalk its prey—unhurried, unconcerned, and with an insolent ease that infuriated Starbrite.

Good. Overconfidence is the first step to failure, Starbrite mused. He feigned helplessness for a few moments, deliberately rolling head over head a few times, as though the rebounding from the U-cord had caught him unaware.

The black figure rose like an apparition from the strut it was holding, expertly maneuvering its jet pack. It seemed to hover as Starbrite tumbled, then moved forward gently, avoiding the mistake of overshooting its target. In the faint light given off by the distant sun of Benera, the figure seemed like a mephitic spirit of destruction, a dark force of hate and terror.

It looked at Starbrite with its glowing, crystal eyes and moved forward.

Starbrite saw the move and feigned confusion, groping wildly with his free arm as though to try and grasp his U-cord.

The CryKon idled forward, moving steadily toward its prey. It came to within five meters, watching with venom the convulsions of the human. Then a warm feeling of satisfaction filled its mind. This was one creature that would pay for the humiliation it had caused—and pay dearly.

The CryKon paused, ready to guide himself in any direction that the bit of organic matter he stalked might dart to. But suddenly the figure had stopped its confused convulsions, and was pointing something. And at that second, the CryKon knew it was in jeopardy and signaled his jet pack to blast forward in attack.

Starbrite squeezed the thumb trigger as the black figure made a sudden rush. He felt a slight recoil and knew that now his life depended on the mechanism—one rarely used in these days but highly prized in bygone eras.

It had been developed seventy years earlier as a rescue tool and the heart of the device was an extraordinarily strong steel-mesh net, the last meter of each thin strand being highly magnetized. The net spread out in flight, then enveloped its target. A thin metal cable connected the net's middle to the gun.

The net shot forward, opened, and struck the dark figure hurtling toward it. The net's end lashed around the CryKon and tightened, the magnetized tips gripping those of their nearest neighbor.

The dark figure, still speeding toward Starbrite, struggled wildly in its steel mesh cage. But even its cybernetic arms, hands, and legs were no match for the thin steel filaments, which tightened their hold at each move. Amazingly, one of the CryKon's flexed arms pushed hard enough against one small square of the net to snap a steel strand. Two more settled in place as he struggled.

Starbrite jetted back a few meters, tightening the line from the net to the net gun, the CryKon's body moving with spasmodic jerks inside the web inclosing it. Starbrite hauled himself toward the air lock a few meters at a time, taking up slack on the U-cord with one hand, holding onto the net line with the other. He reached the air lock and opened its hatch.

Half inside, Starbrite gasped for breath, partly from exertion, partly from sheer relief that his plan had worked. Then, wearily, he hauled in his catch hand over hand.

Close up, even in deep space where vision often plays queer tricks through a helmet, Starbrite could see that the thing wasn't from the world he knew.

He had found extraterrestrial life. Or rather, extraterrestrial life had found human beings.

And they weren't a friendly group at all.

Chapter Ten

"Mostly it's mechanical. But it's got an organic brain much like ours. Almost exactly so."

Vac Orion's hushed voice betrayed his awe at the dark figure lying on the cot in the softly lit compartment. Thumbnail-sized transducers peppered the head and body of the creature. Wires from each transducer led to a small machine that Vac now watched intently. The CryKon was motionless now, still firmly wrapped in the magnetic net.

We'll treat it gently, ask some questions now," Vac whispered, contributing to the solemn aura that filled the compartment while Lyra, Adrian, and Starbrite remained in the background.

"What are you called?" Vac asked quietly.

The CryKon stared at Vac Orion, each crystal eye glittering in the faint light. It seemed to Starbrite that the creature hesitated a moment, as though deciding a strategy. Finally a low, metallic hum of a voice answered. "CryKon is my title and my namesake. I come from a distant place. To meet your kind."

The small group huddled closer around the creature.

"Do you come for conquest or to meet us as friends?"

"As friends," hummed the reply.

Starbrite remembered how this very creature had held Lyra on the rooftop in Benera; how it had attacked him on the hull of the *Cetus*. *Vac isn't asking the most intelligent of questions,* Starbrite thought, bristling. *He's ignoring the facts.*

"What is your purpose for meeting us?" Vac asked.

Starbrite opened his mouth to speak. He felt Lyra's hand on his arm. He looked at her, anger plain on his face. She made the age-old sign for silence, one upright finger on her lips, and Starbrite swallowed his objections. From just in back of him he heard Adrian's steady, deep breathing. *He's probably furious, too,* Starbrite thought.

"To gain and exchange knowledge. To trade. To open horizons for all peoples," the metallic voice responded. Starbrite thought he heard a stronger note of confidence in the electronic modulations of the voice. He gritted his teeth.

"Do you come from this galaxy?" Vac asked.

Better, thought Starbrite. *That's a question I'd have asked right off.*

"From another corner of this galaxy. We are only a small band."

When will the real questions start? Starbrite exhaled heavily and felt a warning squeeze of Lyra's arm.

"Have you known about earthkind for more than fifty years?" Vac asked, his voice a model of unperturbed patience.

Then Starbrite noticed that Vac wasn't looking at the creature when it replied. Instead, he stared intently at three dials on the small box monitoring the transducers covering the figure's body. Starbrite saw the needles flicker, dart nervously to one side, then swing gently back and forth as the creature answered.

"For ten years we have known you. Until now we didn't think you were hostile to kinds other than your own." The mechanical voice had an almost soporific tone.

That space scum. Accusing US of being hostile. Starbrite's muscles tightened in fury. Lyra gave his arm another frantic squeeze. She stood on tiptoe and whispered into his ear."

"Be patient, Quas. You'll understand later." Starbrite calmed. At least Vac would be certain to follow up on that question of hostility.

He didn't.

"For how long do you intend to visit with us before returning to your homeland?"

"Shortly. After making first contact. I am the only scout. We have many single scouts traveling in different directions throughout the galaxy."

A nice answer, thought Starbrite. *A clever answer, even if it is a lie.*

"How many of earthkind do you know?" Vac asked.

Vac's voice held a tenseness that indicated to Starbrite the importance of this question. Funny way to phrase a query, he thought to himself.

The creature hesitated longer than before. Starbrite felt Adrian stir.

"Few. They said you were an enemy of any alien race. They said that before I could come in peace the enemies of alien races must be put in a safe place."

"And the names of four persons you know?" Vac Orion asked.

The creature hesitated, emitting a low staccato hum.

It never had a chance after that moment.

With a wild, animallike bellow, Adrian bulldozed through Lyra and Starbrite, his massive bulk casting Vac aside like a leaf. His giant hands grabbed the creature by its metallic neck. Adrian's face contorted with blood hatred and he yanked the creature from the cot roaring with uncontrollable rage.

"The names of some traitors, ya fiendish, lying scum. The names of those that are helpin' ya rape our planets."

Adrian's voice boomed through the small room as he lifted the creature and twirled it in a frenzied circle, its body knocking Vac's delicate instrument to the hard duralloy floor.

Starbrite and Vac grabbed at Adrian. It was like trying to subdue a maddened gorilla. In desperation Starbrite clenched his fist, raised the knuckle of his forefinger to a sharp point, and gave Adrian a rabbit shot in a nerve center at the side of his collarbone.

Adrian looked up in shock and in a second recovered

his composure. Abashed and contrite, he lowered the creature to the cot easily, though not with notable gentleness. He shook his head as the red flush receded from his face, rubbing his shoulder at the same time. "Lost control at the thought of this—machinery—causing the trouble it had. And trying to sabotage my ship in the bargain."

Vac bent to pick up his instrument. He shook it gently, a look of annoyance flashing over his face. "Enough till we get this repaired."

"There's a man who's interfered too much," Adrian apologized. "And that one's me myself. Sorry, Vac."

Starbrite, annoyed at Adrian's tantrum, tested the magnetic net. Firmly in place. The creature, no matter how strong, wasn't leaving.

For a brief second Starbrite stared at the CryKon. The malignant glow of the creature's eyes dimmed and Starbrite felt the hairs on his neck rise. A shiver rippled through him. He left the chamber slowly, consciously repressing an urge to run, as though he were a child suddenly frightened by one of hell's devils.

They were in Vac's cabin, a large room considering the tight space aboard any starship. Starbrite had never seen the man look so worried. Deep furrows ran across his forehead. His mouth was grim, his eyes frightened. He looked ten years older.

"That thing's lying. Practically everything it said was a lie," Vac exploded.

"How can you tell that, Vac?" Adrian asked.

Lyra filled in. "Dad's instrument gets a magnetic profile of the brain," she began as both Starbrite and Adrian looked at her intently. "Every electrical current has a magnetic component. The brain works with electrical currents—nerve impulses. That instrument picks up the magnetic component."

"What's the advantage of the magnetic component of the brain over just recording the electrical impulses directly?" Starbrite asked.

"The magnetic variations are highly localized. You can't spot from *where* an electrical signal is being given off, but you can with a magnetic signal. So Dad can pinpoint from *where* in the brain a given signal comes. In fact, down to a millimeter."

"An' that tells us what?" Adrian asked.

"That tells us if someone is lying or not, among a dozen other things," Vac said. "The brain has visual centers, a pleasure center, an emotive center. Different brain areas control different functions, sometimes in combination." Vac wiped at his face, then continued.

"For example, when you think abstractly, certain brain areas are more active than others, giving off a more intense magnetic field. If you're looking at a picture, a combination of yet other brain areas becomes more energetic. Lying takes energy. So certain areas of the brain have a different magnetic fluctuation when a lie is told than when truth is spoken."

Adrian objected. "That works for humans, maybe. But for a creature like that it wouldn't necessarily hold true."

Vac shook his head. "My first questions established its magnetic profile when telling the truth. It had no reason to lie about its name."

Starbrite began to understand the apparent absurdity of the question sequence.

"Obviously the thing is hostile; it tried to kidnap or kill Lyra. My second question was designed to solicit a lie; I got a magnetic profile of its brain when lying.

"Then I asked some pertinent questions," Vac continued. "Checked my lie-truth profiles from time to time with obvious questions, but more out of habit than necessity."

Vac turned to Adrian. "So you see, Jost, that creature's brain is close enough to ours for me to zero in on its veracity. An amazing coincidence, really."

"And it told us a pack of lies," Adrian said.

Vac shook his head. "More than that. By knowing when it lied, we can see what it *isn't*, what it *doesn't* want."

Starbrite's brow furrowed.

"For example, I know it doesn't come to meet us as

friends. Nor does it merely want to gain and exchange knowledge, to trade, or to open horizons.''

"What about where it came from, Dad?'' Lyra asked.

Vac paused. "I asked the thing if it came from this galaxy. The creature said it came from our own Milky Way.'' Vac paused again. "That was a huge lie. So, it doesn't come from *this* galaxy.''

Lyra reacted with an awestruck murmur, "A gateway. They've found a gateway.''

"Go on Vac. What else?'' Adrian asked in an ominous rumble that drowned out Lyra's words.

Vac sighed. "All the answers are on tape, in the instrument. I'll go over them later, but I doubt I'll find anything I don't already know.''

"Go on, Dad,'' Lyra urged. Obviously Vac didn't like what he was about to say.

"Probably a lot of these creatures exist, and they've known about us a lot longer than ten years. The thing isn't a lone scout, and it doesn't intend to return soon to wherever it came from.''

A long silence greeted this news. Starbrite asked, "And how many of our own kind are aiding it—them—whatever they are?''

"Whatever he said was a lie. He used up a lot of metabolic energy to create that statement. So I'd guess lots of humans are involved. In fact, I'm morally certain that the entire sedition movement can be traced one way or another to that creature and its cohorts.''

Vac slumped back in his chair and stared at Lyra, Starbrite, and Adrian in turn. "We've got our outside factor. But being concerned about sedition in the Nether Quadrant now is like''—he groped for words, his hand rising and then falling wearily in his lap—"worrying over a hangnail when you've just been shot full of a deadly bacillus.''

"When can we find out some solid facts about who's helping them? Starbrite asked.

"Once the instrument is repaired, which won't be hard. We have spare modules for anything that breaks. There are ways of asking questions that point more directly to what is going on. I'll wring real answers from the thing."

"Dad's good at it," Lyra said matter-of-factly. "It's been his field for years."

"An' now is none too soon for me," Adrian added as Vac shook his head.

"It'll be several hours, Jost. At least. Got to do some thinking before we start again, but I'll have hard facts an hour after we start. Guaranteed."

Adrian nodded, somber faced, and left.

Starbrite, exhausted from all his efforts, left too. It seemed like a year since he had dragged that dark figure into the air lock.

Starbrite headed for his bunk. A bit of sleep before the next interrogation. Five seconds after reaching his cot, Starbrite dozed off.

A dream of some sort—a ship jostling from side to side, out of control.

"Quas. Wake up, it's important." Lyra was shaking him violently, her eyes wide. It took a second for Starbrite to remember where he was. He sat up with a jerk, alert again.

"It's dead. That creature has a burn hole through whatever passed for a skull. Dad said its brain was simply baked."

Starbrite was on his feet and heading toward the creature's room in an instant, Lyra close behind. Vac, Adrian, and Questin crowded into the small space. "Its brains were scrambled by a laseblast," Vac said rising from his knees.

"Murder? On board the *Cetus*?" Adrian growled.

A long silence followed, and Starbrite's stomach knotted. Again. A traitor who could slip in and kill their most valuable source of information.

Adrian flushed and angry, turned to leave. Starbrite stepped back to let him out. In the narrow corridor outside the room Adrian paused.

"Roaring shame that," Adrian muttered again. He looked sympathetically at Starbrite. "An' it held the secret to other galaxies. Something you'll be sorely missing I expect, with your craving an' all.''

Starbrite nodded, as the *Cetus*'s captain turned and limped away. He and Lyra had talked about their aspirations for a gateway on a rooftop in Benera. Eons ago.

Then Starbrite's stomach churned and his scalp prickled. He slumped against a bulkhead, suddenly weak. His left hand began to twitch and his breath came in short gasps.

For suddenly Starbrite knew with absolute certainty who had nearly killed Lyra and himself, who had maneuvered the kidnap attempt on Benera, who had helped with his near capture outside the *Cetus*, and who had murdered the black cyborg.

Quas Starbrite also realized that he hadn't *wanted* to know before. For days he hadn't *wanted* to believe that Captain Jost Adrian was a coldblooded killer; that a man recognized for his courage and fortitude throughout the Federation could be a traitor. It was a self-deception that had cost dearly.

''A gateway, something that you'll be sorely missing,'' Adrian had said. *How had he known?* A gateway was a dream that Starbrite had never mentioned to another save Lyra and that statement inevitably linked Adrian and the black biped.

Adrian was still less than ten meters away when he stopped in mid-stride, as though suddenly aware of his mistake. He turned around slowly, a look of longing desperation in his eyes.

The two men stared at each other, and Adrian's huge face became a white granite block. He spoke:

''You'll never know what mutilation is like 'till it happens. To know how your dreams depend on mortal flesh. An' then to have an escape from the time bomb our body is, to be able to flee death.'' Adrian whispered the sentence in resonant tones that barely carried to Starbrite's ears; he wasn't sure if Adrian was talking to him or to himself.

Then Adrian turned and slowly walked away, his gait

more uneven than ever before, as if now his infirmity didn't matter.

Starbrite leaned back against a bulkhead, emotionally overwhelmed by the pity of it all; Adrian, a planetary legend whose perverted dreams had become a galactic liability. Starbrite's eyes squeezed shut, his jaw muscles spasmodically contracting. He heard the metallic snap of a bulkhead door's latch lever and as his eyes—narrow, calculating—snapped open he glimpsed Adrian disappearing into one of the many service corridors that paralleled the *Cetus*'s main hull. Before Starbrite moved more than a meter he heard the door being dogged from inside, sealing Adrian inside a network of channels as labyrinthine as the workings of his own mind.

The others exited from the room, startled by the feral look on Starbrite's face. In halting words Starbrite told them what he knew. And, strangely, it was Questin who seemed the least surprised and the most resigned.

"He knows everything about our defenses, our starship's power sources, supplies, tactics. He's got to be stopped," Questin said. Noting Starbrite's look, Questin added, "Choice, laddie. Sentiment or justice. Jost opted for one thing. Not going against him is the same as being with him."

Questin let that sink in and Starbrite guessed that the lieutenant had long suspected that Jost Adrian had been more than the image he projected.

"He'll try for that ship that's plagued our tail since Benera. The ship that shot out the module," Questin added with a certainty that Starbrite didn't doubt. "Best stop him now." Questin stared at Starbrite. No crew member could be trusted to capture or harm Adrian. Questin was needed inside the ship. That left. . . . Starbrite nodded, acknowledging the fact that Adrian was probably starting his own EVA at that instant.

And, outside the *Cetus* fifteen minutes later, Starbrite caught sight of Adrian, glittering in his silver spacesuit. The man was obviously preparing to jet off, waiting a bit longer till the second ship got closer, avoiding as much risk of freewheeling through space as possible.

Starbrite cut to the communications frequency used between starships and EVA personnel and heard a strange voice say, "Acceleration up, Adrian. Give it another few turns of the chronometer."

"Jetting off in one turn. They'll be out here soon," Adrian replied, bending his knees to clear the *Cetus*'s hull before jetting to meet his approaching rescue ship. His voice sounded weak, like a child pleading for aid, a guilty child.

Starbrite spoke. "Don't jet off, Jost. You can be of help to us. Your own kind. Nothing you've done can't be repaired by the help you still can give us."

Even as he spoke, Starbrite reached into his space bag and quickly retrieved the small but powerful lasegun, the one that shot a needle beam.

Adrian turned to face Starbrite. He reached down with one hand to his own space bag.

"Captain. We can use all you know. Don't waste it," Starbrite shouted into his mike. He raised his own lasegun without hurry. No need to rush. He was a crack shot even on moving targets.

"Blast you, Starbrite, and all others who'll take life from meeeeee. . . . ."

Adrian pointed a shiny metal object toward Starbrite.

Starbrite fired, and a filament of iridescent blue light streaked from his weapon.

The beam penetrated Adrian's spacesuit. The suit collapsed like a burst balloon, and the man shrieked once before he began his last convulsive movements, a prelude to death in a vacuum. Adrian, encased in his coffin, began to gently float away from the *Cetus*.

Starbrite had killed a living legend.

Chapter 11

KraKon stood staring at the city below him. In a thousand years he hadn't felt anywhere near the frustration he now experienced. Never before had his plans gone so far awry.

In a vicious spurt of anger, KraKon stamped the floor. The room shuddered.

His CryKon *killed*. Not that something as worthless as that pseudo-cyborg meant anything. There were a multitude to fill its place. No, it wasn't that. But a creature—an *alien* creature—actually *capturing* one of his closest servants. The indignity of it drove KraKon into an even deeper fury.

He reminded himself of the true acolytes he had made in that world and the rumble in his voice box quieted. There had been fewer than anticipated from previous experience. Even the elders of that accursed race hadn't been as susceptible to the promise of eternal life as to temporal power, an anomaly he was hard put to comprehend.

Fools! At first he had been faintly amused at their refusal to betray their own race for immortality but willing to do so for power. Amusement had quickly turned to vengeful ire as he came to realize that some of the leaders accepted his offer of help because they believed they could then shed KraKon's hold. Those idiots on Benera, for example. They welcomed the KraKon's emissaries as allies in breaking what they considered some sort of minor tyranny by the Galactic Federation. But it was revolt that interested them, not the Fellowship.

KraKon had helped them with their puny efforts more to create confusion than with any real expectation that such a paltry band could succeed. It was confusion that later would be put to his advantage. Except—

KraKon thought of the few realists he had converted, those thirsting for immortality. The human called Adrian had willingly joined KraKon's Fellowship. The floor shuddered under another blow from his foot.

Adrian, one of the most valuable contacts made among those fools. *Dead.* One of his most trustworthy and appreciative servants killed just minutes from safety. Murdered by another of those worms, someone with a name that was absurd even by humankind's low standards: Starbrite.

His plans had been set back by months. All Adrian knew had been lost and much of his knowledge had not yet been communicated. Yet, there was one more pristine source, perhaps one even more valuable.

A caution replaced KraKon's ire.

He had suspected resistance as soon as that accursed woman had leaped at him. This race had a controlled aggression unlike any other he had conquered. Not that they could succeed against his Dark Hordes, his mass of armies enlisted from a dozen alien races. They would, ultimately, be smashed. And—

KraKon's mind filled with anticipation. His voice box purred. The toll he would exact from those beings who dared to question his supremacy! The price he would demand for the indignities they had caused!

Already he savored conquest.

Obviously his CryKon had been an utter fool. To be captured and *questioned*. The shame of it, the dishonor to his own eminence, brought KraKon to the verge of another rage. But he could reverse this annoying trend. He would *personally* direct the subjugation of the Galactic Federation and inflict punishments on that miserable race.

The idea of harsh retribution put KraKon in a mellower mood, one in which he suddenly wished to taste the coming pleasures. He signaled an attending CryKon.

"I want to see the female. The one captured forty of her years ago. Now."

The CryKon hummed an ultrasonic salute and left hurriedly. Anything that might appease KraKon's month-long fury would be welcome. It was decidedly dangerous to be around when he was in such a fuming temper.

KraKon relished the coming sight.

That woman and her mate had been the first of their race to be initiated into the Fellowship, forced though it was.

The man served as first guinea pig. KraKon's cyborg conversion specialists had torn that piece of flesh apart cell by cell, analyzing enzymes, hormones, fluids, and tissues. And to repay the woman's insulting attack he had made sure she was in a cell close to the dissecting chambers. The man's screams had nicely tortured the female. But that was nothing to what followed.

Given the skill and vast experience of his conversion teams, one of those humans had been enough to profile the race's biological parameters. The man had served as the expendable source of this information.

The woman became the first prototype.

Over a period of five years she had become a full cyborg—or nearly so. As alloy arms, chest, torso, and legs replaced her natural ones, the reports of her moans and shrieks were enough to make the KraKon gloat with satisfaction as he remembered how that single puny woman had attacked him, tried to hurt him.

A CryKon had once asked if she should be given analgesics during the more trying times of her conversion, especially as nerves in the artificial limbs and organs regenerated.

It was then that KraKon had hit on the most appropriate of punishments. He ordered the woman's cell lined with mirrors so she could not avoid seeing what she was rapidly becoming. But KraKon had his most exquisite revenge when they went to work on her face. Flesh yielded to alloy, features were eliminated and replaced with mechanical and electronic equivalents, until her face was a featureless black oval with glowing crystal eyes.

Then KraKon, during a moment when he gazed out over his crystal city, thought of yet another touch. It was a time when a memory of desolation deep within him attempted to surge outward, a phantom he exorcised by thinking of his captive.

He had called in a CryKon, the one assigned to cybortize this race.

"Her skull. Has the flesh been removed yet or does some remain?" he had asked.

"We have left that for last, as usual, master," came the reply. "The internal alloy—tissue grafts have taken nicely, the regrowth perfect. Our teams have been highly efficient," the CryKon had added, a bit nervous about the attention KraKon was paying to this creature. He thought of the vengeance KraKon displayed toward inefficiency or even to simple mistakes.

"Then save half her scalp. Leave it and the strings attached to it."

"Yes, revered KraKon," the CryKon had answered, amazed at the order but certainly not about to question it.

KraKon, put in good humor at this thought, felt an urge to share his satisfaction with his CryKon. "That female is an involuntary member of the Fellowship. And, with those strands she calls hair left, she will always have a reminder of what she was like." KraKon's voice box hummed in amusement. "And her knowing that and seeing herself constantly in her mirrored room, will bring about adequate compensation for her insults to me."

The CryKon had left, more careful than ever to avoid mistakes and attract the wrath of his KraKon, the most powerful cyborg in the universe.

Now, this same CryKon issued orders to a few of the Dark Horde who roamed the labyrinthine quarters. The woman was brought to him and he ushered her to the KraKon's chambers.

As when he first met her, KraKon faced his city as she was brought in. He heard his CryKon's voice announce their presence. His anticipation grew and he delayed for a brief moment the time he'd whirl and see an image and likeness of *himself*. No more would that creature resemble someone else. No longer was she there to coax out dreaded feelings of desolation and loss.

The KraKon whirled and stared at the cyborg he had created. He hadn't seen it for thirty years of her time, and she—it—was more complete than ever.

Glittering black torso. Legs and arms of sturdy alloy. And the head was like those he knew here—steadfast crystal eyes, a voice box rather than a mouth.

But yet there was that reminder. The one he had cleverly thought of. KraKon hummed in satisfaction.

On the woman's head a scrap of scalp, still nourished by remaining biological blood vessels, had grown smoothly over the alloy skull. This patch of flesh covered only the left side. And on it grew hair. Hair that fell to the shoulders, still silky and straight, but steel gray from age and worry.

Those strands of hair were the last physical vestiges of the woman's humanity.

KraKon had one last indignity to heap upon this creature. A new thought, but one that fit his mood. She, the first of this race to oppose him, would participate in the downfall of all others.

This creature would personally witness how he conquered alien civilizations. And she would be a participant in her people's bondage. Willingly or not.

In her forty-year captivity, the woman had learned the language spoken by KraKon.

"Your race and their planets are near to becoming members of the glorious Fellowship, kindred of free spirits," KraKon said.

"Kindred of devils," the woman shot back.

A flash of anger traversed KraKon's brain. The mirrors, the constant witness to her conversion, the last vestiges of her hair, the constant barrages by CryKons hadn't daunted her insolence.

This *thing*. All she delivered was opposition, without a thought to what benefits compromise might bring.

And with that shock came the first thin finger of fear. This race clearly wasn't like any others. They were far more stubborn than anticipated.

All the more reason for directing their conquest personally.

"You will witness your compatriots' disaster. And," he taunted, "your race will change just as you have. To become, slowly, initiates into a Fellowship of eternity."

"A year with my own kind I value more than an eternity with you, madman," the woman answered.

Rage again inflamed him. The interview wasn't offering him the pleasure he had anticipated. Instead of a meek and pleading subject, he faced insults and insolence.

"You will go to Earth with our spearhead outpost, where our Dark Horde members of a dozen alien races even now assemble."

KraKon's voice shrilled even higher.

"And from that cursed planet will spring the invasion that will reap a harvest of blood. Those that are left will be forever the menial servants that will be assigned even to the lowest order of Dark Horde warriors."

KraKon paused for words, collecting his thoughts. The woman—the cyborg *he* had created—seemed unafraid, as though it didn't care about its fate any longer.

"Your dreams are your doom," she retorted.

KraKon shrieked. The door to his quarters burst open as a CryKon and three Dark Horde warriors rushed in.

KraKon slowly lifted an arm, an alloy finger pointing. The arm arched up till the finger grew even with the cyborg, its long gray hair hanging motionless.

"Take this offal to Earth. Use her to frighten the troglodytes into submission. Later she will go on exhibition throughout the organization they call the Galactic Federation. After her limbs have been removed."

The CryKon nodded and two Dark Horde warriors dragged the cyborg from the room, her hair wafting over her shoulders.

The CryKon was about to leave when a short burst of ultrasound stopped it in its tracks.

"Yes venerable KraKon," it said nervously.

"I am taking personal charge of our conquest. Make arrangements for me to be aboard a warship passing through the gateway. I will quarter on the planet they call Earth.

Notify our chief agent on New Earth of this plan through established channels.''

The CryKon knew better than to offer a single comment on such an unprecedented order. In two thousand years the KraKon had never before taken interest in personally leading the Dark Hordes into battle.

The CryKon left. There would be countless battles to relieve the current monotony and the carnage should be enormous, another bonus. The conquest would be as ruthless as any before, with each subject planet at the mercy of a Fellowship governor. And he, as a head CryKon, would almost certainly gain a governership.

A blood lust filled what was left of the CryKon's organic body. Ah, yes. The coming months were something to anticipate.

Chapter Twelve

A trim wrinkled man surrounded by green plants.

He was still trim. He was still surrounded by green plants. And he was more wrinkled than ever before. Ivor Croost, Supreme Commander of the Galactic Federation's Spaceforce. In fact he looked like a ghost of his former self, Starbrite thought. His complexion was a grayish white, and his expression less vibrant than Starbrite had ever seen.

They all sat in silence—Starbrite, Lyra, and Vac. One large chair remained empty—the one Jost Adrian had sat in so many cons ago.

Starbrite saw a new plant on Croost's desk and studied it for a moment, not wanting to look at the empty space. The plant had pronounced ridges on its waxlike leaves and where leaf joined stem grew a multitude of small violet berries.

"The Lacadia plant. Recently got a specimen from one of our colonized planets," Croost said evenly, noting Starbrite's glance. Starbrite wished they could discuss the Lacadia plant, to learn everything about it. To be able to talk about *anything* but what was foremost on their minds.

Lyra moved her lips as though to speak, thought better of it, and lapsed into silence. Vac's ruddy face showed weary resignation. He, too, stared at the extraordinary plant.

"It's unpleasant, I know." Croost began broaching

the topic they all wanted to avoid. "But for our record"
—he leaned forward to hit the start button of his office's
recorder—"we have to have an official summary. It can
be transcribed and signed later." He turned toward Vac.
"Your results?"

Vac grimaced, his eyebrows rising at the word *results*. "Exogenous factors are responsible for the spate of
insurrectionist activity. These factors appear to consist of
an alien and hostile life form. I doubt that every human
supporting the insurrection is an ally of these aliens, but
they form a theoretical and active nucleus around which
insurrection crystallizes."

Vac stopped. Croost gave him an expectant glance.

"What I've said is almost my complete report. I have
supporting data from interviews my crew obtained from
observations and other sources. But Quas here," Vac nodded toward Starbrite, "had the most experience with this
alien life form."

"And not a very pleasant experience at that," Croost
added, turning his swivel chair to face Starbrite. "Captain,
will you add what you know about our so-called antagonists?"

"They're not 'so-called' antagonists," Starbrite corrected firmly. "They're actual, clear, and present dangers
to our Federation."

Croost nodded agreement. "We'll note for the record
that there's no doubt of their hostility. Could you elaborate
on what they're like? We'll have a more technical debriefing later on."

Starbrite gathered his thoughts. "The alien life form
appears incredibly strong for its size. And incredibly light.
This indicates a high technological achievement in artificial muscular development—"

Croost interrupted. "No conclusions, please, Captain.
Just facts about the creatures."

Starbrite reddened, murmured an apology, and continued. "They seem—they *are*," he corrected, "intelligent.
They appear motivated and directed in a hostile but clever
manner. Their limbs are articulated like ours." Starbrite
looked at Lyra and Vac. "Quite a coincidence I'd say."

"We haven't all that much time Captain," Croost said gently.

"Well, there's no doubt about their intelligence. They can plan and adapt to situations. The fight outside the *Cetus* proved that," Starbrite added, looking at Croost's expressionless face. "On board the *Cetus*, after we captured the alien, it responded in speech, in an intelligent manner. Vac can tell you more about that than I."

"Before then. Did you ever see more than one of these aliens?" Croost asked.

Starbrite pursed his lips. "Can't say for sure, Commander. The alien on the rooftop might have been the same one that I saw outside the *Cetus*. Probably it was."

"So in all likelihood, there was only one example of this robotlike creature you've described."

"That's probable, Commander. But what it told us, or rather *didn't* tell us when Vac interrogated it, is vitally important. It indicated that there are a lot more of its kind around."

Croost turned to Vac Orion. "About how many would you say? Ten? Twenty? One hundred?"

"Anything over ten would be a guess. Up to thousands. We only can tell from the tape that the thing lied."

"More importantly, Commander, the thing lied about where it came from. That's *vital*," Starbrite interrupted. "No matter how few or how many are now in our galaxy, there'll be plenty more if we don't find out where they come from."

"You're still missing a key point, Quas. Where they come from *is* important. But not as important as something else." Lyra looked up slowly. For the last week she had seemed particularly withdrawn, almost morose. They had talked in clipped sentences, exchanging information when necessary, then parted.

"And what is more important than uncovering the origin of these thugs?" Croost asked evenly.

Lyra's fingers ran through her long hair. "We know where they come from," she said calmly. The others stirred in amazement. Croost opened his mouth to speak, then closed it just as quickly. Lyra turned to Starbrite and saw his puzzled frown.

"Oh, not *exactly* where they come from. But that's unimportant." Starbrite's frown deepened. Everyone else looked as puzzled.

"Lyra, could you come to the point a bit faster?" Commander Croost coaxed.

Lyra nodded.

"We know they aren't from our galaxy. That came out as an obverse of the thing's statement about its origins. If it comes from another galaxy it has to be using a method of hyperdrive we haven't yet conceived of. That's the 'how' of it all." Lyra paused. "If we can't come up with a drive system equal to theirs, we'll always be at their mercy. But what they've given us is incalculable."

"*Given* us!" Commander Croost's voice rasped. "You sound positively grateful. For what?"

"They've given us the knowledge that travel between galaxies *is* possible. That a hyperdrive method far superior to our own *is* possible. We know, now, that something far better than our 5000-light-year hops is possible. That's a big discovery."

"Leaving only the problem of finding out how they do it." Vac added wryly.

"But settling the question of its possibility," Lyra retorted. "And what's more, I have an inkling of how it's done."

A moment of stunned silence greeted this comment. Croost's face went from a gray color to a pasty white. Starbrite's mouth opened in astonishment. Vac simply stared.

"If so you've stumbled onto a vastly important secret," Croost whispered.

Lyra glanced around with total self-confidence then continued. "You all know I was looking into the large gravitational flux that appeared in the Nether Quadrant. Well, over the last few days I analyzed the data our probes recorded. The data shows the locus of the magnetic flux at navigational points N1426-T3Q56-150008.9." She paused, as though those points should convey some meaning to the others. Seeing no reaction she continued.

"That location corresponds to an isolated black hole, one discovered by my grandmother shortly before she disappeared more than forty years ago."

Starbrite began to get a glimmer of Lyra's reasoning, and he grimaced at its implausibility. Commander Croost's eyes narrowed in bewilderment. Vac bit on his lower lip, knowing what his daughter was about to say, but not really believing it himself.

"They're using that black hole as a wormhole to our universe. They've found out—"

"*Wormhole*?" Croost interrupted, his jaw setting into a firm, unbelieving line.

"Physicists call it a wormhole. A passage or a gateway from one universe to another through a black hole."

"And just how is this done?" Croost asked.

Lyra shrugged. "I don't know exactly—nor does anyone, other than those creatures. But the huge gravitational flux indicates strong disturbances in the region. And calculations show that starships passing through a black hole could cause those fluctuations."

"But *how*? How can you use a black hole? Everything would be crushed."

Lyra shrugged again. "I don't know. But we are sure that within a black hole there *is* no time and space. Massive theoretical studies show the possibility of a wormhole—a gateway—from one universe to another by using those areas. Travel between galaxies would be instantaneous."

Lyra sat back, her features taut from strain. "I think that's how they're doing it. I can't *prove* it. But I'm certain they've found a way to tap a black hole as an intergalactic gateway."

"Interesting theory," Croost said doubtfully. "I wish we could prove it."

Lyra sat up suddenly, her face showing intense determination. "We *have* to find out. We're at their mercy if we can't find out how they get to our galaxy. And"—she paused dramatically—"if we can show that they *are* using black holes to get here we might be able to plug their entry."

"Stop them? Stop their traveling? How?" Vac asked,

incredulity plain in his voice. Starbrite shook his head, trying to absorb it all. The tips of Croost's white mustache twitched spasmodically.

Lyra leaned forward in her chair. "That's why *where* they came from isn't as important as *how* they got here. Plugging their time tunnel is effective no matter where their galaxy is. If we can learn even more, we might be able to get to their home, to travel through the universe ourselves."

"For the moment, however, let's concentrate on our current danger before we voyage throughout the universe," Croost said dryly. "How much more would you have to know to be able to plug up a black hole gateway?"

Lyra shrugged. "I don't know. *No one* could. But there's one place that I think holds a lot of answers. Answers discovered a thousand years ago, which are lying in an ancient computer."

"And where might that be?" Croost asked, half knowing the answer.

"It's on Earth," she said sadly.

It was Lyra's day for dropping bombshells, Starbrite thought as he swallowed hard, admiring her courage for broaching a topic that was a mighty taboo.

Earth: a paradise killed by ineptitude: green, healthy planet that humankind sickened by poisoning its atmosphere with nuclear and industrial wastes.

Ultimately there came a decision to abandon the planet, beginning a hegira to a replica of Earth, scouted by the nucleus of the Galactic Federation's now extant Spaceforce. An entire people migrated across a galaxy, vowing to avoid the stupidity of their forebears. It took one hundred years before the Great Migration ended. At its termination only a few, relatively speaking, persons remained on Earth. From accounts of survey ships, which periodically visited the planet, the descendants of these survivors had reverted to a primitive and rudimentary state: troglodytes, quietly protected by the Galactic Federation out of ancestral guilt.

The shame from having desecrated a habitable planet lived in the migrant's consciousness until talk of Earth or even referring to it became a social taboo.

On leaving the planet—like miners restoring a mountain from which they're taken ore—humankind had left it as orderly as possible. Buildings were restored, cities swept, museums that couldn't be transported refurbished, and technical and medical centers left in perfect repair. It was as though someday, sometime, humankind would return.

Commander Croost showed the least emotion at Lyra's comment. "Why on Earth? What could have been left on that unfortunate planet that has any use to us?"

"Data," came the quick, sharp reply. "After we left Earth," Lyra explained, "careful records of what was left were brought along. And, among these I found references to research on black holes done in the 1980s and 1990s. It was on a giant computer complex in one of their cities. It should still be there. And that data might hold the key to what we're after—plugging the gateway of the aliens now threatening us."

"What could they have known that our own scientists haven't discovered?" Starbrite asked.

Lyra's eyes flashed. "You've listened to the fugues by Johann Sebastian Bach, haven't you?" she asked, while answering one question with another.

Puzzled, Starbrite nodded his head.

"Well, those fugues were written on Earth thousands of years ago. The music he wrote is still wondrous."

Starbrite started to offer a logical objection that art and science are different. Lyra waved down his comment in an impatient gesture.

"So, too, there was a lot of amazing research that went on. Some of the finest speculative minds of science lived during that epoch. Albert Einstein was alive a few centuries later, in case you don't remember," she said, "and the Einstein Parallax, which was named for him, led directly to hyperdrive.

After our exodus, science emphasized all aspects of hyperdrive and anything relating to it. It took up all theoretical and experimental energies. So the nature of black holes was ignored, the research done on it shelved as unimportant. But that research is there, and historical data records I've looked through indicate it's a lot more complete than anything done since then.''

"Go, then,'' Croost said with an intense and decisive voice. He glanced at them one by one. "Take the *Cetus*. We'll work out the legalities later.''

"Adrian must have been a madman,'' he continued. "Under that jovial exterior was a desperate person. The creatures he was helping must be stopped. And if an ancient computer on a desolate planet can be of help, then so be it.''

It wasn't a complete change of mood for Croost, Starbrite thought, but it certainly was a right-angle turn. Croost's next statement came as an even greater surprise.

"Starbrite is still officially liaisoned with your mission. For bureaucratic reasons we'll still consider its official purpose researching the causes of discontent in the Nether Quadrant. I believe that it would be in your interest for Starbrite to be included.''

"Commander, any help you offer is more than welcome,'' Lyra said.

Croost nodded, his face palpably less concerned. Somehow, the chance of plugging the aliens' entranceway to this galaxy appeared to afford him tangible relief from his worries.

"A favor, Commander?'' Starbrite asked. "I'd like to equip the *Cetus* with some weapons, especially a spacefighter. A Whippet could easily be adapted to an empty port bay.''

"Done,'' Croost said. "I'll give you a letter of authorization. But you'll have to arrange everything with the Quartermaster.''

Starbrite mentally groaned. Quartermasters were notorious for protecting equipment in their charge and that meant only relinquished it with the utmost reluctance and days of interminable paperwork to get the Whippet aboard.

"Right, sir,'' Starbrite said, feeling somehow that something remained out of kilter. It was more than Adrian's treachery; for example, how the man had undoubtedly cut his and Lyra's lifeline after the mosquito blast, retying it when he knew Starbrite was looking, and then pretending to be their savior. It was the *motive* that remained so elusive, like a missing number that prevented an equation from adding up. Yet, Starbrite mused, he didn't even know what the equation *was*. So what remained was a vague sense that some nebulous fact of some unrecognized problem was vital to their welfare.

And Starbrite's amorphous sense of unease couldn't have forecast what awaited them more accurately.

Chapter Thirteen

Earth—the mother planet of the millions who had settled throughout the Galactic Federation—filled their viewscreen. The *Cetus* was in parking orbit, and over a period of little more than an hour, every part of the planet could be viewed.

It was partially covered by brilliant white clouds and the swirling shapes of incipient hurricanes could easily be distinguished. Turquoise oceans could be glimpsed through the clouds and occasionally a patch of dull green could be spotted—a vast expanse of forest or grass-covered plains.

The beauty of the sight belied the reality.

As nuclear plants had exploded, become disabled, or malfunctioned, it had been generally concluded that their development was a noble effort but a dismal failure. Technologists had gone to work on new power sources, using combustible fossil fuels as an interim measure. Then came the discovery of hyperdrive and most energies of Earth's technologists polarized on this fascinating phenomenon. Humankind plunged into a ghastly paradox: it was experimenting with time travel yet still using Earth's remaining fossil fuels to power its industry.

By the time scientists became alarmed at the amount of carbon dioxide in the atmosphere, it was too late. The critical level had been reached, and each carbon dioxide molecule was acting as a mirror, reflecting heat radiation back to Earth. More bounced back to the planet than escaped into space, causing a phenomenon popularly known as the "greenhouse effect."

Within a time span of only twenty years, Earth had warmed enough to melt the polar ice caps, inundating major coastal cities. There were drastic weather changes: Fertile areas became deserts, deserts experienced monthly floods, and, everywhere, water rose to a higher level, destroying the world humankind had known.

The rising water seeped into caves where radioactive wastes had been stored. It unearthed caches of toxic chemicals. It leached out poisons from vast tracts of land. And, in two separate instances, violent tidal waves roaring over inland areas swept away pounds of plutonium, the most radioactively toxic material ever created.

Humankind fled, or at least the lucky ones did. New Earth had already been discovered and it became a refuge for a mere ten percent of Earth's once teeming population.

"The ice caps formed again, once plant life turned carbon dioxide into oxygen and restored that atmospheric balance. The relatively few survivors became troglodytes," Lyra explained while giving a short briefing of what she knew of Earth to Vac, Starbrite, and Questin.

"Their descendants barely resemble human beings now because of the radiation-caused mutations. But some, so I understand, can be quite intelligent."

Starbrite glanced again at the viewscreen, its picture of Earth clear and vivid. "Social service ships reporting?" he asked. Periodically New Earth sent supplies and medical teams, more as an expiation of conscience than a practical measure.

Lyra nodded. "Read a bit before leaving. No one likes to talk about Earth. Some of the social service personnel say that many troglodytes are in primitive tribal states. Civilization is beginning again.

"However, it's the data left behind that we're after. Shouldn't take more than a few days. Then we can leave," she added firmly, hoping that the time spent on Earth would be less. Most of all Lyra wanted to avoid the troglodytes, rovers that melted through forests and cities like malformed ghosts.

"Descend any time now," Questin said. Since Adrian's death, Questin had assumed command of the *Cetus*, a welcome decision for everyone. He knew the ship intimately and was trusted by its crew.

"According to all the old records, the matrix computer that would have the ancient's data is in an old city on a river."

"What was it called?" Starbrite asked.

"Washington. It was one of the co-capitals of the federated Earth government they had formed. Lots of scientific records there, especially when space exploration began."

Starbrite distributed weapons, hand-held laseguns. It was believed some troglodytes would kill or loot. Though the team would make every effort to avoid violence, going unarmed was unwise.

They descended by shuttle ship to a landing field near the old capital of Washington. Lyra, efficiency personified, even had a copy of an area map she had found in New Earth archives. They exited, each one experiencing a welling of emotion from breathing the air of their race's home planet. Hot air, sultry with moisture, yet air with the variegated smells of tropical plants, riotous blooms, and damp loamlike soil. Earth was healing, and the wild explosion of vegetation, which fed on carbon dioxide and released oxygen as a byproduct, had restored a balance to the atmosphere. Slowly. Over eons the scars were healing—except for those mephitic localities where radioactive debris or plutonium deposits still released their invisible and deadly rays—areas that were, and would be for thousands of years, lifeless wastelands.

Lyra breathed deeply, beads of sweat already dripping from her brow. She unfolded her map. "This used to be"—she turned the map—"National Airport at the time of the exodus. And we have to travel to"—Lyra bit on her lip as she measured the distance with her finger—"International Science Foundation, which is . . . right . . . *here*," she pronounced triumphantly.

"How far?" Questin grunted, his narrow eyes continually circling the area they had landed in. Faint trails that once had been major highways meandered through the thick foliage. It was going to be dangerous walking through all of this, he thought.

"I judge it at twelve Km's. Quite a walk."

"I'll get the autocart," Questin said, sweeping a sheen of sweat from his bald head with an open hand. A few standby crewmen remained on the shuttle ship. He motioned for them to roll out a small wagonlike vehicle powered by fuel cells.

"That'll carry provisions for overnight, our power generator, other odds and ends," he explained.

Vac, his face flushed from heat and wet with sweat, finally spoke. He had studied their surroundings as though drinking in history. Earth's sky was an even deeper blue than that of their own homeland, and huge white clouds scudded across its horizons like white, aerial beasts. "A planet lost by stupidity and greed," he murmured to no one in particular. Starbrite shot him a glance, their eyes met and Vac said more gruffly than he had intended, "Let's get going. We've lost this one by ourselves. Let's make sure we don't lose all the others to a pack of hostile aliens."

They marched, then trudged, then rested and marched again, never seeing any sign of the primitive Earth people. More evidence of a beautiful city greeted them as they neared a white dome that glistened through the sultry atmosphere. Buildings, most without obvious damage, were encased in vines and weeds. The narrow path turned into a wider trail with patches of a harder undersurface showing through the trees, plants, and growth that had poked through its length. The number of monuments and buildings increased as the trail widened.

"A people of imagination and art," Vac exclaimed on passing a particularly large shrine of some sort. Rectangular, with the cracked statue of a giant man sitting in a chair, tall stone columns supporting remnants of a domed roof. The sight was impressive, even awestriking, despite the ever-present vines that grew over the structure.

Finally they were in the city proper. The avenues and buildings had better resisted the onslaught of vegetation. Greater expanses of open spaces showed between the buildings, which ranged in rows for blocks on end.

"Strange how they built in those days," Starbrite murmured. "Building after building sitting together, rather than in clusters."

"The paths we're on were much wider. Used for mechanized transportation. No people-movers then. They actually had vehicles in the center of their cities," Lyra explained, thinking of how tolerant those people must have been to live with such great activity, movement, and confusion. Vehicles and people just meters from each other. Lyra shrugged once then glanced down at her map.

They had been marching for five hours now and the sun beat unmercifully from above. The heat sucked energy from them all. Vac sat on a stone pillar to rest while Lyra turned her map, trying to find their location from the position of the buildings, each of which was indicated on the map she had had copied.

"If we only knew what streets these were," she said, squinting. "There. There's a corner just ahead with a post, and the signs are still on," she said, amazed. On leaving Earth, nothing had been destroyed. And, apparently, even during the eight hundred years of the planet's abandonment its population hadn't bothered to destroy buildings—or street signs.

"We can look, but after all this time—" Starbrite said doubtfully.

It was barely legible—and only because the sign was of a thick, solid metal with the names cut into it. He traced the letters of the encrusted plaque and read aloud the letters he could make out "C—O— —N—E—C—T— C—U—T—A— —E."

"Connecticut Avenue!" Lyra said triumphantly, looking at the map. Now the other side, Quas."

"There's a one and a five next to two letters. One is S. The other—"

"Fifteenth Street. That means we're only a quarter Km from where they left the computer."

"Crazy. Just doesn't make sense," Questin murmured, thinking of a time hop, then a trudge through jungle to get to a computer, for some esoteric research that mightn't be stored there after all. Providing the computer could be made to work after all this time. Crazy, he told himself again. It made no rational logic.

But he knew that it made emotional sense. He had seen organized scrambles when spacers had had to flee a planet. He knew that after some basic items were rushed aboard a shuttle there was a crazy, patchwork reason for taking other things. Items that were apparently useless suddenly would be considered treasures, while valuable items would be left standing. He once saw a spacer nearly get killed to save his good-luck charm while ignoring a precious communicator lying beside it.

And flight from Earth, even if it had taken a century, was—given the enormity of the task—a scramble. And some things were left behind. Including information that wasn't considered valuable, just as old letters are carefully stored away, then left unread. In this case data ancient theoreticians had accumulated on black holes and stored in the treasure house of a computer memory.

Maybe.

They reached the building, a tall ominous stone structure that was in the middle of many other similar edifices. "Seen jails lookin' better," Questin said to no one in particular as he jockeyed the autocart up the long flight of stone steps.

They entered after Starbrite and Vac shouldered open a door. Another strange feeling: entering a building that probably no one had been inside for centuries. A waft of cooler air greeted them along with the echoes of their footsteps.

But the incongruity didn't end there. Lyra whipped out yet another map, this a detailed plan of the building. "Now, why'd they save building plans and not just bring along the computer memory?" Questin asked.

Starbrite, too, was thinking the same thing. He met Questin's eyes. They both shrugged at the same time.

"Leaving Earth was an emotional time for the human

128

race. Maybe some clerk just crossed out the computer memory on a list of things to take," Vac said. "Maybe he added a carton of geranium seeds instead. Everything was judged according to its weight versus its worth, so the legend goes."

"So we have to make a dangerous trip to Earth to find data to stop aliens from entering our galaxy because of geranium seeds." Starbrite retorted impatiently.

"When you leave your mother planet forever maybe a carton of geranium seeds *would* be more important," Vac said gently. "Frankly, I think so."

"Well, I like flowers, too. But right now I'd rather pry loose some information about black holes." Luckily for us someone included a detailed catalog of what was left on the memory cores," Lyra hesitated as she held up the floor plan in front of her. "Up a flight. Probably that stairway there," she said, pointing to a long row of wide, stone steps.

At the head of the stairs she turned the map, squinted, looked up, and pointed directly ahead. "There. That should be the computer room."

Lyra led them into a vast chamber. Rows and rows of square machines lined the room in silent, monolithic columns. "So much knowledge here. Maybe things that we've totally forgotten," Lyra whispered.

Questin added, "There've been research teams who've used this room in the last one hundred years. So those machines can still probably be made to work."

"Let's do it then," Vac added, plainly disturbed at being on Earth and the history it represented to him. "Lyra, you have the record of which machine?"

"Anyone'll do, Dad. They're all tied into the same memory cores. Let's get one working."

Starbrite prowled through the room, down one corridor, its sides made of the huge modules holding computer memories of a past civilization, then up again. He felt vaguely depressed and equally nervous. Lyra accidentally dropped her maps and he spun around, hand to his lasegun. He couldn't have said why he expected danger. But he knew that his skin felt as though it were crawling from his body.

Questin had maneuvered the autocart into the room and now set up a power feed, something Lyra had anticipated. They began hooking up the wires to a computer bank, Lyra again tracing the connections from ancient records.

"Can't understand," she said with admiration, "how they could mess up an entire planet yet leave everything so neat that eight hundred years later we can just plug in. Weird."

But both Questin and Starbrite could well comprehend the seeming contradiction. As spacers they knew the primeval compulsion of a crew to clean their ship when they had to abandon her, provided any time was left. Everything was put in as perfect working order as possible. Then the crew took off in lifeships. It wasn't necessarily rational to spend so much time leaving a derelict ship which no one would ever see again, in pristine condition. But it was understandable.

The compact power plant Questin had brought drove magnetic impulses across stationary coils, with electricity the result. Varying the rate and intensity of magnetic pulses determined the voltage and current. Again Lyra squinted at a data sheet. "We need one hundred twenty volts and sixty cycles per second. That's what the computer feeds on."

Questin toyed with the power pack. It hummed nicely. He threw a feed switch, and the computer in front of Lyra began clicking.

They stood, pleased and amazed. No one had really expected the thing to work on a first try. It was like witnessing a resurrection after a practice incantation.

With noticeable reverence, Lyra began to punch out preliminary instructions on a keyboard jutting from the computer's retrieval control bank.

The clicks increased in intensity, a friendly staccato sound that echoed around the giant room. Some keys began to chatter and with the tinkle of a bell, a sheet of opaque plastic shot from a slot of a printout module.

"We'll need holograms of the data. The plastic sheets are too brittle to carry," Lyra said. Starbrite took a palm-sized camera from his belt. They'd planned to photograph the data with the holographic crystal inside and examine the results later on a viewscreen. A single crystal the size of a pea held thousands of separate snapshots.

After a few more preliminaries with the computer, Lyra began searching for data on black holes. Thousands of research papers had been written—an almost impossible number to request. But Lyra had selected certain key topics she was particularly interested in and ordered the computer to deliver them in batches. The keys chattered now at an enormous pace. Sheets of data streamed from the machine. A second printout automatically activated to fulfill their data requests, then a third. Starbrite rushed from one to the other, photographing every page, each one filled with mathematical formulas.

"Just interested in time-space discontinuities," Lyra murmured once, her tunic drenched with perspiration, her hair pasted to her forehead. She worked continuously, checking catalog sheets, punching furiously at the retrieval keys, scrambling from one machine to the other to glance at the printouts that Starbrite, equally harried, photographed. Questin stayed with the power pack, monitoring its performance every second, knowing that any alteration of voltage or cycles could shut down the sensitive computer.

Vac served as "go-fer," holding up the readouts for Starbrite to photograph, carrying notes Lyra scribbled furiously on a pad, checking off on the detailed catalog the data they'd already retrieved.

And then, after five hours of steady work, they were through. The chattering slowed to intermittent pecking. Only one or two readouts slipped from the printout modules, then none. The keys became silent.

"Time to clean up," Vac said, tired. He glanced at his chronometer. "We should leave the place as neat as we found it," he said.

"Mebbe a snack to stem the growls my belly's making firs . . ."

Questin didn't finish. He stiffened, back straight.

Starbrite shot him a glance then followed his line of sight and his stomach convulsed.

Lyra uttered a short screech.

"My god," Vac exclaimed, feeling his knees buckle.

They froze, paralyzed by the sight of the black figures at the end of the corridor, watching the other shadows filter out from behind the memory modules and form a solid, silent phalanx.

Another dark figure suddenly strode through the doorway, and Starbrite felt a rush of panic. A long black cape swept the floor behind the biped. He moved in arrogant strides until he was just meters away. No one had yet made a sound. Then, slowly and almost with obvious pleasure at their fright, KraKon, his eyes glowing, raised an arm and pointed at the four humans.

Chapter Fourteen

The power pack that Questin had brought was no taller than his foot and could easily be circled by his hands. Starbrite could hear its hum in the ominous silence following KraKon's appearance. Then, through that hum, he heard an almost inaudible, high-pitched whine. Before the whine faded, five of the dark figures rushed forward, as though on some unspoken command.

One of the Dark Horde soldiers dashed from between the memory matrixes where the power pack lay. The figure's foot brushed against it. The dark biped stumbled forward another few steps and tripped over its own two feet. Its strange-looking weapon slid across the floor. Another whine screeched through Starbrite's brain. The four remaining figures running toward them swerved toward the fallen biped, one of them sweeping up the discarded weapon.

Starbrite, his surprise fading, acted on the momentary distraction. His hand flashed to his holster and gripped the lasegun as he bellowed out a hoarse cry to Questin. The gun slid free and arced toward the obvious leader—the black biped with the long, dark cape.

It was then that a stationary figure well to Starbrite's flank pressed a lever on a weapon that resembled a square barrel connected to a large box.

Starbrite never heard the discharge. But suddenly he felt as though half his insides had leaped sideward while his body remained stationary. Then, with an unbelievably swift jolt, he, too, jerked a few centimeters to one side while his head seemed to cave inward. The world grew gray, dimmed—and then disappeared.

Cool. The hard floor was cool. Stone, perhaps, because it felt rough. A glowing figure wrapped in a cape pointed a steady, accusing finger at him. It grinned maliciously. No, that wasn't right. Starbrite groaned. That figure: no smile at all. No mouth. No ears.

Just like that black biped on Benera.

Starbrite sat up and felt rocket blasts scorch his brain. He groaned again, feeling someone support him from behind.

"Alive and functioning. Maybe better than we'd thought." Questin's voice.

"Quas. Nod if you can hear. If you can understand the words." A low, whispered voice. Female. Lyra. Starbrite tried to nod, then waited until the pounding inside his skull tapered off.

"He's trying to follow directions. Could be only a stun." Male voice. Vac sounding frantically concerned.

"Where are we?" Male voice. Weak but steady. Tremulous, as though recovering from a long sickness—or a sudden blow.

His own voice.

"Quas. We're in some building. Deep down. Can you open your eyes?" Lyra's voice.

"What happened?" His own voice again. He knew because he felt himself speak. Felt the effort. He opened his eyes and was grateful that the light was low, soft, and flickering. A bright light would have seared right through his head.

"You got zapped with something. Never saw it before. You were standing in one spot, then a microsecond later you'd been jerked to one side. Don't know what it was, how it works." Questin answering.

"Quas. There are a lot of them. Lots. Just like the thing we saw on Benera. They're everywhere," Lyra told him, fright plain in her voice.

Starbrite nodded, testing the reaction. Only a dull pain charged through his head. Better. He breathed deeply then stiffened as his chest seemed to rip apart. Worse. Felt like a meteor had bounced off his ribs. But no sharp pains. Better again. Sharp meant puncture. Dull pain meant bruises. And bruises were better than punctures.

Things were looking up.

Starbrite glanced around.

Things looked bad again.

They were in a cavern of stone, or so it seemed. Arches dripped water, each drop sounding like a small tinkle as it fell to the stone floor. "Read about dungeons and dragons in books when I was a kid. They seemed just like this," Starbrite said, slowly looking around, avoiding any sudden jolts to his head and body.

A huge wooden door, thick and heavy, was firmly fixed by huge metal hinges. A small light plate glowed dimly, shedding the only illumination inside the tall, cavernous room. A bucket lay in one corner. No food, water, blankets, or other amenities. It took no great imagination to realize this prison, an old storage area, was a staging depot. Not meant to keep them for long.

Then what?

Separation, for sure, Starbrite guessed. Something to be avoided at all costs. Once they were apart, once communication was lost, they'd not stand any chance at all.

"We have to get out of here," Starbrite said, his words hollow in the stone room. Vac looked up and nodded weak agreement as Lyra sighed.

Questin explained. "You've been out a couple of hours. We've all looked this place over. They dragged us down right after you were zapped. No explanations, no talk, no nothing. Just threw us all in and left. We searched everywhere. Not even an insect could fit through that door, and there's no other exit."

Starbrite, now sitting on one of the cots, checked his belt. The hologram camera was in its case, as were his compass, light, communicator—for all the good it would do—first aid pack, everything but the most important item: his lasegun. He slapped his hand against the empty holster.

"Took 'em all," Questin said disconsolately. "No

weapons left. Didn't have a chance to draw my gun. They knew proper what weapons were. Left everything else.''

"Quas, I'll take the hologram crystal,'' Lyra said.

Starbrite handed her the camera. Essentially, its lens focused light on a crystal which turned slightly after each exposure. The crystal was a standard size, interchangeable with holographic viewers everywhere.

Lyra snapped open the camera, flicked out the pea-sized crystal, and stuck it in a pocket of her tunic. "They might take the camera. But with this''—Lyra patted her pocket—"we still have the data we came for. The trip won't be wasted.''

Given the circumstances, Starbrite thought, Lyra was expressing a lot of faith in the future.

A scratching at the door caught their attention. Questin was about to speak when Vac silenced him with a wave of his hand. They heard the sound of metal being fitted to the ancient iron lock. More clicks, surreptitious and halting, then the solid scrape of a turning key and the clunk of a spring lock.

The door swung open. Questin dashed to one side and—without the need for words—Starbrite to the other.

In the dim light a dark figure walked hesitantly into the stone room. Another of those—*things*. Questin had slipped his belt free, the heavy buckle hanging loose. He raised his arm and started to swing.

Then his eye caught a thick mat of gray hair that streamed from one side of the creature's head. He paused, confused. The hair seemed almost human. Still, the thing had the same dark carapace of all the others, the same smooth and almost featureless head. He raised his arm again.

"Be quiet. Close the door, quickly,'' the creature said.

Something akin to an electric shock stilled Questin's arm.

Starbrite, trusting his instinct, reached the door and closed it swiftly. Lyra let out a bewildered sigh and Vac sat.

"I can help. Maybe. But quickly,'' the thing said. By

now the others had noticed the long silver hair streaming from the creature's head.

"You're human, aren't you? You're a human being?" Vac asked in a whisper from where he sat on an ancient cot. He was the first to grasp what that long hair meant. A human being transformed into—*what*? And where there was one, there might be many.

"I was. I can talk to you without a cartridge," the creature said, forgetting that the others had no idea of what she meant.

"Who are—what's *happening*? What's going *on*?" Lyra stammered out, regaining some composure.

"Quickly. Don't know when they're coming." Anxiety crept into the mechanical drone of the cyborg's voice.

"Who is *they*?" Starbrite blurted, desperately coveting any information that would tell them what they were facing.

"Quas. Lyra. We'll take it step by step," Vac said, quickly assessing the best way to glean the most information in the least time. "This—" He paused. What *should* one call the biped? Vac improvised. "This—friend has things to tell, in its own way."

Questin, his back to the wall, regarded the dark figure warily, the belt firmly in his grasp.

The biped's smooth alloy legs moved forward in a jerky kind of step until it was in the middle of the chamber. "I was human. Years ago. This is what they want to do to everyone—"

"Your name," Vac interrupted. Later a name would place a missing person at some location and at a given time and perhaps lead to the circumstances that transformed him or her into what it had become.

"I am—I was called Lisa Orion. Was captured—" Vac groaned. The biped stopped speaking.

Vac covered his face with his hands. Lyra stared for a moment and collapsed onto a cot. Starbrite and Questin looked on, comprehension slowly dawning.

The creature, Lisa Orion, was puzzled by the tense silence. Then she asked, with a hope plain in her voice, "Can that name mean something to you?"

Vac raised his head, his face haggard. And, with a

bravery that the others appreciated later, said, "Orion was a famous scientist. Name's known. But continue."

He waved down Lyra's exclamation and ignored her look of stunned surprise. He knew that telling this creature that she was his mother, that Lyra was her granddaughter, would only delay the information they so desperately needed.

Vac Orion swallowed, his face lined with emotional pain. "Continue. Please tell us what you know." His voice was gentle and compassionate.

Lisa Orion, her brain sharp and lucid, spoke rapidly, the mechanical tone of her voice almost hypnotic.

She told of KraKon, a tortured monster that had no pity, compassion, or honor. She detailed its insatiable ambition to dominate the universe.

One by one, her rapid-fire explanations filled in huge gaps of the jigsaw puzzle. And gradually it became clear to the stunned listeners what they were facing. Especially after Lisa Orion described what KraKon offered to the organic beings of a dozen different worlds he now owned.

"Eternal life. Mechanization of the body, an everlasting brain. He'll trade that for freedom and independence, knowing that few beings can resist avoiding death. And power—he grants power to those who follow him." Lisa Orion's tone conveyed her strong loathing.

Starbrite, his stomach churning, then knew what Jost Adrian's last words meant, why he had betrayed humanity.

"Your involvement. How? Especially how did you get here?" Vac asked, his questions short and pointed.

Lisa Orion spoke again for a few minutes, condensing years of mental torture into short paragraphs. How she had spent decades on KraKon's planet, being transformed into a cyborg. How the KraKon through some perverted vengeance wanted her to witness his taking over Earth, how he brought her here, how she overheard some of the minor Dark Horde soldiers talking about newly captured humans. She found out where they were, mixed with the Dark Horders of the guard group, stole a key, stole back their weapons and came to see them.

To do *something*. To *somehow* thwart any of KraKon's plans.

"Could you outline those more precisely?" Vac interrupted, wanting an overall view, to help anticipate events to come.

"Invasion of the entire Federation. Forcefully taking over each planet. That's his style, his way of operating. But for us—" Lisa Orion paused dramatically, suddenly remembering what she had become—"for *you*, humans, KraKon has more animosity. He's leading the invasion personally, with advice from traitors. Don't know who—"

"The insurrectionist movement—just a facade," Starbrite murmured.

"Weaponry. What's their weaponry like?" Starbrite asked, jumping Vac's next question. Now that they knew they faced a Galactic-wide invasion he *had* to know that.

Lisa Orion paused, then her voice box hummed: "Based on gravity. Their science focuses on gravitational rather than electromagnetic or nuclear forces. They can distort gravity and their warships have gravity cannon. I don't know more than that."

It was enough. Starbrite remembered how his insides seemed to jerk to one side. A gravity gun? Distortion of a gravity field so that things accelerated from one point to another almost instantaneously.

Lisa Orion unwrapped a small packet. Inside were their laseguns, puny, weak laseguns, brought more to frighten Earth's troglodytes than to kill.

Then Questin asked the next logical question. "Do they know how we got here? By the shuttle ship and the larger ship above?"

"They know almost everything. But they won't attack or capture it. They're afraid the ship will give off a warning. They don't want that. They're not ready yet. I've got the impression they need another few days or so but I don't know why."

Pure luck. An event in their favor. Something positive in a situation that seemed nearly hopeless.

"When do they plan to attack the Federation? Any idea at all?" Vac asked.

"Nothing definite. But soon. More Dark Horde troops

come each day. I don't know how you missed seeing them. They're streaming into our galaxy."

Lyra unconsciously touched the small crystal in her tunic pocket. It would be one of the absurdities of their era if the information on that crystal could tell them how this KraKon and his Dark Hordes carved out a gateway to their universe. One of the greatest scientific secrets of the universe in her pocket.

Starbrite, his mind racing, his hopes revived, asked about guards. Lisa Orion could tell them little, other than the Dark Hordes made periodic sweeps through this building, mostly to make sure no Earth's inhabitants had sneaked in. One of their sports, it seemed, was ripping these creatures apart with their weapons on full force. Most troglodytes had fled the area. Some had been particularly bellicose and fought back. One had shot a Dark Horder with an ancient weapon called a bow and arrow.

"An arrow against their guns! What happened?" Starbrite couldn't resist asking.

"It bounced off. They shot to either side of the thing with their guns. It tore him in half, each of his sides jumped away from the middle. It looked like he was cut in two with a sword."

Vac brought them back to the present. "Can you lead us out? Do you know an exit?"

Lisa Orion pivoted her head toward the door, her long gray hair swirling behind her. "There's an unpatrolled exit. But lots of Dark Horders everywhere. They're all cyborgs, members of KraKon's fellowship. Many alien races. He saturates them with destruction, with hate."

As the drone of her voice box stilled, Starbrite thought of how much more she could tell them. KraKon? Cyborgs? Fellowship? Other aliens? His emotional system was now saturated with surprises. Later there would be rivers of time to digest all Lisa Orion knew. Later.

If they made it.

And if they didn't, then whatever more they learned wouldn't be of help anyway. Starbrite holstered his lasegun. Lisa Orion moved toward the door, walking in a stiff but quick step that characterized KraKon's cyborgs. After one pace into the dank corridor she motioned for them to follow.

They left their cell, stomachs knotted, senses at high edge, murder in their hearts, and laseguns in their hands.

For all the dangers surrounding them, extreme caution was necessary only once while they were inside the building. A troop of what Lisa Orion had called Dark Horders were gathered in a chamber they had to pass. Soldiers passing time, careless because of confidence. So much so that they never noticed the dark shadows flit by the open door. But Starbrite noticed that they were atypical in that all they did was stand quietly in a circle; no drinking, carousing, boisterous laughter. Just silently standing, staring ahead at an invisible point. They may *have eternal life, but they look bored as hell*, Starbrite thought to himself as he dashed past the open door.

Questin moved past the door, then stopped abruptly. He jerked his head for them to wait and, silent as a panther, rushed back to the door where the Dark Horders were quartered. Starbrite saw him bend down, then scoop up something.

"Got me an idea. Mebbe help a bit later," he said, rejoining the group. Starbrite grimaced. In one arm Questin was carrying their small power pack. "Saw our stuff as we passed. They just threw it at the entranceway," Questin added, oblivious to everyone's annoyance at his using precious time.

They moved ahead, following Lisa Orion's stiff but sure gait out of the building and into the muggy air. *She knows the area well*, Starbrite thought, glancing around in the twilight. For a moment Lisa Orion hesitated. Then she lifted her arm and pointed down a vine-choked pathway. "We'll take that one. Leads to a bigger path, then a narrower one. I think it will end near your ship."

The cyborg saw Starbrite's suspicious look with her stark, crystalline eyes. "I have freedom here. The Dark Hordes don't understand about taking initiative, such as scouting an area without a direct order. They'd stand all day unless directed. They assume I'm on official business unless told otherwise.''

Keeping up a fast, distance-eating pace, they moved into the darker shadow of the vegetation. Then Starbrite called a halt. "Let's try the ship," he said, pulling the communicator from his belt.

The return answer came quickly, the crewman on the ship's communicator frantic with worry. Starbrite silenced him with a sharp command. In thirty seconds he briefed them on their danger, ordering a swift takeoff as soon as they arrived. He got a curt and efficient reply and signed off.

They all felt better. The ship was there. The crew was ready. They might still make it.

They turned to follow Lisa again—and saw two darker shadows standing in the pathway. Even in the dim light Starbrite noticed that they both carried the strange guns with square barrels. He shot Questin a glance and saw that he, too, had recognized the danger.

Lisa Orion, her brain animating her cyborg body with a determined courage, walked forward. Starbrite felt a high-pitched sound in his ears. And even as he moved toward the left, he saw Questin move toward the right in a standard guerrilla maneuver.

The two sentries showed a momentary confusion as they heard Lisa. The large square barrels of their guns faltered. Then, as Starbrite continued moving to the left, they recovered. The barrels steadied, and an eerie whine filled the air.

Then the space just meters from Starbrite imploded into a deadly gravity void that would have sucked in an elephant like a feather.

Chapter Fifteen

Two streaks of dazzling red light preceded the whine from the gravity guns.

Starbrite had darted to one side for a clear shot at the Dark Horde soldier on his left. Questin dashed to the right for a good shot at the other. Each had winged off a laseblast while still moving. And each needle-thin beam had pierced the hard chest of a cyborg, fusing interior circuits only milliseconds before they squeezed the release on their gravity guns. It had been close—but time enough to destroy perfect aim. The sharply focused gravity beams missed their human targets only by meters, destroying trees, bushes, and vines instead.

Starbrite raised himself to his knees, still stunned by the implosion. His chest ached more than ever. He realized then that the gravity charge that had decked him in the computer room must have been a small fraction of the weapon's full force.

From a corner of his eye he saw motion. Questin. Also on his knees, clearing his mind with short, violent shakes of his head. Questin blinked two or three times as though surprised at being alive. He exhaled a long, heavy sigh and peered around. He spotted Starbrite and gave a quick thumbs-up sign.

Questin rose slowly and picked up the power pack he had dropped.

"What's that *for*?" Starbrite asked.

The others crowded around and before Questin could answer, Vac said in worried tones, "Got to move, Quas. Your radio transmission was probably monitored as a matter of course. They knew we're out."

Lyra helped Starbrite rise and as if to confirm Vac's worry Lisa Orion moved closer, her voice box humming. "Get to the ship quickly. They'll be coming now. They'll knew that two of their own are gone."

In her metallic-like hands Lisa Orion held one of the gravity guns. Starbrite picked up the other then dropped it in amazement. The gravity gun was heavy, almost a quarter of his own weight. It was nothing he could cart around with any speed. He saw the apparent ease with which Lisa Orion nestled the heavy weapon in her arms and again realized how powerful the cyborgs were.

The group broke into a fast trot, following Lisa Orion's swift but ungainly gait. Twilight was rapidly descending, but even in the penumbra Lisa Orion easily followed the path, her artificial eyes amplifying the dim light.

Then, on a rise that overlooked a flat glade, in the last vestiges of daylight, they saw the faint outline of their shuttle ship.

Just then, Lisa Orion came to a sudden halt. Her head swiveled back and forth, like an antenna trying to pick out the direction of a faint signal. Then she stood absolutely motionless for a brief moment. "Dark Horde troop is following us. Still some distance away, but behind us. We must hurry," she said abruptly.

They ran. Sweat poured from their bodies, soaking their clothes. They breathed with huge gulps, their chests stinging from the effort.

The path narrowed and low-lying branches whipped at their faces and bodies. Then, abruptly, the trail ended and the group burst into the spacious glade. At the far end the outline of the shuttle ship still could be seen in the twilight.

They paused, gasping for breath, hands on thighs and heads hanging. "To your ship. They're close now. Not long before they're in range," Lisa Orion hummed quickly. From behind them, along the path they'd just left, came the faint sounds of branches being broken and leaves being trampled. "Hurry," Lisa exclaimed again, urgency plain even in her mechanical voice.

They ran again. Except for Questin, who knelt at the spot where the path ended and the glade began. Starbrite looked at him, annoyed. Questin said tersely, "Got something to do. Be there in a second. Go." Starbrite followed the others at a full run, hearing the loud hum of the power pack start while yet only a few meters away. He glanced around and saw Questin bending over the thing.

Starbrite yanked out his communicator as he ran. He tried to talk as he moved but had to stop to make the words come clearly. *Transmission, keep a clean transmission.* The words echoed in his mind. "We're approaching ship. Hostiles following," he gasped out. "You'll be under attack. Use light amplifiers. Shoot to kill any pursuit. Be careful not to hit us." The reply was short and reassuringly pungent.

Then Starbrite heard Questin's gasps behind him as the man sprinted to join the group. He glanced over his shoulder.

Dark Horde soldiers, ominous as black ghosts, flitted from the path sixty meters or so behind them and tumbled into the glade. Starbrite spun around and squatted, two hands holding his lasegun for a steady shot. It was probably futile, he knew, but anything was better than total inaction.

Questin rushed past Starbrite, skidded to a halt, returned and grabbed him by the shoulder, desperately motioning him to follow. Starbrite jerked at Questin's hand angrily and looked again at the bipeds tumbling into the glade.

Tumbling?

As each Dark Horde soldier moved into the clearing it seemed to stumble before falling to the ground. For a brief instant Starbrite stared. He felt another urgent tug at his shoulder and heard the desperate gasps of Questin's breathing. Completely mystified, Starbrite ran toward the shuttle in tandem with Questin, not looking gift horses in the mouth for more than the fleeting second he'd already wasted.

From under the shuttle ship came the bright glow of warm-up engines. Their gentle rumbled rolled across the glade. Still a chance, Starbrite thought, as he neared the ship. Two streaks of brilliant light darted from the shuttle, accompanied by the loud snapping sound high-powered laserifles made. Three more streaks in staggered sequence pierced the dim light, darting toward the other end of the glade. Attackers from both sides in a pincer movement, Starbrite thought. He mentally cheered on the shuttle ship's crewmen as four more laserifle blasts snapped through the clearing in quick succession.

Starbrite and Questin reached the bay entry of the shuttle only moments behind Lyra, Vac, and . . .

Starbrite glanced wildly around. Lyra and Questin were helping Vac up the steep ladder into the ship. The dull boom of a gravity gun reverberated over the dull roar of the shuttle's warm-up engines and Starbrite knew that only seconds separated them from defeat.

Three more blasts of a laserifle cracked in rapid succession, followed by another huge boom of a discharged gravity gun. Vac was nearly inside the ship. Starbrite risked another second to look for Lisa Orion.

She was ten meters or so from the shuttle, the gravity gun cradled in her arms pointed toward one end of the clearing. She fired. Starbrite heard the piercing whine of the discharge, saw Lisa Orion recoil from the shot, and almost immediately afterward, flinch at the roar of the gravity blast. He started forward, then felt a brush against his arm as Lyra dashed past him to her grandmother's side.

Starbrite rushed forward, frantic with worry, his lasegun in his hand. Then he spotted two Dark Horde soldiers emerging from the gloom, strutting toward the shuttle. They stopped, each biped raising its gravity gun.

Lyra shouted frantically at Lisa Orion, her words

obscured by the roar of the shuttle's engines and the cracks of laserifles. Lisa spotted the two soldiers at almost the same instant as Starbrite. She swept Lyra back toward the ship with one hand and spun toward the closest Dark Horde enemy. Lyra backpedaled, stumbled, and fell from the force of her grandmother's blow. Starbrite skidded to a standstill and took aim with his lasegun at the far cyborg.

Lisa Orion snapped off a gravity charge and the dark figure fifteen meters ahead of her evaporated. Starbrite fired as the second Dark Horde cyborg jerked his gravity gun toward Lisa. The air filled with the simultaneous sounds of a weak snap from Starbrite's weapon and the reverberating boom of a gravity gun on full charge.

Lisa Orion's torso jerked a meter to one side while her legs and head remained stationary. The effect was like seeing someone explode in space. The Dark Horde soldier Starbrite had shot staggered then dropped as another blast pierced its chest.

The laserifles had begun a steady staccato snap above them, a covering fire that was their last defense against the cyborgs advancing toward the ship.

In the next few seconds Starbrite half dragged, half carried Lyra up the ladder of the shuttlecraft. Her face was wet with tears of sorrow and frustration and she was nearly helpless from exhaustion. Starbrite saw eager hands grabbing Lyra and yanking her into the ship. And even as her body disappeared into the entance hatch Starbrite rapid-fired his lasegun at random toward the glade around them. Then he, too, was hauled in, a yank on his arm almost dislocating his shoulder.

Even before he was fully inside the hatch the shuttle ship's engines metamorphosed into a rich roar. During the single second between full thrust and liftoff Starbrite reached the shuttle's interior. Someone slammed the hatch closed as the ship lifted from Earth.

Starbrite was pinned to the floor by the swift acceleration, the force flattening his body and face against the hard surface. He could do nothing now except hope. At this point—he gave it five seconds—they were the most vulnerable. A swiftly accelerating ship was a difficult target but one that couldn't fight back.

The ship lurched once, proof that a gravity charge had exploded close by. Then it wobbled and that gentle shake meant to all aboard that they were no longer in range of the cyborg's weapons. The acceleration slackened as the engines backed down to normal thrust.

They regained the *Cetus*, sweat and grime covering their bodies, their clothes torn, their mood dispirited and angry. Immediately after a quick hype hop to avoid any Dark Horde spaceships near Earth, they gathered in the *Cetus's* bay for a memorial service for Lisa Orion. From an air lock they ejected an empty spacesuit into deep space, a symbolic tomb for a fellow human being whose intrepid spirit had survived all adversity and who had given her life to save them and the Galactic Federation.

At least now they had a perspective.

The *Cetus* floated through space a short time-hop from Earth, safe from discovery from the aliens' warships in the vast sea of emptiness. In the observation deck Vac, Lyra, Questin, and Starbrite sat licking their wounds.

"Insurrection? A few hotheads tricked into softening up the Federation thinking they're fighting for freedom. Flies on a spider's web have more chance of freedom than they'd get," Vac growled with unprecedented venom.

"But actually they were delivering information about our defenses, the Federation's reactions," Lyra added. "But I'll bet most don't know there's anything like that— KraKon thing. Or Dark Horde soldiers. Or aliens ready to take over the Federation."

"Some're true traitors, wantin' power and long life. They're the ones leadin' the others on." Questin swallowed a great sorrow. "Like Jost Adrian. A fine man once. But I seen him turn into something else. Can happen to others."

"We know what they intend. Thanks to your—mother, Vac. Now, it's a question of what we're going to do about it," Starbrite said.

One of their first steps was to get a coded message outlining what they had back to Croost. The reason they had come to Earth in the first place was barely a half notch below a message to Croost on the priority scale.

"What about plugging their black hole gateway?" Starbrite asked Lyra.

She shrugged. "I have the holographic crystal. It'll take days to sort out the information I need. But if I can use the *Cetus*'s main computer—well, it'd help."

"It's yours. Priority time, 'cept for trouble," Questin added and Lyra nodded her thanks. "She'd been your grandmother, then," Questin said. "That—cyborg. . . ." It wasn't a question he was asking but rather a confirmation of something too extraordinary to be believed at one mental gulp. Lyra nodded again. Questin breathed out a sigh, as though a bad dream had been confirmed. A story like this wouldn't be believed in any of the fifty spacer bars he knew throughout the Federation. *He* wouldn't believe it if someone else told him the details.

Starbrite summed up. "We agree, then, that plugging the gateway is our primary goal, once Croost is alerted."

"It's a logical move, Quas, for several reasons," Vac answered in rational, scholarly tones.

"From what Moth——Lisa Orion told us, we're just one of many civilizations that this KraKon thing has attacked. He *needs* his own base for such aggression. Even the threat of sealing off a return to his own world would send him—*it*—fleeing. Like protecting its escape hatch. That's one good reason."

Vac looked upward as if collecting his thoughts, then added, "KraKon's got to need supplies, weapons, and equipment troops. I doubt if it expects to take over without some losses, probably a great many. So resupply is another reason that closing the gateway would destroy its plans."

Starbrite swiveled his chair to face Lyra. "It's your move. Viewers, hard copies of any papers you want, computer time, help, whatever. All our resources will be funneled in your direction."

Lyra stood, her face lined with strain. "First things

first. I'll start the viewers going after a nap. Shouldn't be hard to sort out the important data from the fluff. Even in the twentieth century, scientists padded a lot to get something published.''

Lyra left and a long silence followed, during which Starbrite felt the tension of the last days flood through him. He stirred in his chair, knowing that he'd fall asleep right there if he didn't rise. Getting a message to Croost and putting the Federation on a war footing was his first priority.

"Can you get us near a shipping lane?" Starbrite asked Questin.

Questin chewed on a lip. "I'll check with the navigation computer. Shouldn't be too long before we hit a time hopper going toward New Earth that'll take your message." Questin made a gesture to rise from his chair, a laborious move that indicated his exhaustion. He sat back as Starbrite spoke again.

"How'd you immobilize those Dark Horde soldiers chasing us, right at the edge of the glade?"

Questin grinned, grateful of another few moments before having to rise. Vac shot them both a surprised look. "Immobilize? Any weakness they have is important."

"They've got a lot of weaknesses, Vac," Starbrite said. "They're not omnipotent. But there's one I can't explain. Questin can. The Dark Hord soldiers seemed to tumble into the glade, as though they couldn't walk. Otherwise we wouldn't be here now."

Questin nodded, his bald head reflecting patches of light. "Magnetic fields did it," he answered, with a relaxed exhale. "Just before you got stunned in the computer room one of those black suits of armor passed the power pack and collapsed. That little gadget sends out a high-intensity magnetic field. So I figured they were all sensitive."

"Quite a chance you took, Questin. Suppose it hadn't worked?" Vac asked testily.

"What's to lose?" Questin answered patiently. "I put the power pack on ful! so it generated maximum magnetic field and put it where they came out single file. As they swept by the field one by one it messed up whatever circuits those electronic junk heaps use. A chance? Sure. Why not?''

"Of course," Vac said, simply.

For four hard-paced days they helped Lyra Orion in whatever way they could. Four days of steady drudgery, sorting out information from the holographic crystal, analyzing relevant data on the ship's computer. After the second day they lived on no-sleep drugs, their nerves raw and tempers short. On the morning of the fifth day, Lyra stumbled into the observation deck where the others were assembled.

She had never looked so haggard. Her face was a blotched medley of different shades of white. Her skin was drawn and dark puffs under her eyes added years to her age. Her movements were weak and lethargic. She seemed animated only by pure mental energy, a kind of furious determination that ignored the demands of her body for rest.

"Got something that might help. You won't like it, but it might help," she began, slurring her words. The no-sleep drugs could be taken for only so long. Lyra was two days over the maximum limit prescribed.

The others said nothing, waiting for her to speak, too exhausted themselves to respond with more than a grunt of encouragement.

"A rotating black hole can be used for time travel. A stationary one can't.'' No one asked why. Full explanations could come later.

"Inside the singularity—that's just where the surface of a black hole begins—time and space are crushed out of existence by gravity. Those gravitational forces are enormous but delicate. Anything that can resist getting crushed, even for a microsecond, can pass to another galaxy. Those— creatures have found a way to suspend gravity for at least that long. A way of avoiding being crushed.''

The importance of what Lyra reported cut through

their fatigue. "I don't know how they do it. But it's a marvelous secret."

Lyra grasped a cup of steaming black coffee with her two hands and sipped slowly. Her voice dropped to a whisper as she continued. "The countergravity force they use, whatever it is, has to balance the gravitational force of the black hole exactly. Just enough for just so long. Too much or too little and they'd end up in another galaxy, or another universe—or no-place with no-time."

Lyra sipped again on the coffee, as though draining strength from the cup to keep talking.

Starbrite stretched his neck muscles and looked at the ceiling of the observation room, awed at a technology that could create such a countergravity. To have it would open up the entire universe. It was *possible*. Those creatures had done it.

"Sensitive business then," Questin said after a time.

"Very much so," Lyra answered. "And that's maybe how we can plug up their gateway."

It was as though they all got a second wind, brief though it might be, from Lyra's conclusions. Even Questin showed some animation as he raised one eyebrow a millimeter or so.

"We can't change the tuning or countergravity forces of their ships," Lyra continued. "But if we can disturb the gravitational characteristics of a black hole even the slightest, then their ships would end up—well, who knows."

Starbrite saw the obvious flaw. "But then they'd simply readjust their countergravity forces and hop through their gateway to our galaxy again."

Lyra shook her head, her long hair undulating. "No. Not if we could disturb a black hole at will in a random way at any time we wanted. No technology could cope with that."

"How?" Starbrite asked for all of them.

Lyra took another long sip from her coffee mug. "That's the part you won't like too much," she answered and later Starbrite thought this might have been the understatement of the entire mission.

She sipped again then added calmly, "Only one way I can think of. Antimatter. By sending antimatter bombs right into their gateway, right into the black hole they're using, the one near Benera."

Chapter Sixteen

They slept on it, too bone weary to even think more about Lyra's suggestion. Questin ordered maximum thrust drive, setting trajectory toward the nearest shipping lane. And, while the *Cetus* pushed through deep space, they slept.

Questin awoke to the sound of an alarm bell in his cabin. He hadn't the slightest idea if it was minutes, hours, or days since he'd headed the *Cetus* toward shipping traffic. But he knew they'd scored since the bell was an alarm set off by the intercept radar. Another ship nearby, to carry their reports to Croost.

Questin rose, went to the observation deck, and sent out an identification request. The message sped from the *Cetus* on a laser beam, lancing through space at the speed of light, repeated on the beam several hundred times a second. All the receiving craft would need for its electronics to snatch the message from space and display it on a viewscreen was a fraction of a single second of contact with the beam.

A minute or so later an alert tinkled and Questin read the contact ship's ID.

It was the *Capella*, a trade merchant about a time hop to New Earth.

Questin inserted a tape cassette of Starbrite's coded message to Croost in the transmission unit. It was prefixed a Spaceforce priority rating and destination, so the *Capella's* captain would know its importance. Then Questin shoved in his own cassette message, one he'd quickly prepared, letting the *Capella's* captain know of invasion by the Dark Hordes and the threat to the Galactic Federation.

Questin was groggier than he'd thought.

A few minutes later, longer than normal, a reply from the *Capella* hit the *Cetus's* reflector antennae, designed especially to receive lasebeam messages. The contents flashed across the viewscreen, preceded by the tinkle of the alert bell.

"What drivel you're using communications lines for, *Cetus*! You're going under report for abuse of comm time. Cut down on the drink. Soon you'll be seeing little green men wandering over your hull. Coded message will be forwarded as per regulations: along with report about *you*. OUT."

Questin grinned slightly. He didn't blame the *Capella's* captain for not believing the story of Dark Horde soldiers and alien invasions. Croost would get the coded message soon enough. He imagined a lean-jawed captain on the *Capella's* deck ranting right now at junior officers about abuse of communications lines and the dangers of intoxication.

Questin glanced at the observation deck's chronometer. One full day had passed since they'd been in flight. Time for everyone to get moving. Questin yawned and stretched widely, feeling the pleasant strain on his back and neck muscles. One day's worth of sleep had done wonders. He rang for a crewman and told him to wake the others.

Antimatter bomb? A ticklish matter, that. Best thought of after a hearty meal, black coffee, and another stretch. Questin began the sequence with the stretch.

It was Vac who needed explanations. Starbrite and Questin knew some details about antimatter and its terrible force. Lyra filled in for her father, wondering how someone so educated otherwise could have missed learning something so fundamental as the nature of matter and its counterpart, antimatter.

They were on the observation deck again, the room having become their general headquarters. The remains of a meal lay on fold-up tables and steam rose from several mugs of coffee. Lyra spoke.

"Well, everything is made of atoms, we can start from there."

Vac grimaced and put down his coffee mug. "*That* much I know Lyra," he said, plainly embarrassed.

"OK, but just to make sure. The nucleus of each atom has a positive electrical charge. Electrons spin around the nucleus. They have a negative electrical charge."

Vac nodded patiently, but with concentration.

"Big question. Who or what says that the nucleus *must* have a positive electrical charge? And that the electrons spinning around the nucleus must have a negative electrical charge?"

Vac almost blushed. "Guessing games, Lyra? The Galactic Federation is under siege. Just say what antimatter is, if it's important at all."

Lyra combed her hair from her brow with a quick stroke of her hand. "It's important. Just making it simple. The answer to my question is nobody said it *had* to be that way. In fact, possibly half the atoms in our universe have the electrical charges in reverse. The nucleus has a *negative* electrical charge. The spinning electrons carry a *positive* charge. That's antimatter."

Vac's eyebrows rose slowly into almost perfect arcs, as though he were slowly digesting the importance of some arcane but vital fact. Finally his lips formed the outline of a single word.

"So?" Vac's hands spread out to his side, palms up, as he spoke.

Lyra continued gamely. "When matter and antimatter meet the two annihilate each other into pure energy. The explosion is the most powerful known. *All* mass goes into energy. It makes nuclear reactions and nuclear bombs look like fireworks."

Vac's mind churned. "If some atoms are antimatter and others regular matter, how come we're here? How come we haven't been turned into pure energy yet?"

Questin gave a slight exhale. It was his equivalent of a long, hard groan. He knew what was coming. And he didn't like it at all. Starbrite felt the same way.

"Dad, I won't go into details. But, overall, matter and antimatter separated at the start of the universe. There are antimatter galaxies out there. Our galaxy is matter—mostly. But there are remnants of antimatter. Beds of the stuff that still exist in the form of small asteroids and debris. Questin and Quas know where those beds are because they're charted in all navigational books."

Vac looked to Starbrite and Questin, as though for confirmation.

"Most dangerous stuff in the galaxy. Most spacers avoid even going near antimatter beds. An antimatter meteorite the size of a rice grain could disable a ship the size of the *Cetus*," Starbrite said.

"Most spacers. But not all. Right, Quas?" Lyra retorted.

Questin nodded regretfully, answering for Starbrite. "Did it once. With Jost Adrian. Scientists experimenting with the stuff. Combining matter and antimatter in controlled doses. Wanted it for new drive systems."

Lyra leaned forward in her seat, intense and direct. "We have the technology to contain limited amounts of antimatter. And that stuff's powerful enough to disturb even a black hole's symmetry. If we can drop enough into KraKon's gateway, we can close his entrance to our galaxy."

Vac's mouth formed a discordant grimace. "What happened to that experiment? When they mixed matter and antimatter to develop drive systems," he asked Questin.

Questin scratched the back of his neck. "Never heard from 'em again. Jost and I just brought the stuff to 'em. A space station. Left it an' ran. Heard later they all disappeared in one big white flash of light."

"If the stuff is so dangerous, if it just *touches* matter to explode, how'd you get it anyplace?" Vac asked.

"Magnetic bottles, Dad. Antimatter is suspended in a strong magnetic field. It doesn't touch anything. The magnetic field doesn't react to antimatter because the field isn't made of atoms."

"Simple enough," Vac murmured, nodding his head in comprehension.

Starbrite and Questin exchanged quick glances. *Simple enough*? Suspending the most volatile material made by nature in a magnetic field; keeping the field perfectly symmetrical; guaranteeing that every *atom* of the stuff was confined. Containing a handful of dust on a plate during a hurricane was simple in comparison.

"Jost an' I. We carried back a few specks of the stuff. " 'Bout the size of a fingernail. How much you be needing?" Questin asked cautiously.

Lyra looked skyward, lips pursed. Then, her head facing Questin, she glanced toward Starbrite. *Here comes the part we really won't like*, Starbrite thought.

"A few kilograms at least," Lyra said.

"That's the part I don't like so much," Questin said abruptly, folding his arms and leaning back against an instrument panel.

"It is possible, Questin?" Lyra asked.

Questin remained silent for a long time, calculating the problem. A few clicks from the navigational computer making a slight course correction sounded like laseshots. Finally Questin gave a barely perceptible nod of his head. "Just possible. Have to tap some of our hyperdrive capacity. To force a stronger magnetic field for the large container. Can be done." There was no doubt from Questin's tone that it was a reluctant admission.

"Dangerous, I suppose," Vac commented blandly, not really understanding half the problems. "What happens if a bit of the stuff gets loose?"

Starbrite gave a quick exhale. "Remember the team that was experimenting with antimatter drive systems? Went up in a big white flash? Well, we'd go up in a bigger white flash. Simple as that."

They hype-hopped to the closest antimatter bed, a feat of navigational virtuosity. The bed was a mere five Km's in diameter, composed of tiny nuggets of antimatter iron.

"This is the one Jost and I mined," Questin explained. "Got rich from that one job. Now mebbe we just get dead, eh?" he added with a gallows grimace.

Vac ignored Questin's pessimism. "Good luck that the stuff's all in a tight patch. No loose nuggets floating around," he said.

"Not luck, Dad. Gravitational attraction keeps them close together. Nothing else is out here to drag the bed apart."

They began mining the bed that day.

Reluctant crewmen took a shuttle ship to within a few score meters from the bed of nuggets while the *Cetus* lay dormant a hundred Km's or so away. Then, during an EVA, they would coax one small nugget into a cryogenic bottle with a magnetic wand. Each bottle was the dimension of a man's forearm and chilled to zero degrees. At that temperature the electrical current that induced its internal magnetic field churned through the bottle's wire coils without resistance. That field held each antimatter nugget at the bottle's center.

It was a traditional method of confining the material. Questin had found five cryogenic bottles stored in a rarely visited stowage compartment, the same ones he and Adrian had used a decade before. Four were still functional. And each sortie from the *Cetus* brought back four additional antimatter nuggets.

The collection was confined in a huge cryogenic magnetic container Questin rigged up in the hyperdrive chambers, tapping the drive coils to achieve an enormously powerful magnetic field.

"I'd rather move a whole hive of bees, one by one, with my fingers than get near this stuff," Questin murmured to Starbrite on the third day of mining.

They were near the hyperdrive coils and Questin was using a hysteresis field to coax an antimatter nugget from its smaller cryogenic bottle into the larger container. His face was like white parchment and they both had the acrid, stale smell caused by constant high tension.

By the seventh day, Questin called for a rest. "Strain's too much on all of us. Mistake time coming up without rest," he explained.

Lyra calculated the amount of antimatter they had accumulated and asked for at least another day's worth, preferably two or three. Already they'd gathered enough of the material to destroy ten planets the size of New Earth. They were the biggest floating bomb humans had ever constructed.

"Three more nuggets of the stuff is all I'd want in that container. The magnetic field is doing a lot of work already. Got to have *some* safety margin," Questin told Lyra, his tone uncharacteristically testy.

Strain, thought Starbrite. *It's the strain we've got to watch for*. He voiced his agreement with Questin despite Lyra's annoyance. Not because of a safety margin but because chances for mistakes grew geometrically with time. In another day or so there'd be a slip someplace. After that—one big, white flash.

They rested for one day. Then practiced teams of crewmen took the eighth day's shift of three trips. And it was on that eighth day—while one team was at the fringes of the antimatter bed—that Questin spotted the attack formation heading toward the *Cetus*.

They hadn't neglected security. In fact, given the tribulations they'd experienced, every electronic alert on board had been at full power during their mining expedition. And it had been the long-range intercept radar that caught the four fast-moving objects streaking toward their ship.

"Comets, maybe? Meteors?" Vac asked after Questin summoned them to the control room and pointed out the four white blips on the long range viewscreen.

"None of those. Fighter craft. An hour away, still," Questin answered firmly, fiddling with the dials to sharpen the view.

"Then where's the mother ship?" Starbrite asked. "Can't have short-range fighters without a supply ship nearby."

"Can if they have hyperdrive. They shot onto the screen. No analog warning. One minute—nothing. Then they were there."

Starbrite's mouth opened as he stared at Questin.

Lyra and Vac looked on bewildered. "We don't have hyperdrive capacity for our fighters," he said flatly.

The conclusion was obvious.

"Full alert. I'll recall the mining crew. Bad news 'cause we can't get out of here for at least three hours."

"Well—maybe it's not—" Lyra stammered weakly, hoping that Questin could withdraw his sentence.

"Our fighters can't hype hop. So those specks are part of those Dark Horde contingents. Don't doubt it for more'n two seconds," he warned.

Lyra shrugged weakly.

A steady pinging sound erupted from somewhere on the control panel. Questin moved rapidly, manipulating a swarm of dials. The pinging stopped. "They've got us on their locater radar. Our sensors picked up their beam an'—"

Questin paused, his mouth dropping as he stared at the viewscreen.

"Now there's only three. One's scrammed." He bit furiously on his underlip.

"Hype-hopped back to the base ship. To get reinforcements. They're not taking chances with us. These three will head on in, and others will follow," Starbrite growled. "Determined bastards aren't they."

Then Starbrite calmed, as though a decision had been made. He stretched his neck, moving his head in muscle-loosening swings. "How long now before arrival?" he asked Questin.

"Less'n an hour."

"The Whippet. I'll meet them as far from the *Cetus* as I can. Meanwhile you get ready for an instant hype hop. When I rejoin the *Cetus*, we'll crash out of here. Might just beat them yet."

When I rejoin the Cetus, Starbrite had said. But he— and everyone else—knew they were words that carried a lot more hope than expectation.

Chapter Seventeen

The fighter craft that Starbrite had pried loose for the mission was a chef-d'oeuvre of New Earth's technology and contained radical innovations in both flight maneuverability and electronic camouflage. It was the first of these innovations that Starbrite initially used against the Dark Horde spacefighters now streaking toward the *Cetus*.

The Whippet was an ungainly craft, with a shape that resembled two crossed sticks with a pilot pod at the intersection. It was the tips of these four ends, each of which expanded into a bulbous shape, that held much of the Whippet's virtuosity. For, in each bulb, were a pair of gyroscopes which gave the craft an unprecedented maneuverability in deep space.

Starbrite had dressed in a compression suit and eased into the Whippet's cockpit minutes after leaving Questin. There had been a brief, poignant moment with Lyra, when they had realized how the threat to the Federation also threatened them personally. Their time together might come. But not without first warding off the most clear and present danger: three Dark Horde fighters bent on their annihilation.

Starbrite's fingers moved over the preflight check controls with delicate, almost reverent, gestures. The control stick had a familiar feel and look, and the cockpit itself carried warm remembrances of the times he had carried out mock maneuvers with many of his colleagues in the Space Academy.

He pressed a sequence of controls and the Whippet ejected from its pod on the *Cetus*. In a burst of admittedly childish exuberance, Starbrite whirled the Whippet at an almost right-angle turn, past the *Cetus*'s control tower, then into another sharp arc and set trajectory toward the three Dark Horde fighters. From the corner of his eye, Starbrite glimpsed the sheen of the shuttle ship returning from the antimatter beds. It would be almost another full hour before they berthed at the *Cetus* and unloaded their deadly cargo of nuggets. The Dark Horde fighters would reach them well before that.

Unless. . . . Starbrite gunned the Whippet forward, feeling the comfortable pressure of added acceleration against his form chair. He took a deep breath—a physical prelude to the coming battle. He checked his comm systems with the *Cetus* and got the three aliens on his craft's viewscreen.

A tight formation for deep space. Flying in series: one, two, three. Each fighter not more than one Km from the other. Bearing ahead at a steady pace.

Then he heard Questin's voice, calm and deliberate as ever. "Closing time to target fourteen minutes. Vectors add head-on. Target stable. Approach accelerating."

"Thanks Questin. Keep up the data feed. Might not have time for personal calculations," Starbrite answered. In fact, the Whippet had constant readouts of all the data Questin reported. But it was reassuring to have a familiar voice in the background. *Keep talking, Questin. Glad to have you aboard*, Starbrite thought.

Then he thumbed a switch, and two neutron rockets streaked from the Whippet's undercarriage, their pinpoints of exhaust growing smaller by the second.

Neither was aimed to hit an invader. Starbrite doubted if he could disable a craft at this range, even with the density-seeker warhead guiding each weapon to its target. His intention was to break up their formation, then possibly take out at least one attacker at long range. The two neutron rockets were a skirmish punch.

The alien formation scattered, the first two ships peel-

ing off to the left and right. The third began a slow arc
upward. They had no other choice, really. Not when potentially lethal missiles could knock them out all at once,
as a single grenade might kill a group of huddling warriors.

"Eight minutes contact time." Questin's voice again,
announcing the moment for a second, more deadly, strike.
Now that he was closer, Starbrite went for a knockout with
two more neutron missiles. One he aimed above the third
alien ship, the other below.

The first two missiles sped past the three ships harm-
lessly. The third Dark Horde fighter, still arcing upward,
continued in its trajectory. It might have headed down, but
it made no difference. For, having successfully dodged the
first two missiles, it was nicely caught by one from the
second salvo.

Starbrite had timed it to near perfection, electronically
arming the missile to explode where the alien would be at
its present speed. The rocket exploded in what looked like
a bright flash from a stroboscopic light, dousing the enemy
craft in a bath of neutrons, causing every electronic circuit
in the fighter to stop functioning. The craft began to
shudder, then wobble, and then begin an end-over-end
tumble that meant death in any language of any galaxy.

One out, Two to go.

"Enemy behind. Closing fast with acceleration burst.
Another returning in slow arc. Make it fast." Questin's
voice, uncharacteristically anxious.

Starbrite's eyes raced to the Whippet's viewscreen
and a millisecond later he had snapped the ship into a
sharp, right-angle turn. The Dark Horde fighter was a
mere ten Km's away and even as Starbrite gritted his teeth
at the tremendous G-forces created by the turn he felt his
Whippet shudder with a near miss.

"Enemy starting a curve. Passed you by. Whippet's
evasive maneuver successful. Other enemy approaching in
series." Then, in a more personal aside, Questin added,
"Quas. Try for a quick end. They learn fast. They'll
coordinate an attack now. Be on the lookout for quick
maneuvers."

The two alien fighter craft were darting toward him in

tandem now, and at this close range he could make out the strange asymmetrical shape of their ships, as though a basketball had developed a cancer the size of a baseball on one side.

Asymmetrical or not, their weapons were deadly and Starbrite gave his Whippet an acceleration burst, hoping that another feature of his craft would now pay off: the electronic camouflage.

He yanked back on an eject lever. A tiny capsule, oriented by pinpoint rocket jets, tumbled from a hatch on the Whippet's rear fuselage.

Suddenly there were three Whippets, one following the other.

The pursuing Dark Horde fighters zoomed apart, their pilots momentarily confused by the sudden appearance of two more high-performance craft, their alarm signals flashing.

Those additional Whippets were highly accurate simulacra of Starbrite's own, designed to confuse even the most sophisticated of detection and alert mechanisms. The ejected capsule was a holographic projector and for the next few minutes it followed Starbrite's craft, creating a three-dimensional image on the solid matter of his exhaust jets.

Whatever confusion the Dark Horders experienced, they recovered quickly. Each craft attacked a Whippet. One arced toward a simulacrum, and the other closed in on Starbrite's ship. Better if they had both gone for a simulacrum, Starbrite thought. But then, one couldn't ask for everything.

Starbrite pulled up his Whippet in the sharpest bone-crunching curve he dared impose on the craft, his pressure suit equalizing the G-force over all his body. Still, his chest felt like a lead vest. He could barely breathe. Red and black spots darted before his eyes. Then, more by instinct than instrument, Starbrite straightened his trajectory: a Dark Horde fighter lay in the center of his gun sights.

Effectively, Starbrite had looped in space, the final tail of his sharp arc forming a tangential line with the wider arc of the Dark Horde fighter.

Starbrite clenched both hands on the side handles of one boxlike control stick. Both handles had to be depressed within a half second of each other for the lasecannon to fire.

Two thick bolts of speckled red light streaked from the Whippet in quick, stroboscopic bursts, raking toward the alien craft. Then the dazzling bright flashes caught up with the attacker's ship. The lasecannon poured an even faster tattoo of red fire into the Dark Horde fighter.

It disappeared in a bright ball of orange light that quickly faded to a dull glow before completely darkening in the icy cold of deep space.

"Your tail, Quas. Other alien. Closing with acceleration burst."

Questin's warning had hardly died out before Starbrite jerked back on the control stick, cursing himself for the seconds wasted watching his first close kill of the Dark Horde invaders. The gyroscopes whined and the Whippet wheeled up and to one side in an instantly conceived evasion maneuver. Any intricate trajectory pattern would do—any twists or turns to avoid being targeted in the enemy's sights.

The Whippet lurched with enough force for Starbrite to feel his neck bones crackle. For a sickening moment the craft wobbled violently, then rapidly regained equilibrium as it resumed its course. Starbrite, surprisingly calm after the hit, glanced at the damage report panels.

One of the strut-damage lights blinked ominously. Starbrite glanced through his canopy. The bulbous tip of the right strut wasn't there—cleanly amputated by the gravity beam of the invader ship.

"Close. But a miss is a miss is a miss," Starbrite murmured, gently moving his hand-operated control stick, finding out how his maneuverability was affected by the one missing gyroscope mechanism.

"An' miss he did. But not by much. He's arcing toward the *Cetus* now. No sight of any others. Suggest haste. Arrival time is nine point zero five minutes." Questin's voice again. Starbrite grimaced as he remembered his words were broadcast on an open comm line.

He concentrated on his own computer display of relative vectors. To compensate for the lost gyro, Starbrite flipped in the total logistics manual override, another special feature of the craft.

The override permitted the pilot to make all tactical decisions, allowing his intuitive insight to come into play, an intangible, fugitive factor that computers couldn't duplicate. With the Dark Horde fighter streaking in a wide arc and the *Cetus* at an intersection point less than nine minutes away, Starbrite fudged in a way that would have driven a computer to madness.

The gyroscope controlling the Whippet's pitch was gone. Under override, Starbrite maneuvered the Whippet on its side. Then he activated the gyros normally governing his yaw orientation. The Whippet began a tight circle toward the *Cetus*, Starbrite forced to one side as though a giant, invisible hand were shoving him into his chair's side.

"On course Quas. You'll be driving right toward us. Give another five seconds." Questin's voice. Starbrite eased back on the turn. That hand shoving him to the side backed off. He maneuvered the Whippet to a horizontal position relative to the *Cetus* and glanced from his cockpit. The base ship lay directly ahead, a silvery splinter in space.

"My arrival time relative to enemy craft," Starbrite snapped out, gunning the Whippet to maximum acceleration.

"Enemy four minutes. You're a scratch less, fifteen secs or so."

Just fifteen seconds: on that bit of time hinged the *Cetus*'s safety, the success or failure of their entire effort. Starbrite relinquished all emotion. His mind became an intuitive machine, drinking in numbers, accelerations, and locations while spewing out evaluations, probabilities, and maneuvers.

Starbrite aimed for the starship. It was more than likely that the Dark Horde pilot assumed he was disabled or dead from the hit. The *Cetus*'s bulk would hide his approach and what he'd lost in maneuverability he might gain by surprise. In any event, he'd have only one chance for a kill.

"Times, Questin. Fast."

"Enemy two minutes from target. One minute fifty secs for you." Questin's voice hardly trembled.

Starbrite eased up the Whippet's nose with a touch of his yaw control, aiming to skim over the top of the *Cetus*'s hull. If Questin's calculations were correct, the Dark Horde fighter would be ending his parabolic arc and closing for his kill a few seconds after the Whippet streaked past the larger ship. He'd meet the enemy a Km or so beyond—a speck of space and a sliver of time away.

The *Cetus* enlarged with enormous speed. Then the ship filled his window and rolled under his Whippet as Starbrite skimmed his craft over the hull. Staring at his gun sights, he aimed his lasecannons as he dipped the Whippet slightly.

The Dark Horde fighter was a green blip on the sight screen, about 3 Km's away and off to one side of Starbrite's trajectory. Starbrite jerked the Whippet into a course correction, squeezing his cannon triggers at the same time. Bright bolts of red lasefire leaped from the craft, the loud snaps reverberating throughout the cockpit, the dazzling stroboscopic flashes almost blinding him with their intensity. The bright bolts swept an arc through space as the Whippet turned slightly then zeroed in on the asymmetrical fighter ahead. Puffs of vaporized metal spouted from the dark craft as a dozen rapid strikes from the cannon stabbed into its hull.

The Dark Horde pilot was good. But the factor of surprise had overriden his reaction time. From a leisurely safe shot at a huge, nearly defenseless starship, the pilot had to cope with the sudden apparition of a Whippet streaking over the hull and heading toward him with lasecannons blasting.

The alien craft began to wobble and vibrate simultaneously, while beginning a sickening lurch that quickly evolved into an end-over-end spin. The stress forces were too great for any structure to support and the ship broke apart into rapidly tumbling segments that would whirl forever in the vast womb of space.

"Sit now, you can't do more," Questin commanded. Starbrite slumped into a form chair in the observation room. It had taken him only a few more minutes to berth his craft, a record for docking time. Controlled pandemonium seemed to fill the ship. The mining crew had just returned from the antimatter beds and was now transferring their last nuggets into the larger container. Some of the crew helped Starbrite to the observation deck; on leaving his ship, Starbrite's body began trembling uncontrollably, turning him into a near invalid. He wouldn't have made it to the form chair without the support of two crewmen.

"Balance that feed to the coils!" Questin rumbled into a communicator as he scanned the instruments monitoring the charging rate of their hyperdrive coils. Starbrite had never seen Questin so rattled.

"Few minutes behind schedule," Questin shot to Starbrite, without specifying what schedule he was referring to. "Lyra an' Vac, they're helping get those last nuggets into the big container. Docking crew took more time, too. Time—

An incessant, jolting ring interrupted Questin's words. He regarded the large viewscreen impassively. "Can't say they're unexpected. Best leave soon."

A bevy of dots had suddenly appeared on the screen and Starbrite didn't bother to count them. Just one of those dots coming close to the *Cetus* would be enough. There was no fight left in him or his Whippet.

Questin made some quick mental calculations then opened all comm circuits, broadcasting his words throughout the ship.

All here now. Enemy fifteen minutes distant. In twelve minutes I activate hyperdrive. One minute's warning bell."

Questin leaned back against the edge of the control panel and faced Starbrite. Then his thin lips actually expanded into a narrow smile. "A ship full of antimatter. Getting ready for a hype hop in minutes when it usually takes hours. An' a half-dozen or so alien fighters bearing down to cut our throats." Questin's mouth broke into an even broader grin as he glanced leisurely at a chronometer. "If we make it, it'll be a story of a lifetime. Jost would have loved it. This was his kind of operation."

Then Questin dipped his head to Starbrite in an almost solemn nod, a gesture of camaraderie if they were successful, one of farewell if not.

With a slow majesty and an occasional glance at the chronometer, Questin turned to the control panel and began preparing for the coming hyperdrive flight. At one minute before full activation he pushed the hype-hop alert signal. The *Cetus* filled with the sound of a clanging bell.

The dots on the viewscreen had grown to the size of bumblebees. A few gnat-sized specks left the larger dots, quickly outpacing them.

"Some kind of rocket fire heading our way," Questin murmured to himself as he inaugurated their hype hop.

The dark of deep space in the port windows seemed to shimmer and slide into a vacuous gray, as though the ship had been immersed in liquid mercury. In the last instant, just at the point when the shimmering gray hadn't yet wiped out the dark velvet of true-time, Starbrite thought he saw a bright burst against the darker background. A bright burst that was quickly engulfed by a shimmer, then a duller uniform gray, and then by another shimmer. . . .

And then by the dark velvet of deep space again, light years from the Dark Horde rockets that were now exploding at the point the *Cetus* had occupied a few microseconds before.

Chapter Eighteen

They exited near Benera.

The planet was a reasonable hype hop for the charge Questin had forced into the *Cetus*'s hyperdrive coils. In addition, Benera was a way station where they could get news of the Galactic Federation's alert as well as make a precise navigational fix on the alien's black hole gateway, a mere 1000 light years away.

But only a hulk of a planet remained.

They began a quick reconnaissance of the colony. The short-range optical scope had picked out city after city. The smaller municipalities were nothing but black, smoking pits. Larger cities still showed the skeletal remains of buildings. No sign of organized civilization remained.

The apocalyptic sight had answered one question at least: whatever alert the Galactic Federation had received, it hadn't been soon enough. And Benera's doom certainly meant that other of the Federation's settled planets had been attacked—or soon would be.

"A space scan. Get a quick scan," Starbrite said to Questin, his voice tremulous. Even before he had finished Questin was tuning in the multiple sensors that were the *Cetus*'s long-range eyes and ears, looking for the marauders, for any threats lurking in the deceptive tranquillity of far space.

The *Cetus*'s own microwave radar probed the vastness around them. Sensor units on the ship's hull picked up any signals that radiated in their direction. The giant viewscreen combined this data into a composite image. And, at maximum magnification they saw two groups of tiny dots on the vast screen.

One group was a few hundred Km's from the other. Both groups were a few thousand Km's from the *Cetus* and drifted across the screen in a barely perceptible motion.

"Pursuit. Someone's chasing someone else," Questin said slowly, more for the others' benefit than his own, for in those impersonal dots he and Starbrite read the story of a ravaged planet, of attempted help, of failure and then flight. Those dots meant a major space battle was taking place, with the Federation's ships in full retreat.

The chirp of an alarm bell caused them all to jump. Questin's hand was poised over the general alarm switch when a crewman whose face had been chiseled from an ebony block called over: "Got a quick ID. It's a Whippet."

"Keep at it Spica," Questin said, relaxing a bit. Spica had been manning the domestic sensors, those that gave a closer picture of space around the *Cetus*. Radio, infrared scans, short-range radar, and optical scopes.

"Just emerged from behind Benera's horizon. Got a fix on us. P'robly was circling the planet," Spica added.

"Guide it in. Take over its docking," Questin murmured to the crewman. It was an incongruous event—one Whippet circling a ravaged planet. But in war, strange events were the norm. "But keep our lasecannons on it, just in case," he added with venom.

"Got the pilot," Spica called out. "Female voice. Sounds authentic. She'll be docking in a few minutes." Questin nodded. The pilot's verbal report would be invaluable.

They waited in the observation deck while the Whippet docked. Starbrite gazed wearily at the newly arrived craft. It was scorched, torn, scratched, and dented. It had been through hell.

The panel to the deck slid open and the pilot entered. Starbrite's mouth dropped. The pilot's eyes opened wide.

And in the next seconds they were in each other's arms, whirling around, Starbrite lifting her off the ground in unrestrained glee. They backed off from each other, hands clenched together, with the satisfaction of trusted friends suddenly renewing acquaintance.

"Rhinna. Rhinna Treaver," Starbrite said, as though to confirm what he saw, his eyes glistening. Rhinna Treaver bit on an underlip self-consciously, her eyes wet. They hugged again in a sudden, spontaneous burst of affection.

"Old friends," Questin murmured, a twinge of a grin on his face as he got a good look at Rhinna Treaver. She had a robust beauty complemented by natural poise. She was short and a stylish V-neck tunic enhanced a full, graceful body. She had tied a silk scarf, patterned with green polka dots, around her neck, a feminine highlight. Her manner was understated, almost hesitant. When Starbrite introduced her as an old friend at the Space Academy, one with the highest spacefighter kill-scores in its history, Questin knew that her apparent ambivalence was a surface feature that masked a fiery competence. For her to have survived in a fighter as badly scarred as the Whippet indicated a skill anyone would envy.

Starbrite led Rhinna to a form chair, relieved to note that warm way she and Lyra greeted each other. Vac remained morosely silent, as though overwhelmed by incomprehensible events that threatened the foundations of some cherished beliefs.

Rhinna filled in with a tired voice, at first in bursts of words punctuated with hesitant pauses, then finally in an almost stream-of-consciousness narration.

The Spaceforce fleet had got a Yellow Alert. The wing to which Rhinna was attached had been sent to scout the Nether Quadrant. They hype-hopped to the vicinity of Benera. The planet was under siege, its spaceport sending out frantic calls for help.

"Some of us thought it was a practice mission, with a dash of realism added for effect," Rhinna said, shaking her head in a slow, disbelieving motion. She remained silent for a moment, her mouth grim. "Then they swarmed over us."

The Dark Horde fleet had pounced on Rhinna's wing of the Spaceforce fleet. Whippets leaped from their berths, expecting some sort of ultra-real exercise. A dozen or more were torn apart in space before the others actually fought back. At the same time giant space cruisers bombarded Benera from an orbit high above, destroying its cities with what Starbrite and the others knew were gravity cannon.

"Whose ships are they? Pirates? Some kind of settlement wars our Intelligence Division hadn't heard of?" Rhinna asked.

"Later." Vac spoke in a commanding voice, halting Starbrite's answer. In calm, almost fatherly tones, he added, "Your commentary first. It would only be confusing if you interpreted the events by what you learned now. Another few moments, but go on."

Rhinna's voice lowered as she remembered the last details. Benera had been effectively destroyed. The Spaceforce fleet regrouped into a smaller area, allowing its fighters to offer better cover for its escape. They were still running.

"Hype-hop. Why doesn't the fleet use their hyperdrive units to get away?" Lyra asked, her face lined and tired.

Starbrite answered. "Old tactics, really. You harass the larger ships. They have to send out fighters to combat the enemy. You can't hype-hop with all those fighters out. Not until the very last. No commander wants to be responsible for that kind of sacrifice."

"The fleet's still running. With the Dark Horde ships just behind. They need more space between them to make a hype hop to safety," Questin said.

Rhinna's eyebrows rose, and she grimaced. "*Dark Horde* ships?" She looked around, bewildered.

And that look spoke volumes to Starbrite. For a week now the edges of his consciousness had been prickling, as though fighting for a larger panoramic view of something he was closely involved in. There was something out there, something a broader perspective would illuminate. He felt

176

it as an unease, a frustrated annoyance. And now, his consciousness was in turmoil, as though *some* fact would fit a lock and open the door to a still obscure awareness.

Lyra explained and Rhinna ran her hands through her dark hair, trying to absorb in minutes what had taken the others weeks to assimilate.

Starbrite rose from his form chair. "How'd you end up here, Rhinna?" he asked, his voice holding a sudden metallic coldness. Lyra glanced at him curiously.

"Took on some of those lopsided ships. Got two, hit another. But the last blasted me with a kind of weapon I've never seen—"

"Gravity cannon, we call it," Questin interjected as Rhinna paused for breath.

"Knocked *me* out but somehow not the Whippet. When I came to I was orbiting Benera. The fleet was too far to reach with the fuel left. So I figured to orbit as long as possible before crash-landing on Benera. Then my radar spotted the *Cetus*. Been on that Whippet for three solid days. I need a shower," Rhinna added incongruously.

Starbrite nodded. "Lyra will get you a berth. Let's take a few hours maintenance and rest time, then meet here." It wasn't a suggestion. Questin looked at him curiously. Lyra seemed annoyed at his perfunctory tone. Vac appeared indifferent and Rhinna grateful.

"The fleet—well," Lyra said tentatively. "Can't we do *something*? Help *some* way?"

"A few hours from now. We'll talk then," Starbrite said firmly. Lyra's eyes blazed and tears of frustration welled in her eyes.

"Time won't be wasted. Lots to catch up on. Check our magnetic container for sure," Questin said, pouring a bit of oil on troubled waters.

Starbrite's mind churned now, absorbing all his energies, leaving no room for social amenities. He stalked from the deck without another word and entered his cabin. Then, his eyes blazing as comprehension slowly emerged, he sat on his bunk and slipped a music cassette into a receptacle player.

The melody was a sweetly haunting tune that rolled

from a wooden flute. It was a Celtic air, preserved from Earth and accentuating its gentle rhythms was the strong beat of a bodhran, a Celtic drum. The subtle rhythms and lyrical tune was one of Starbrite's favorites and it wiped his mind clean of thought.

His unconscious worked mightily, free now to invade the clarity his mind had become. An idea simmered, grew, and—while the lilting strains of the tune haunted the room— emerged into Starbrite's consciousness.

The epiphany was like a physical shock, but a shock that relieved a gnawing frustration. There was nothing he hadn't known. But now he *experienced* the truth: phantoms became incarnate problems; vague worries turned into concrete concerns; unsubstantial impressions metamorphosed into convictions.

The melody segued into a bright, ornamented series of notes and gently ended as Starbrite schemed with renewed intensity, creating plans from reality rather than false assumptions. Assumptions everyone had made about their situation. Assumptions that were diametrically opposed to the truth.

Starbrite formed priorities from his knowledge: First, help the Star Fleet now under attack. A practical idea emerged, fit in nicely with a secondary plan and tied into plugging the black hole gateway. No, not quite correct.

Starbrite grimaced at the irony.

Plugging the gateway was *not* a priority. Having KraKon flee back to where he came from was the objective. And now the two—plugging the gateway and making KraKon flee into it—weren't quite the same thing. And on that distinction hinged his plan.

Starbrite rose, his weariness gone. They still had a good chance. A chance based on understanding what *really* was taking place.

He strode to the observation deck. Questin was there and Starbrite asked that the others be sent for, meanwhile giving the man a preview of his scheme. They were a tightly knit team by now. They had a right to know what he planned, but not yet to learn what he'd discovered. That would have to keep.

"Rhinna, too. We'll need her skills before we're done," Starbrite said crisply. Questin sent for the group, himself feeling a satisfaction at Starbrite's decisive manner. The situation seemed to have been fading from their control. Now it looked like they'd be on an offensive course again. It was a posture Questin liked best.

"I think we can give the fleet some breathing space. Enlarge the distance between it and the Dark Horde ships. The fighters can land, and then the larger ships can hype-hop to safety," Starbrite said to the assembly. Everyone noticed that he seemed less tired and more alert. The attitude was infectious, and morale began to build. Even Vac Orion, who had seemed beset by a constant depression during the last several days, perked up.

"Details, Quas, just fill us in quickly," he said, hope plain in his voice.

"We have antimatter aboard. I'd like to sow it in a wide swath between the fleet and the pursuers. Break it into motes—tiny particles. When the Dark Horde ships hit the antimatter swath they'll pull back. Just puncturing a few hulls will be enough. And even a mite of antimatter will do that."

"How much will you need?" Lyra asked cautiously.

"Almost all of it," Starbrite said firmly. Lyra shook her head.

"Quas. We need it for the black hole. What's the sense of saving a fleet and losing the Federation?"

It was the moment Starbrite dreaded. He couldn't tell Lyra right then. Perhaps never. He couldn't let her know *THAT IT MADE ABSOLUTELY NO DIFFERENCE IF THEY PLUGGED THE BLACK HOLE OR NOT.*

"We'll have to make do, Lyra. We'll use a good part of it now. I'm sure the rest will be enough," he temporized.

"Idiotic. You haven't made those calculations. *I* have," Lyra shouted at him.

"The decision isn't negotiable," Starbrite said coldly. Lyra's mouth trembled with fury. Then Starbrite elaborated with forced calm.

"Questin and I already talked over how to deliver the

antimatter swath. Complicated but possible. We'll contain most of the material in a cryogenic bottle. Questin can rig up a magnetic pulser that will release one nugget at a time.''

Vac cut in with an obvious question. ''Quas, we only have larger nuggets. Maybe twenty or so. How can we break them up so they deter an entire fleet?''

Starbrite silenced Vac with an impatient wave of his hand, irritated at his own dictatorial bearing and defensive at its necessity. ''One of the *Cetus*'s shuttlecraft has a defensive lasecannon. We'll blast each nugget with a lasebeam. It'll turn to dust specks and be spread over a wide area at the same time.''

''It'll explode. When it touches matter. You said—''

Starbrite shook his head. ''A laser beam is electromagnetic energy, not matter. Just like light waves. No, it won't explode the antimatter. It'll break it up into dust specks,'' he reiterated.

Questin added, ''Getting the lasegun to blast each nugget is the easiest part. There's an automatic tracker. We can juice up the sensitivity. Should hit even a nugget at that close a range as easy as a pirate scow at a greater distance.''

Questin didn't mention the enormous difficulty in rigging up a magnetic pulser, getting the antimatter into a large cryogenic bottle, and affixing the mechanism to a release hatch on the shuttle. Now *that* was an ad hoc engineering problem whose solution would merit a few boasts.

A short time later Starbrite got off a terse lasebeam message to the fleeing fleet, asking them to make a tight formation and outlining his intention of providing a protective screen of antimatter particles while they berthed their fighters.

Starbrite added a postscript for delivery to Commander Croost once the fleet hype-hopped to New Earth. In a few brief sentences he summarized their attack while at the antimatter bed and detailed their intention to get to the black hole gateway.

Chances were it would be the last message beamed from the *Cetus* for ultimate arrival at New Earth.

At least the communiqué would let posterity know that they had done their best to abort the alien plague now ravaging the Federation.

Chapter Nineteen

It was to be a complicated piece of celestial navigation.

The shuttle ship would sweep out an arc behind the fleeing Spaceforce craft, spreading the deadly antimatter motes like a sheltering umbrella. It took all of Questin's skill to program the shuttle's autopilot for such a flight, and even then they needed someone in the cockpit.

"Too tricky. Rigging an automatic sensor to trigger the lasecannon three seconds after the pulser ejects an antimatter nugget. No time to foolproof it. Someone's got to go," Questin announced dourly.

"But it's so simple after all the other things you made," Lyra answered, bewildered. They were just minutes from making the short hype hop to the fleet. The shuttle ship would bolt from the *Cetus* for its sweep behind the fleet seconds after arrival.

Questin bored into an upper molar with his tongue, then replied, "Simple's often the hardest. No way out. Not with our time schedule." His tone plainly told them he regretted his own conclusion.

"There's an obvious candidate for that job. Me," Vac Orion added.

Starbrite's mouth opened for an objection, then closed slowly. Only Lyra voiced a weak no. But Vac's suggestion made sense. Regretful sense, but sense nonetheless.

"It's a simple job. I'm plainly the most expendable

person on the *Cetus*. Everyone else has a precise function. I'm relieved to finally be of concrete use,'' Vac said.

"Dangerous trip, Vac. No problem for one of the fleet to pick you up. Programmed a curve at the end of the sweep that'll carry you near the ships. Standard rescue after that. But. . . ." Questin's voice trailed off.

"You're saying a lot could go wrong before the end of the shuttle's flight. I know that. The same dangers hold for anybody. But this is a job I *can* do without depriving the *Cetus* of a skilled crewman," Vac added, his voice vibrant. He seemed more animated than at any time in the past week.

"We'll alert the fleet to have rescue craft out. You'll join them back to New Earth and report to Croost personally. He'll want to have a firsthand account," Starbrite added.

They rushed to the shuttlecraft, arriving just as an engineering crew finished adapting it to an antimatter mine layer. Questin and Vac covered contingency operations for the most probable malfunctions. Starbrite listened, thinking again how often the human mind had to take over from even highly sophisticated machinery. Whatever Vac might have to do would be simple—a button here, a switch there. An intelligent child could learn any of the procedures in minutes. But *when* to use one contingency plan rather than another? *When* to substitute a red button for a green or a blue for a yellow? Human judgment: no machine could yet duplicate its legerdemain.

They hype-hopped to the formation, which had gathered in as tight a grouping as logistically possible. The shuttlecraft, with Vac inside, leaped from its pod and streaked into trajectory, the glow from its thrust slowly shrinking as its distance increased.

An escort of Whippets buzzed to the sides and front of the shuttle, protection against any Dark Horde fighters that might try and avert their seeding space with antimatter. From the optical sensor, Questin saw the quick flicker of a bright red light. "Lasecannon fired. First nugget must be motes by now," he reported.

Then came a flash of brilliant white light. Questin

increased volume on the comm set monitoring the frequency band used by Whippet pilots. ". . . down. One got it. Tried for a kill from behind. This stuff *does* work," came a flat, tinny voice from the speaker.

"They'll have broken the code for the message we sent to the fleet. They'll know we intended to spread a minefield. Now they'll know we actually have," Starbrite said. He turned to the group. "They'll *have* to pull back now. Give the fleet time enough to berth the fighters and hype-hop to safety. Our turn now. On to the black hole gateway."

"Lot of good, Quas. We haven't but a few nuggets left," Lyra spat out bitterly.

"It'll do *something* Lyra, distort the gravity a bit," Starbrite said, aching at her anger. *It doesn't make any difference what we send into the black hole. It doesn't make a difference,* he screamed to her in his mind, feeling dismal over tricking everyone, necessary as it was.

"*Something?* Quas, those nuggets we have left will be like a wart on an elephant's rear. *That's* the effect they'll have," Lyra shot out.

Starbrite, his face a stone mask, turned to the controls. Questin shot him a glance of wry sympathy. Rhinna looked on, confused. Lyra had told her about the black hole gateway and their coming attempt to plug it. It didn't seem like Starbrite to confuse a mission, not to have a reserve trick somewhere. He had become famous at the Academy as an ingenious innovator, winning score after score on test maneuvers by sheer cunning as well as strong determination.

A strained silence filled the deck while the *Cetus*'s hyperdrive coils charged. A message on Fleet frequency indicated that two more Dark Horde craft had disappeared in a burst of brilliant white light. Streaking Whippets manned by pilots with renewed hope were fast annihilating the Dark Horde fighters remaining in the area. No new ones seemed to be entering. The battle-scarred fleet was getting its breathing space.

It was at a moment of surging optimism that disaster struck Vac Orion's shuttlecraft. His long arc of a trajectory had nearly finished and the shuttle was about to eject its last antimatter nugget and turn toward the fleet.

"One from ahead! Serat missed. Converge before—" The voice of an escort Whippet pilot screaming out a warning to his partner.

"Something's ahead of me. Not firing—" Vac's voice, tinny over the speakers and characterized more by curiosity than alarm.

Questin's hand flicked to a dial and the speaker's volume increased even more just as Vac's voice was drowned out by a sharp, rumbling sound that faded into an eerie silence.

"Head on. Crash kill. Sneak's cannon didn't work. Crashed into shuttle. Return to base ships." An anonymous Whippet pilot's voice in an impersonal account of Vac Orion's death. Lyra stood stock still, her face white and taut. Questin, as ever, seemed unperturbed. Starbrite felt his heart thump with hammer blows. Rhinna moved toward Lyra, offering whatever comfort she could.

"Fleet's going to hyperdrive out soon's the Whippets berth. Matter of minutes. We better be gone," Questin said tersely, using abruptness to mask his own sadness. He hit the hype-hop warning signal.

The viewscreen showed that the alien fleet was far behind now, with only one or two darting dots left in the immediate area: Whippets, either returning to base or polishing off the remaining few alien fighters. There would be some additional casualties. Not every Whippet would make its base ship. But at least most of the fleet would have been salvaged.

"Minute left, that's all. Get into chairs. Got our course set for the black hole gateway," Questin said. They sat, Lyra still too stunned to show emotion. The alarm bell sounded its last-second warning.

The shimmering gray enveloped the observation deck's windows, at first a light, diaphanous veil that rapidly became opaque. Then they felt a quick jerk of nausea and knew that the *Cetus* had entered null-time. They were nowhere, again beyond the space of time. Then the ports cleared, the silvery gray fading away into the black velvet of real space.

Starbrite leaped to Questin's side, helping him activate all scanners, long- and short-range, for a quick glimpse of their new neighborhood. Spica was already at the navigational computer, calculating the exact location of the black hole relative to where the *Cetus* had exited from hyperdrive time.

"Got a reading. Six thou Km's. Easy range of ion drive," Spica reported in a rasp of a voice. Questin's navigation, typically, had been quintessential. That was the good news.

"Company. Might not have spotted us yet, but I wouldn't give it more than a few minutes," Starbrite grumbled. The viewscreen showed a white blip. Relative to the *Cetus*, it was further away than the black hole gateway.

"That ship's trajectory heading is right toward the gateway. Fast too," Questin muttered. More good news, although only Starbrite knew the real importance of the blip.

Several more blips appeared from behind the larger white dot and slowly separated. "A fighter screen. Enough to protect as well as attack," Rhinna commented in a tone of cool, professional appraisal. And that, definitely, was bad news.

It became a matter, now, of close timing and precise action. It was a question of getting a smaller craft loaded with the remaining antimatter. But more important, it was vital to get that craft to the black hole without being obliterated by those fighters. Then, whatever margin of luck remained would be used to flee from this gateway with whatever hyperdrive time was left in their coils. That's how Starbrite saw it.

The others, knowing less, had more obvious questions.

"Who's making those blips?" Lyra asked.

"Trouble's making 'em," Questin retorted. "No friends would be here. Too much activity closer to New Earth." Questin actually grimaced. It was the most motion Starbrite had seen his face make. "But why? Why a cruiser along with escorts running to that gateway? A puzzler, that one.''

Because the KraKon is inside, fleeing. And he'll con-tinue running unless we, or whatever ship we send into the black hole, is wiped out, Starbrite thought.

''Probably a messenger ship, maybe a casualty load. Something like that getting back to its hellhole of a world,'' Spica growled gratuitously. It was an acceptable reason as any. Starbrite said nothing, letting Spica's conjectures sat-isfy curiosity.

KraKon saw them exit from their hype hop on the massive viewscreen. ''Destroy them. Instantly,'' he or-dered, collecting the shreds of composure by a mighty exertion of will. He stood on the raised dais in the execu-tive command quarters as he addressed his starship's offi-cers, his body starkly immobile. Even the uncontrollable trembling that had lately wracked his limbs was quieted. It took a mighty effort to forge such calm but he knew that now he was fighting for his very existence.

KraKon viewed three of his Klyster fighter craft—the *last* three under his immediate command—accelerate to-ward the far starship. In that craft, he knew, was a human pestilence with an obscenity of a name toward whom he focused his massive frustration and hatred: Starbrite. The KraKon's control faltered as he thought of Starbrite and he roared, unnecessarily, to his officers, ''Obliterate that ship. Him as well. NOW.''

He flapped his ceremonial cape to underscore his words as he thought that he—the KRAKON—might be impris-oned in this hellhole galaxy. *Forever*. That those worm-colored specks of organic life had uncovered a weakness in his gateway, one his own scientists had analyzed centuries ago. That the Earth scum had uncovered the means of destroying a black hole's symmetry by antimatter bombs was nothing less than fantastic luck given their imbecilic minds. But they had and in that ship was enough of the deadly substance to maroon him in this world forever.

KraKon's control cracked again at the thought. ''De-stroy them,'' he screamed in ultrasonic tones. His officers,

their gun-metal patinas gleaming dully in the light, scur-
ried from one bank of instruments to the other, hoping that
varied movement would appear as determined action, trying
to pacify their KraKon by any means.

"Aggghh." KraKon's voice box ululated spontane-
ously. By all rights those pestilent creatures now threatening him should have been annihilated. Long ago. And
those under his command who allowed their escape would
soon feel a lingering death. Only that thought calmed
KraKon and his voice began a low, vibrant hum of satisfaction as he contemplated the savage revenge he would
inflict.

Because of these reveries KraKon missed the sudden
stillness among the command crew. The score of gleaming
officers and crew froze in fright as they saw on the giant
viewscreen two tiny blips edge away from the target craft
and head toward their black hole gateway.

Then, KraKon saw them, too. His voice became an
ultrasonic snarl, holding disdain for his subordinates and
fear for his existence. "Have the Kysters eliminate their
craft. Accelerate toward the gateway." The officers stirred
uneasily. They knew that there would be a dark revenge
waiting for some of them even if they did pass safely
through the gateway before those blips, and the antimatter
bombs they carried, obliterated their passage.

Unless. . . . There was not one cyborg on the deck
who didn't yearn with every neuron of its organic brain for
the success of those three Klysters.

It seemed to Starbrite that events had now gained a
momentum of their own. Somehow he felt as though all
moves of a chess game had been decided on—and that he
existed only to move his pieces in their preordained manner.
He had made a plan and, except for minor contingencies,
it was now being played out move by move.

Starbrite and Questin conferred hastily. They would
drive the *Cetus* so it skimmed the black hole—a body a
mere one hundred Km's across—their momentum countering
the massive gravitational attraction. Meanwhile, they would
be charging their hyperdrive coils once again. The speed

gained from the acceleration toward the black hole would help them circle the dense body of Benera, like a comet skimming past the sun. That added impetus to their hype hop would save them hours of charge time.

"I'll fill one of the smaller cryogenic bottles with the remaining antimatter nuggets," Questin said as a postscript.

"For whatever good it'll do," Lyra said with venomous sarcasm.

Starbrite shot her a pleading look. "It'll work, it'll get the job done," he said intently, trying to *will* her to believe him. *It's not the event, but the illusion that counts*, he shouted to her with his mind.

Lyra's jaw tightened and she looked away. "I'd like to know how. That's all. Just *how*," she muttered. Questin was probing that tooth with his tongue again, wondering the same thing. While Rhinna looked on curiously.

The broad outlines of their efforts were well formed. It was the contingencies that Starbrite was worried about. The variables that immediate tactics would have to cope with so that overall strategy remained preserved.

The shrill ring of an alarm bell coupled with Spica's bellow of warning announced that such a contingency had occurred.

"Three craft. Moving fast. Heading our way," Spica shouted.

Questin studied the viewscreen for a moment. "Give 'em fifteen minutes," he announced as though intoning a death sentence.

Starbrite hadn't overlooked this problem. He had expected to be spotted, had *wanted* to be noticed. But not so soon. And not by a ship with a fighter escort that could launch such a quick attack on the *Cetus*.

Starbrite stared ahead, his mind whirling for the right response to this immediate emergency. Oily beads of sweat appeared on his forehead. His mouth tasted like burned cotton. This time there would have to be some deliberate losses. He didn't like the idea, especially as it was his turn to become expendable.

"Rhinna, can you run interference?" he snapped. It wasn't really a question. She gave him a quick, wide smile and her eyes squinted, as though in pleasure. It was answer enough. For no logical reason at all Starbrite registered the fact that she now wore a maroon silk scarf around her neck.

He spun toward Questin. "Maximum acceleration for a trajectory tangent to the black hole's singularity." Questin dashed to the control panel and was coaxing every bit of thrust possible from the ship's engines before Starbrite finished his words.

Starbrite glanced at the viewscreen. The three blips were larger now. Thirteen minutes away, maybe a little less. "I'll be taking that bottle of antimatter nuggets in on my Whippet. Can you have it delivered?" he asked Questin.

Everyone seemed to freeze, except Lyra, who whirled toward him, her face red and her hands tight fists.

"It's a *waste*, Quas. There's no reason. That little bit of antimatter won't make a difference," she pleaded, her voice husky with emotion. "We can hype-hop out of here and come back later."

Starbrite, his heart pounding and his lips dry, stared at her. "Lyra, I've got to. It's not futile," he pleaded. Then, seeing her misery he added more than he wanted to tell. "The KraKon's on that cruiser. He won't leave 'till he sees one of our ships getting close to the gateway. Once he's gone the invasion will collapse."

Lyra swallowed, her eyes wet and her neck muscles taut.

"Why's that mechanical mess in the vicinity at all?" Questin asked slowly, half guessing.

Questin would have to learn the entire story, Starbrite thought. He'd explain it all on the way to his Whippet. He had planned to send in a drone ship, one of the last shuttle-craft, but the Dark Horde fighters would easily blast it from space. His own Whippet—damaged as it was—still offered a lot of maneuverability. With Rhinna running interference, he'd stand a good chance.

From that moment, events moved so rapidly that Starbrite scarcely remembered the sequence. Spica took over the control room, reporting the Dark Horde fighter positions every thirty seconds or so. Other of the ship's crew helped Rhinna into her Whippet.

Starbrite reached the underside of the pod holding his own craft and faced Questin. "Antimatter bottle aboard?" he asked, one hand on the air hatch leading to the Whippet.

Questin nodded. "Don't need it, but it's aboard." There was a moment's pause. Before Starbrite could speak, Questin added, "Just want you to know. Got a first-class qualification for piloting the Whippet. Jost an' I. Both ran 'em one time or another." A first-class qualification was low on the scale and such a pilot couldn't utilize even half the craft's capabilities. But, then, Starbrite's Whippet was to be used as a mere transport, one that might dodge a bit, but nothing more.

Starbrite ignored Questin's comment, his face an annoyed frown. "Quick now. Got to tell you a few more things. About the Dark Horde invasion and why—" He stopped, irritated as Questin silenced him with a wave of his hand.

"Know time's short, Quas. Know there's lots to explain. But you know all the details in fine tuning an' can act on them better'n me. Got an inkling myself." Then Questin said a few more quick sentences.

Starbrite's jaw bunched once. "Right," was all he said. When Questin finished. "Take care of it for me. For the Federation." His hand went out and gripped Questin's shoulder in a quick, affectionate gesture.

Questin gripped Starbrite's arm tightly with his left hand. "Best if you handle it, Quas. More efficient. I might not be able to in any case," he repeated.

"Thanks. But I'm taking the Whippet in." Starbright's tone left no room for argument.

"Not with that flange hanging loose like that," Questin said flatly, jerking his head up toward the air lock door. Starbrite whirled to look.

Questin's right fist connected solidly with Starbrite's jaw, just at the nerve plexus in front of his ear. Starbrite's world went black and he felt his mind disconnect from his body. He sensed pressure around his waist, felt his feet dragging, heard Questin bark out some orders to nearby crewmen as red and black spots did a tango in front of his eyes.

Starbrite awoke on the observation deck. He shook his head and the red and black spots did another slow dance before settling in place and fading away. "Two minutes to arrival time," Spica's husky voice intoned. Starbrite sat up quickly, his head clearing. It had been a skilled rabbit punch, placed for a short-term blackout with little aftermath.

A bloom of orange fire on the *Cetus*'s outside deck caught his eye. "Questin's just taking off. Rhinna's been up awhile," Lyra said flatly. Questin's Whippet banked, quivered once, then darted in a straight line for the black hole's singularity—the point at which gravity began to crush time and space into abstractions.

"Enemy close by," Spica said nervously. "They're heading for us first. Got our cannon fixed on 'em. But. . . ." His voice trailed off, his words broadcast on an open comm line to Rhinna and Questin. Lasecannon on large starships were notoriously ineffective against high-performance fighter craft.

Through the port windows Starbrite saw Rhinna Treaver pull a stunt that pushed her Whippet far beyond its design limits. The craft, accelerating after Questin, shot sharply upward. Its rear skidded toward the black hole as its front pitched toward the *Cetus*. In the space of a few Km's the Whippet had reversed direction and was streaking back toward its ship.

Like a hellion avenger, Rhinna swooped to head off the first Dark Horde fighter approaching the *Cetus*'s rear. She streaked toward the observation deck, bright pulses of lasecannon blasting from her Whippet's gun ports and puncturing the alien craft closing on the *Cetus*. At the last possible second, Rhinna undercut the enemy fighter, diving between it and the *Cetus*, missing the massive hull only by meters. Chunks shed from the Dark Horde craft and in a sudden frenzy of shudders it burst apart a mere Km away.

* * *

"One Klyster craft im—mobolized," stuttered Kra-Kon's chief of operations.

"Send the squadron officer to me," KraKon hummed, watching the four remaining smaller blips dart across the command viewscreen. One blip headed in a direct line toward the gateway, no doubt the one holding a literal time bomb of antimatter. Two of the Klyster fighters remained active and KraKon took no great comfort as he saw one edge toward that streaking craft. To have even a single Klyster destroyed was galling. The inefficiency and failure had become a personal insult that threatened the very majesty on which the Fellowship—his creation—had been built.

A dark figure approached from his side, his extremities twitching in uncontrolled fear. KraKon turned slowly from the viewscreen. "A Klyster failed. It was under your command."

"Fortunes of war, a lucky blow from an inferior enemy, Immortal KraKon."

"A weak explanation and a worse excuse." KraKon shrilled a peculiar ultrasonic command. Two massive Dark Horde CryKons, who served as his imperial guard, seized the squadron commander by his alloy arms. KraKon moved closer, savoring even this moment of redemption—payment for the insults of failure.

"An accident, Master KraKon. The two Klysters will more than compensate—" The cyborg saw its dreams of immortality fade as the KraKon approached, ominously silent. The other officers on deck turned to their consoles, not wishing to witness what they all knew might very likely happen to some of them.

In a swift motion the KraKon clamped both hands to the commander's metal head, snapped open four tiny release levers and whipped off the top portion of the alloy skull. The cyborg's brain was bared, covered only by a clear shield of silicon dioxide.

"The others, Immortal KraKon—they will—"

The squadron commander's piercing wail was silenced as the KraKon, with slow and steady deliberation, plunged one hand into the commander's brain, cracking through the brittle silicon shield. KraKon squeezed, pulping the cyborg's brain to a formless mush. The cyborg body twitched and shuddered, then collapsed to a motionless pile of scrap.

"There will be no more unpaid failures," the KraKon intoned, raising his eyes to the viewscreen and dreaming of the time when he might have the morsel of flesh and bones named Starbrite before him.

The other two enemy ships had been following the first, intending a mop-up action before destroying Questin's Whippet. Starbrite following every move on the viewscreen, realized how vengeful and stupid those tactics were. Their primary aim, he knew, was any craft heading for the black hole. Now, as if to confirm Starbrite's appraisal, the two remaining Dark Horde fighters veered from the *Cetus* on a straight-line trajectory for Questin.

Rhinna whipped her own craft around in a tight arc, latched onto Questin with her sensors, and followed a similar trajectory. On the long-range viewscreen, Starbrite saw the large enemy ship also speed toward the singularity. *Busy time around the old gateway today*, he thought grimly.

The enemy ships separated. One pursued Questin, obviously the kill craft of the pair. The other decelerated in a clear attempt to delay Rhinna. By now they were too far for visual observation. Starbrite activated the short-range sensors, flipping their data on the viewscreen, watching one of the last acts of their mission played out by swiftly moving dots on the large green-tinted screen.

Rhinna coped with the decelerating enemy fighter by the simplest of tactics: she ignored it. Her Whippet accelerated with a burst of thrust, veered to confuse the ship's fire, and hurtled after the craft that was stalking Questin. In that wild, frenzied pursuit, Rhinna opened up the thrust override, feeding more fuel to her engines in seconds than most Whippets used up in hours.

In a quick, evasive maneuver, the Dark Horde pilot swerved from its course at the sharpest curve it could manage, hoping to occupy Rhinna while the remaining alien ship caught up and killed off Questin. It was a standard tactic and Starbrite's lips were white as he watched it on the viewscreen.

It was Rhinna Treaver's skill that annulled the Dark Horde pilots' strategy. She launched her Whippet at the veering asymmetrical fighter like a starving cat pounces on a mouse. Her Whippet's gyroscopes whirred almost to the point of disintegration, but still she coaxed out more rpm's, forcing her craft into a sharp V-turn. The Whippet shuddered under the strain and Rhinna's stomach caved backward, compressing her lungs against her spine. Just before total blackout she cut trajectory arc and thrust directly ahead, the G-forces created by the sharp turn disappearing.

The alien fighter lay directly ahead and it was child's play to take it out with a salvo from the Whippet's lasecannon. By the time Rhinna let up on the gun triggers, the Dark Horde ship had been almost completely vaporized.

Unbelieving, KraKon stared at the viewscreen as the blip that was another Klyster fighter faded and disappeared. The enemy ship quickly veered toward the last Klyster and no doubt the two would clash. But it was too late. Somehow, sense overwhelmed KraKon's hate. He couldn't chance it now. If the last of his Klysters didn't immobilize the craft holding the antimatter he'd be exiled in this galaxy. And, once having departed through the gateway the precious secret of how to block his passageways that the female, along with the cretin Starbrite, had discovered and so far confined would become widespread. He could never again wreak his revenge in this galaxy.

Comprehension came suddenly. Starbrite. A *single* alien creature who would never be punished, who would never redeem his crimes against an immortal intellect. He—the great KraKon—would remain unavenged. And if it happened once, if he just one single time lost such control, might it not happen again? And again? And again?

Memories roiling below the surface of his mind fought for existence: memories of screams from a long-haired female as he, in a blood rage, had squeezed her throat. Control . . . it was fading.

A spasmodic hum reverberated from the KraKon's voice box, periodically ascending into high-pitched keening wails. The officers on the control deck moved uneasily and the Chief of Section signaled a menial cyborg to hit the acceleration controls. KraKon's ship moved faster toward the black hole gateway, racing the three other blips to be the first to reach the singularity, to arrive at a haven before it was sealed forever.

KraKon, immersed in his own horrors, hardly noticed the acceleration as ghostly images now pummeled his mind, driving him into a frenzy. He whirled in circles, hand to his head, as his mind fragmented. He babbled random orders in ultrasonic speech that his own frightened crew ignored. During one slow gyration, in a last remnant of sanity, he glanced again at the viewscreen and screeched so piercingly that he destroyed the acoustic sensors of several cyborgs.

One white blip was closing in on his last Klyster, and KraKon's mind greeted defeat by disintegrating into total insanity. Even as his ship's crew tried to restrain him, he rampaged among them, striking at random, roaring over and over again with each metallic blow the single name: "Starbrite, Starbrite, Starbrite."

Starbrite saw it all on his own viewscreen: one blip that was Rhinna making an incredibly tight turn and closing in on the Dark Horde fighter. Even as this shape faded from the screen, Rhinna arced into another body-punishing curve toward Questin's Whippet. Starbrite's hands bunched into tight balls, the knuckles white. He banged with his fists in an unconsciously steady beat on the control console's edge, knowing that he could never have come close to equaling Rhinna's piloting. He could only imagine what the strain had done to her. . . .

Blood streamed from Rhinna's nose, flowing from a dozen burst capillaries. Her vision had blurred because of G-pressure on her retina. She breathed in and gave a quick screech, feeling a splinter of broken rib prick some inside organ. Still, she held to a sharp turn, her eyes on the craft's small viewscreen, watching for a blurred dot that would be Questin's ship.

A white speck drifted onto her viewscreen and even her faded vision saw it had the shape of a Whippet. Then, not far behind, came the more amorphous outline of the last alien craft making a final dash toward Questin.

In the background of both smaller dots was the vast arc of the black hole, whose edge was only four hundred Km's away—a minute or so at her present speed—a gravity well from which there could be no escape. Then a larger shape drifted across her viewscreen, a cruiser-class starship also diving at the singularity—the edge of the black hole where time began to disappear.

Time.

Still time for her to pull away. For a millisecond Rhinna hesitated. She almost *felt* the warm memories of New Earth: the tinkle of merry voices during celebrations, the gentle touch of a warm wind, the fragrant smells of mown grass and wet forests. She remembered, too, the conversations she had had with Questin during the few hours they'd managed to find for themselves. She remembered, also, the carnage on Benera and the desperate look on Quas Starbrite's face as he told her of blocking KraKon's gateway. And then, Questin again. . . .

Rhinna aimed her Whippet at the pursuing white dot, knowing that power for her lasecannon was unreliable after such heavy usage, realizing with a professional's calm that only one sure means of protecting Questin remained.

She blasted in at a sharp angle to Questin's Whippet, visually sighting the Dark Horde fighter gaining on the ship with each moment. She gagged with pain as she inhaled sharply at seeing Questin's craft lurch from the fire the alien was already delivering.

Long before she had thrown in acceleration override. Her hand now shoved against the thrust lever, twisting it around to slip past the last safety cam and pushing it another few centimeters ahead. The Whippet shot forward with yet increased acceleration, its engines vibrating in their sockets from forces they were never designed to tolerate. Blood whipped back across her face in thin rivulets that looked like a thousand, spidery streams. Vision in one eye blacked out completely and darkened in the other. With the strength remaining in her arms, Rhinna edged her control stick so that the alien craft was square in the Whippet's gun sights. She held a straight course.

Just before collision she closed her eyes.

The skin on Starbrite's knuckles was torn and chafed. His eyes and face were wet and his lower lip bled from where he had bitten while watching two white blips on the viewscreen converge then disappear. Seconds later the huge alien starship had plunged into the singularity along with Questin's Whippet. In a coincidence that defied astronomical odds, the two craft had entered the gateway only a few Km's from the other.

At the instant of their entry, Starbrite had glanced from the viewscreen to the port windows. Later, Lyra told him that what he had claimed to see was impossible. That once anything had entered a singularity it would leave no trace, that such a massive gravity well as a black hole would force even light into null-time.

Yet, Starbrite would always swear that he had spotted a pinprick flash of intense white light. A white light that only the remaining antimatter being transported by Questin's Whippet could have made.

Chapter Twenty

He was still a trim, wrinkled man with pointed white mustache and still surrounded by lush green plants. But now the plants were obscured by darkness, as was most of Commander Ivor Croost's face. Shadows from a single low-lying light flowed over half his features. His eyes, still crystal clear, seemed like pale lamps hovering at the entranceway of two dark caves. Stray light rays shone on the tips of Croost's snow-white mustache, translucent white specks that occasionally twitched in space as though animated by some power of their own.

Starbrite sat opposite the man, noting how his hands were folded on his desk, fingers interlaced, illuminated by an oblong patch of light that slanted across his desk. The hands had remained motionless, as though carved from flesh-colored stone, throughout the entire twenty minutes of his verbal report.

"That's the gist of it," Starbrite finished in a low voice.

"Up until plugging the gateway, anyway," Croost answered with the smallest hint of admiration. "I take it you had no extraordinary trouble regaining New Earth afterward."

Starbrite breathed in slowly, taking time to fill his lungs down to the last lobe. The memories were already easier to absorb now and the events following Questin's and Rhinna's deaths flashed across his mind like the images in a fast-moving kaleidoscope.

No, there hadn't been any extraordinary trouble. They had skimmed around the black hole in a parabolic arc and then hype-hopped as close to Benera as they could. The *Cetus*'s hyperdrive coils were shot and the ship was doomed to remaining in the Nether Quadrant the remainder of its service. There came the eventual approach of a reconnoitering Space Fleet cruiser. Its reconnaissance of the Quadrant's planets showed that some had been totally destroyed while others remained completely unharmed. The starship's captain had told them that the invasion had ceased almost as suddenly as it had begun, with only pockets of aliens still fighting last-ditch battles. They had hype-hopped to New Earth over a week ago.

Then: saying a hasty goodbye to a puzzled Lyra as soon as their shuttle ship docked; fleeing Terra—New Earth's capital city—right from the spaceport; tapping old friendships for quick, furtive favors, his vengeful determination fueled by the memory of people who had died on the mission.

Even now, he recalled their names like a litany: Rhinna Treaver; Vac Orion; Questin; Lisa Orion; Jost Adrian; thousands of settlers and various crewmen who were no less important for being less well known. Each death was a stark reminder of an ambition gone mad.

Then: a hasty return to Terra, a private call to Croost, arrangements for a secretive meeting for tonight, one that he knew Croost would welcome as much as he.

Less than a half hour before he had entered the Commander's office, carefully centered one of the chairs in front of Croost's desk, and begun his quick recapitulation. Starbrite was relieved that Croost had postponed questioning him about his unexplained absence. He had begun his report satisfied at the late hour, at the absence of security guards, and even at the murky shadows of Croost's office. The darkness fit his mood.

With slow deliberation Croost unfolded his hands, leaned back, and laced his fingers behind his head. Shadows moved across his face with the movement, forming new, hard-edged patterns that grew narrower and longer as he rocked back and forth in his chair.

"The strategy you all devised to help the fleet and plug the gateway deserves commendation," Croost said in low, dry tones. "I only regret the deaths of brave men and women to achieve the ends."

Starbrite bored unmercifully into Croost's clear eyes. Eventually he said, "We didn't plug the gateway, you know. It was a ruse. But the Federation *can* block it any time."

Croost's gentle rocking stopped and the shadow patterns on his face stilled. His hands remained clasped behind his head. When he spoke his voice sounded like dry, rustling leaves. "Your message. The one you sent by the fleet. It mentioned you had enough antimatter left to plug the gateway."

Even in the obscure light of the room, Starbrite saw Croost's taut face tighten even further. His own steady gaze challenged Croost as he again remembered: Rhinna, Questin, Vac, Lisa, and all the others. Now *their* moment was coming.

Starbrite's long, unflinching stare was response enough to Croost's comment.

After a time Croost's mustache twitched with slow, thoughtful precision—his only sign of emotion. "How did you find out, Starbrite? It seems I've seriously underestimated you." Croost said it as though he had been caught in a minor administrative error.

Starbrite gave Croost the credit he was due: at least there were no puzzled expressions to sow doubt about his treachery; no rationalizations to excuse his treason; no pitiful excuses to justify his collusion with the Dark Horde forces.

"Lisa Orion told me, among other things," Starbrite answered, his eyes never wavering from Croost's impassive face. Except for more quick flicks of his mustache, the man seemed completely at ease.

"Would you elaborate on that?" Croost appeared genuinely curious.

"Lisa Orion told us she'd been on Earth long before

we arrived. So the aliens hid from us, at least at the start. They knew we were coming. They were warned by someone." Starbrite paused. "Why weren't we captured first thing? Why wait?"

Croost ignored the question, leap-frogging to where his own curiosity led. Starbrite didn't mind. They had plenty of time.

"You hinted there were other—mistakes. Would you care to elaborate, Starbrite? I'm interested when inefficiency creeps into an operation." Croost might have been asking about resupply snags of a berthed shuttle ship.

"Antimatter beds, Croost. You knew we were going. I told you so in code. We were attacked. I assumed it was coincidence at first, but not later. You were in direct contact with that KraKon thing."

"A fact you exploited in an extraordinarily clever fashion, Starbrite. Telling me that you had enough antimatter to close that gateway, knowing that I'd relay the information. Clever boy, you."

"That KraKon *had* to leave. Vac made that clear. It couldn't survive without resupply." Starbrite paused, his eyes never wavering from Croost. "Also, I expect it preferred returning to a world it knew, rather than getting stuck here. Even with you on its side, the Federation wouldn't seem like home."

"Sarcasm, Starbrite? It's beneath you."

"The Yellow Alert did it, too, Croost. Just for the record."

Croost dropped his eyelids in a slow half blink, as though conceding points to an adversary. "I wasn't at all sure the Dark Horde fleet could really cope with a Federation force prepared by a full Red Alert." Croost unlaced one hand and swept it in front of him in a deprecatory gesture. "They're not very good soldiers you know." Starbrite stiffened, then relaxed as the hand drifted to its resting place behind Croost's head.

"When you fight for longevity rather than ideals it tends to decrease enthusiasm for dangerous situations. Especially if your enemy is as vigorous as the Federation can be."

"So you covered yourself politically with a Yellow Alert, knowing it was a half measure that would doom hundreds in the Space Fleet."

Croost remained silent, trying to bore through Starbrite with eyes that had taken on a malicious glitter. Starbrite's query didn't need an answer.

"A question, Croost?"

"Feel free to indulge your curiosity, Starbrite."

"Why Lyra? Why kill her during the mission? Just as easy here on New Earth. In fact, why kill her at all?"

Croost's lips pursed outward, then retreated into a thin line. "KraKon's invasion was imminent. Lyra Orion's discovery of the gateway would have been disastrous. Even any attention directed toward that particular black hole would have been—upsetting."

"So. The instruments monitoring gravitational flux were recording the invasion forces entering our galaxy."

Croost's head moved in an almost imperceptible nod. "Her coming on the *Cetus* was a last-minute thing. It couldn't be avoided. So I told Jost to get rid of her by accident. Didn't want her getting a closer look at KraKon's entranceway."

"Jost Adrian was under your command?"

"Nominally. KraKon authorized Lyra's demise."

"But why the expedition at all? Why send Vac on such a trip?"

"Camouflage, my boy, for political consumption. We could claim that any untoward event in the Nether Quadrant was already being investigated. That paltry insurrectionist movement was a mere flank attack, a long-range distraction. Vac hadn't a chance of really tracing those amateurs to KraKon—Croost's mustache twitched violently. "Under ordinary circumstances at least."

For the first time Starbrite was totally astonished. He hadn't suspected that so many years of spadework had preceded the invasion.

"Why was I included as an escort? You had a better reason than military-civilian liaison."

Croost breathed in deeply before replying. "It was a decision that I admit was inappropriate given your particular brand of enterprise, Starbrite. Basically you went as a troubleshooter. I had you assigned to me years ago for just such an eventuality.''

''To probe for any weaknesses in your invasion scheme and report them directly to you.''

Croost's lips barely moved as he whispered, ''Correct again, Starbrite. You were a mere troubleshooter.''

''Just like Trensk Kattern.''

Croost jerked forward a fraction of a centimeter. ''Been busy I see. *Quite* underestimated you.''

''Trensk. Two years ahead of me at the Academy. Was supposed to have died—''

Croost took over. ''—on Alcans. I know. I planted that story so you'd see it. He was an agent, attached to the intelligence division. He *did* find a tenuous link between the insurrectionists and the invasion plans, one that drifted uncomfortably close to me. Did away with him. Good cover story, I thought, turning *him* into a traitor. But just how did you uncover Kattern's assignment?'' Croost seemed genuinely awe-struck.

''High-level computer search. Military Intelligence code access.'' In answer to Croost's next question Starbrite added, ''Friends, Croost.''

''So there are others who know my role in all this?'' Croost asked calmly.

Starbrite ignored the question. ''You couldn't kill Lyra with me around. So I was added to your private hit list.''

Croost winced at the slang term. ''Not quite correct, Starbrite. You were to be *terminated* because Jost felt your initiatives might get out of hand. A conclusion that, in hindsight, proved all too true. Lyra, it was finally decided, might uncover something of scientific use to us, so we gave you access to Earth's computer. Her safety was assured when the KraKon seemed to take a special interest in her.''

Starbrite felt his stomach pitch toward his throat.

''Actually, KraKon had a particular interest in you, too,'' Croost continued. ''A special animus over your killing Jost Adrian. You were rather lucky to escape Earth, you know.''

Croost sucked on an underlip as though regretting the fate Starbrite would have suffered at KraKon's hands.

Shifting topics again, Croost said, ''So there are others who know of my tendencies?'' He pronounced *tendencies* as though he were talking of minor bad habits.

''Actually not,'' Starbrite replied, his eyes still glued on Croost. ''Couldn't afford to.''

''Perhaps you'd care to explain that, Starbrite. Your thought processes are no less than intriguing.''

''Several reasons added together, none sufficient alone. First, a question of belief. It'd be hard to convince someone of your treachery. I preferred to make inquiries about the Yellow Alert, Space Fleet orders, Trensk Kattern, and other of your activities on the basis of friendships. Saying I was checking on *you*, that you were allied with the Dark Horde aliens, would have put my sanity in question.''

''And, consequently, cooperation from your surreptitious sources. You're quite right about that. More?''

''Second, there are probably others equally traitorous. Exposing you publicly would cause them to burrow deeper. It's going to be hard to find them in any case.''

''If at all,'' Croost murmured, then added, ''Excellent reasoning so far, Starbrite. Continue.''

''Other motives? Exposing another hero besides Jost Adrian. That's a lot for the Federation's moral to sustain. Those are enough.''

Starbrite eyed Croost carefully as the man leaned forward and again folded his hands on the desk, his face in deeper shadow than before. ''Why, Croost? When did it all start? What did you hope to gain?''

Croost responded in tones of total reason. ''When? Years ago. Jost Adrian arranged my first meeting with the KraKon.'' Croost's pale eyes rose and drilled a hole in the space just above Starbrite's head. ''Why? For love of life, Starbrite. To live millenia, to accumulate power. To carry out one's dreams without homage to the fallible opinions of others. A dream, Starbrite, you might someday share.''

If Croost's comment was a subtle invitation it remained ignored.

It had taken a bare second for Starbrite to digest Croost's first words. He asked with an edge of disgust in his voice: "You *met* him—it—the KraKon thing?" Croost offered a flicker of a swift grin back at Starbrite, as though his surprise had gained some moral advantage.

"The pronoun 'it' will do nicely, Starbrite. Yes, I knew KraKon. A rather intense personality, to say the least. Not much charm but extraordinarily forceful. A difficult being to control, actually. I needed to learn more of his technology before. . . . Jost Adrian was going to accomplish *that*. Bah!"

Starbrite, again, was astounded. "You were going to try and control that KraKon. *You* were going to forge a dictatorship from New Earth. You're as mad as that thing."

Croost moved back in his chair with a look of resigned boredom. His hand brushed against a writing stylus. It fell to the carpeted floor with barely a sound. Croost started to retrieve it, then caught up by Starbrite's statement, remained half leaning toward the ground, half facing Starbrite.

"I'm not mad at all. It's the KraKon who is quite insane. It can't last much longer. Makes too many strategically foolish decisions. And, Starbrite, with immortal life as the carrot one barely needs a stick. With intergalactic time travel at our behest, we can use life for its full advantage. That includes, you, too. Eons of—"

Croost paused in mid-sentence to retrieve the writing stylus. His head dipped below his desk top, then reappeared.

Starbrite killed him then.

A bright blue streak of light flashed from the finger-thick lasegun Starbrite had bought on Benera, the same weapon that had killed Jost Adrian. The lasebeam flashed from Starbrite's hand, the needle-thin beam hitting Croost full in the forehead. A wisp of smoke rose from the tiny entry hole as Croost slumped to the floor. The smell of cauterized flesh slowly permeated the room.

After a while, Starbrite rose and went behind Croost's desk. The man still grasped the large military lasegun that he'd taken from the nook underneath his chair. The same lasegun that had undoubtedly killed Trensk Kattern; the weapon that Starbrite had noticed over a year ago when in Croost's office as an aide-de-camp; the same one Croost had intended to use on him.

Starbrite had known that only one of them could leave this room alive. Personally confronting Croost had been a moral imperative. And Croost couldn't possibly let him live with what he knew. In this room, their own loves and hatreds had reduced morality to its lowest common denominator: kill or be killed.

Starbrite grabbed Croost by the armpits and sat him in his chair. He placed the heavy lasegun in Croost's hand and then fired a laseblast into the hole his own weapon had made. The tiny wound was obliterated by the huge channel Croost's weapon burned into his own skull.

Starbrite went to the input keys of Croost's office computer. He programmed a message to be displayed on the office secretary's readout the next morning. It was a short epitaph.

```
HAVING FAILED IN MY RESPONSIBILITIES TO EF-
FECTIVELY ANTICIPATE AND REPULSE AN ALIEN
ENEMY, I NO LONGER WISH TO ASSUME THE DUTIES
OF THIS OFFICE. SELF-INFLICTED DEATH IS NOW
A MORE PALATABLE ALTERNATIVE TO ME THAN CON-
TINUED LIFE.
                IVOR CROOST
```

Starbrite sat at the computer terminal awhile longer, not yet capable of feeling remorse or further surprise. Effectively, his mission was now complete. A mission that had graphically illustrated how the insane ambitions of madmen—or in the case of KraKon, an insane being—could wreak so much havoc on humanity.

It was a lesson, Starbrite knew, that would take a lifetime to absorb.

Epilogue

The horizon was a light turquoise that darkened into a rich blue canopy. Constellations of white, sparkling stars dotted the heavens overhead. Still others slowly emerged at a lower zenith as dusk deepened into night. The rich smell of Terra's forest park wafted over the balcony of Starbrite's apartment, carried by a warm, gentle breeze that lightly brushed against his and Lyra's skin.

Starbrite cursed himself for the sudden awkwardness he felt as he again looked at her, stunning in a pale, yellow tunic, her hair lifting and settling lightly in the breeze. She turned to him slowly, a poignant smile on her face.

"They're ours, now. All of them. Throughout the universe," she whispered, tossing her head slightly to indicate the sky above.

Starbrite had become used to Lyra's cryptic thoughts, a mannerism he'd come to enjoy. It had become a kind of game for him to interpret what she meant. His average was steadily improving. Yet. . . . His eyebrows hunched briefly together at her comment.

"The stars. Those in our galaxy. Those in the entire universe," she explained with a quick smile. "Our scientists are tearing apart the equipment the Dark Horde forces left. Eventually we'll understand their gravitational technology, how they used black holes as gateways. Then the universe is ours."

"How long?"

Lyra gave a playful shrug of her shoulders. "Don't know, really. A few years maybe, a decade at most." She stared again at the stars overhead, her head thrown back, her hair hanging loose, hands holding onto the balcony rail. Then, feeling that this was the most appropriate time and place asked, "There's more to Commander Croost's death than you've told me, Quas. I can feel it. I'm right, aren't I?"

Even as she asked, Lyra noted how much Starbrite had changed since their first meeting. No longer so impetuous or obdurate. He was equally innovative, but his initiatives, even his thoughts, were modulated with a deep inner caution. *Seasoned* was the word that sprang to her mind.

"You're right. There's more to it. I'll be able to tell you someday."

"When?"

"Don't know really. A few years, a decade at most," Starbrite kidded, then added more seriously, "Soon."

Lyra, satisfied at Starbrite's response, held onto the balcony rail and again threw back her head toward the sky, her hair hanging loose behind her. It was a gesture of spontaneous joy and Starbrite, looking at her, sensed how much Lyra had changed. No longer quite so imperious or opinionated, more aware of her own fallibilities as well as her resources.

"It's an even richer universe than we thought," Starbrite said, the meandering comment fitting their mood. "KraKon forced many alien life forms into his service. Made them into cyborgs in his own image and likeness. We know now that the universe is filled with intelligent life, all just sitting there waiting to be contacted."

"Isn't there any hope for them, Quas? They're all dead or dying," Lyra said, compassion in her voice.

Starbrite shook his head. "Fantastically strong machines, but delicate. In need of constant maintenance. And each life form needs a different set of components. No, all we'll have left from the invasion is hardware. The few Dark Horde soldiers we've communicated with don't even know where they came from."

212

"But that KraKon knows," Lyra said, feeling a rash of goose pimples rise over her arms. "And he has the coordinates of our galaxy. But we don't have his. Can he come back, Quas?"

Starbrite drank in the smell of Terra's forest and Lyra's fragrance before answering. "He can, but he won't. Not since we discovered how to plug up a black hole gateway." He tensed as he added, "But we may find KraKon's galactic coordinates from instruments on starships he left behind. A preemptive Star Fleet strike would eliminate all worry."

"War. Not now, Quas. I'd rather think of how we've entered a new epoch," Lyra said quickly, moving from the bitterness she knew Starbrite still felt at the invasion, the deaths, the betrayals. "We're about to begin the most exciting era of exploration ever seen in the history of our own race."

"It's our time, too," Starbrite murmured, consciously moving from the dark mood that sometimes seemed overwhelming to a sense of well-being that flooded over him as Lyra moved closer.

"No more postponements," she added, sliding her hand in his, suddenly becoming serious again as she remembered the last several weeks.

"They only invaded settled colonies. They never even tried to take New Earth. I'm glad, of course. But from an invader's point of view it seemed, well—amateurish."

'. . . *Can't last much longer. Makes too many strategically foolish mistakes . . .*'. Starbrite suddenly remembered Croost's words.

"Settlements were wiped out. But their invasion gave us a technology that will take us throughout our galaxy and into others," Starbrite murmured, again fighting his bitterness.

"At what a price. The suffering of our own settled colonies. The people—"

"Birth is always traumatic," Starbrite interrupted gently. "We can't help that. But the Galactic Federation's tribulations are in the past. And they've given us a legacy that will carry us to the universe. That's what I'd like to focus on.''

''A lifetime left to explore the stars,'' Lyra said, her own twinge of moroseness replaced with a happy wonder.

''Together?'' It was half a statement, half a question.

Lyra moved even closer and felt a warm comfort as Starbrite's arms circled her waist. ''Why not?'' she said coquettishly.

They stood for a time, quietly watching the horizon deepen into progressively deeper hues of blue, watching as yet more sparkling stars emerged from the darkening sky.

Stars that were now their dominion to explore.

ABOUT THE AUTHOR

JAMES BERRY is a writer whose special interest is physics. He is the author of several young adult novels and non-fiction books, as well as science fiction novels. He lives in Brooklyn, N.Y.

FANTASY AND SCIENCE FICTION FAVORITES

Bantam brings you the recognized classics as well as the current favorites in fantasy and science fiction. Here you will find the beloved Conan books along with recent titles by the most respected authors in the genre.